A Girl Called Rose

Kay Seeley

Published by Enterprise Books
Copyright © 2021 Kay Seeley
All rights reserved.
ISBN-13: 978-1-9164282-8-7

TO ALL WHO SERVE:

PAST PRESENT AND FUTURE.

Also By Kay Seeley:

Novels
The Water Gypsy
The Watercress Girls
The Guardian Angel

The Hope Series
A Girl Called Hope (Book 1)
A Girl Called Violet (Book 2)
A Girl Called Rose (Book 3)

All Kay's novels are also available in Large Print

Box Set (ebook only)
The Victorian Novels Box Set

Short Stories
The Cappuccino Collection
The Summer Stories
The Christmas Stories

Please feel free to contact Kay through her website
www.kayseeleyauthor.com She'd love to hear from
you.
Or follow Kay on her Facebook Page
https://www.facebook.com/kayseeley.writer/

Chapter One

Rose stood on Westminster Bridge staring at the imposing building ahead of her. The fear of failure squeezed her chest. She took a breath. The icy air stung her lungs. A sharp, biting wind picked up a discarded newspaper and rolled it along the pavement dropping it to lie, flapping forlornly in the gutter. Frost lingered on the bridge's balustrade. Below her the river swirled, the smell unlike the salty spray of the sea at home. Boats chugged and hooted as they made their way to the docks.

Excitement and trepidation churned her stomach. She'd had to fight to get here and now she'd arrived she was besieged by crippling doubt. Supposing Ma was right, she was too young? Too inexperienced to face what she might encounter?

Ever since she'd read about Florence Nightingale in the Crimea, all she'd ever wanted was to be a nurse; someone who made a difference to people's lives. Now she had the chance. She'd come to London to follow her dream and vowed to make the most of it. New adventures and opportunities beckoned. Thanks to the war the world was changing and she wanted to be part of it, to do her bit.

So, here she was in the greatest city in the world. Her eyes shone with anticipation as her head filled with possibilities unknown. Life would never be the same for any of them. She looked forward to creating a new future for herself, but couldn't help recalling all she had left behind. Could it really be only a few short weeks since she'd stood, looking over the sea, on Christmas Eve? The memory spiralled through her mind:

She'd stood in front of the Addison Grand Hotel, Great Yarmouth, her home for the last ten years. It was her favourite place to watch the changing of the seasons, gazing out across the vast expanse of sea. Today, although it was only late afternoon, pale moonlight danced on the water, specks of stars were beginning to appear in the darkening sky. The whoosh of winter waves as they reached the beach filled the air. Barely a whisper of wind caressed her face. The early dusk had laid a cloak of gloom over the town. No light shone from the pier or the shore.

She'd glanced up at the sky. Earlier in the year a Zeppelin bomb had fallen on the nearby town, causing devastating destruction. Now the threat was ever present. She remembered long summer days before the war when the Promenade buzzed with life, light and laughter from the summer visitors who flocked to the resort. Happy times now gone as was much of the life they'd known and loved.

"Penny for 'em."

Her brother William's arrival brought her sharply out of her reverie. She flushed with pleasure at his presence. "I was thinking how different it used to be," she said.

"And no doubt thinking about the lads across the water. Difficult not to these days," William said. "I wish I could join up. I bet it'll be all over before I get a chance to go."

Rose gasped. They both knew men from the town who'd volunteered and gone to war. Some of them had worked in their parents' hotel. Her mind filled with visions of today's residents; men who'd come to convalesce from serious injuries sustained overseas. She shuddered. "I for one am glad you're too young," she said. "I know Ma is too. It's not the glamorous life you think it is."

"But I want to do my bit. You don't understand, you're just a girl."

Rose's anger flared. "Just a girl? Who is it risking life and limb working in factories supplying munitions for the troops? Just girls, but where would the men be without them?" It was a real risk too. Rose read the papers. There'd been an explosion in a factory a few months ago and workers had been killed. "And the nurses too," she said. "Working at the Front." Rose had wanted to train as a nurse but, like William, had been too young.

She'd shivered again as a chill wind blew in from the sea. William removed his coat and wrapped it around her. "I'd fight to my last breath to protect you, Ma and the little ones," he said.

She saw his cheeky grin and the twinkle in his cornflower blue eyes and sighed. The light sea breeze ruffled his baby blonde hair. She loved him beyond measure, but why did he always have to make her angry one minute and have her laughing the next. Her

3

heart melted a little. "I know," she said. "But I'm glad you don't have to and you are doing your bit with the coastal patrols. Ma relies on you while Pa's away. You're the man of the house."

"I suppose," he said resting his arm around her shoulders. "Not the same though is it?"

They stood in silence listening to the sound of the sea. She felt him take a breath. "Big day tomorrow," he said. "We'll both be sixteen and old enough to leave home."

"Yes. But I can't see Ma agreeing to it," Rose said. "She misses Pa and won't want us to leave too."

"Any idea what her plans are for tomorrow?" William asked.

"I know she was hoping Pa would make it, but it doesn't look likely now." Their stepfather, Gabriel, was overseas fighting the war. She shivered.

"Let's go in," William said. "You look like you could do with a hot drink. If we're lucky there'll be some of Martha's cake left."

Rose turned and walked into the hotel with him. "Aunt Hope and Uncle Silas are driving up in the morning with Olivia and Sean," she said. "It will be lovely to see them again."

Their mother's sister, Hope, lived in London and with petrol being on ration had been unable to visit in the summer as usual. Rose looked forward to seeing their young cousins again too.

William chuckled. "You mean we have to listen to the story of the night we were born all over again?"

Rose giggled. The surprising appearance of twins on Christmas Day was related every year on their birthday. "Wouldn't be a proper birthday otherwise," she said.

When they arrived in the kitchen Rose checked the big kettle for water and moved it onto the stove. William raided the larder and came out with the remains of a cake. Rose made tea and put the pot on the table with two cups and saucers then fetched a jug of milk.

"Do you think Aunt Hope will put in a good word for us?" William asked. "After all Peter's joined up. She'll understand that we want to do our bit too."

Their cousin Peter, the orphaned street-boy Hope and Silas had adopted, was eighteen and with the Artillery in France. Rose had always been secretly in awe of him. He had the arrogant confidence of a street urchin coupled with stubborn determination to resist any attempt to change him. Still, he always had time for them. Time to show them how things worked, time to answer their endless questions and time to play with them on the beach, or do whatever they wanted to do.

"I'm not sure she'll help," Rose said. "I don't know how she felt about Peter enlisting."

"I miss seeing him and the good times we used to have," William said, putting the cake on the table.

Rose poured the tea. "I miss him too," she sighed. "I don't expect he's having much fun where he is."

William shrugged. "No. I suppose not."

"Who's not having much fun?" their mother, Violet, asked as she walked into the kitchen. She plonked a heavy basket of crumpled sheets on the table. Rose noticed the weary look on her face and the worry shadowing her usually bright eyes and felt a stab of guilt for not coming in earlier to help.

"We were just talking about Peter," Rose said. "Saying what a shame it is he couldn't get leave to come home for Christmas."

Violet nodded. "Shame about a lot of things these days." She gave a heavy sigh. Rose knew she meant Pa not coming home. She felt her disappointment. She missed him too, more than she could say. She wished there was something she could do, but there wasn't.

Violet glanced around and tucked a stray curl of copper-coloured hair behind her ear. "Our guests will be here tomorrow. We've still got a lot to do before then." She looked at William. Her brow furrowed. "Aren't you supposed to be on patrol with the coastguard tonight?" William, like many of his friends, spent his evenings watching the skies for possible air raid attacks.

"Just going." William picked up his tea and swallowed it in one gulp. "Don't wait up. I'll see you in the morning," he said and snaffled another piece of cake on his way out.

"I need you to change the beds on the second floor," Violet said to Rose. "There'll be a fresh intake after Christmas and I want everything to be ready."

Rose nodded. She finished her tea and made her way up to the second floor. She was glad the men had gone home but the thought of more arriving filled her with dread. She was acutely aware that people she knew and loved could be among them. She wasn't sure how she'd cope with that.

The next morning Rose woke before dawn. She got up and crept to the window, drew back the curtain and glanced out. In the gloom she could just make out the white caps edging the waves and a light covering of frost on the ground. It was her favourite time of day, everything so quiet and peaceful. She watched a couple of boats cutting through the water on their way to the harbour. Not even Christmas would stop the men fishing. With shortages and much of the food produced on the farms going to feed the army, the herring catch provided much needed relief for the locals.

She glanced at Florence, her five-year-old sister, still asleep in the other bed, her hair a tangle of tangerine curls. The Christmas gifts at her feet were surprises for when she woke up.

After dressing quietly she went downstairs. Martha, the cook, would be in soon and the hotel would come gradually to life. She put on her thickest coat and collected her bicycle from the shed. The icy morning air caught her breath in clouds of mist as she wheeled her bike out to the empty road. By the time she reached town her cheeks were glowing.

"Good morning, Mr Pickering," she said as she came to a halt where the baker stood in the doorway of the bakery. The smell of fresh baked bread filled the air. "Merry Christmas to you."

"And to you, Miss Rose," the baker said. He rubbed his hands together. "It's a cold one an' all. Have you come for the order? I could have had it delivered, no need for you to come out so early."

"I like to get out early," Rose said. "I have something special to collect in town."

Mr Pickering laughed. It being Christmas Day he didn't have to guess what that was. "You go on, then and I'll get lad to put the order together ready for when you get back." He grinned.

"Thanks, Mr Pickering." Rose rode on to the boatyard near the harbour. It felt eerily quiet with only the sound of the lanyards slapping against masts, the rub of buoys against hulls and the slurping and slapping of the water as the boats bobbed on the waves.

She leaned her bicycle against the wall of the boat-shed and went in. Several boats were propped up, their bodies scarred as though waiting to be finished. Ropes and pieces of wood lay all around. "Hello," she called. "Anyone here?"

A grey haired, stocky man appeared from behind one of the boats. His face lit up when he saw her "Ah, Miss Rose," he said coming towards her. "Come for Amos 'ave you?"

Rose smiled. "Yes. Is he ready?"

"Aye. Sorry 'e weren't finished sooner. I 'ad to wait for the paint to dry." He walked to a large trunk next to the workbench, lifted the lid and brought out what appeared at first sight to be a bundle of clothes. When he unfolded them Rose saw exactly what she'd asked for. A wooden carved dummy, about three feet tall, with wide blue eyes, a smile on his face and his hair painted pale blonde. Dressed in fisherman's knitted jumper and coarse trousers, he wore the smallest pair of wellington boots Rose had ever seen. The boatman named all his dolls and Rose was delighted with Amos Little.

"He's splendid, Lenny," she said. "William will love it."

"I 'ope so," Lenny said. Then he went on to demonstrate how to move the head and showed her the lever to use to move the dummy's bottom lip up and down as though he's talking. "Shall I wrap him?"

"Please," Rose said. "It's very good of you."

"Aye, well I enjoyed making 'im. Bit of a change from the usual." Lenny made his living as a carpenter and joiner working on the boats, but he also made wooden toys that sold in the local shop.

When William and Rose were about ten they'd seen a ventriloquist act in the Pavilion on the pier and William had been enthralled. He kept talking about it and saying 'When I grow up I'm going to be a ventriloquist.' Their mother, Violet, soon squashed his enthusiasm.

"I thought you wanted to be an engineer," she said. "A much more useful and worthy profession."

Nothing more was said but Rose hadn't forgotten it and when she saw the dolls Lenny carved in the toy shop window his words came to mind and the idea of the perfect combined Christmas and birthday present for William formed in her head. The fact that William was a brilliant mimic also helped. For years he'd kept her laughing when they walked to and from school by imitating all the teachers, the other boys and the local shopkeepers. He seemed to have a talent for it. Yes, the dummy would be perfect. It had been difficult keeping it secret as William spent much of his spare time hanging around the boatyard, but they'd managed it.

Once Amos was wrapped Rose thanked Lenny, wished him a Merry Christmas and put the dummy into the basket on the front of her bike. As she rode back to the hotel after picking up the bread order, the morning began to lighten. She stopped to watch where the sea met the sky and the rising sun spread its coral light across the water. The sight always filled her with delight and lifted her spirits. A seagull swooped and then soared again against the golden glow of morning where other gulls screeched and circled. She rode on. A few people were out and waved or smiled as she passed.

Back at the hotel she wheeled her bike into the shed and went indoors. Martha was in the kitchen preparing breakfast. Rose wished her good morning and Merry Christmas before rushing upstairs with Amos. She could tell from the noise coming from her mother's bedroom that both Joshua and Florence, her younger siblings, were awake and had already started playing with their new toys. She would have time to brush her chestnut hair into some sort of style and change out of her cycling skirt into a more fetching dress before the day really began.

Chapter Two

Rose changed into a soft, sage green woollen day dress with an extravagant lace collar and cuffs. The skirt brushed her trim ankles. Serviceable as well as decorative, she thought. She put her hair up and, looking in the mirror, saw her cheeks still glowed from the early morning ride. The dress brought out the colour of her emerald eyes making them appear a deeper gentler green. Not too bad, she thought and smiled. Unlike Ma, she didn't usually care much for her appearance but today, being Christmas Day and a milestone birthday, she wanted to look her best.

She didn't want to be late for breakfast so she hurried out to make her way down to the kitchen.

The family lived on half the top floor of the imposing four-storey building in a roomy, self-contained apartment. Staff bedrooms occupied the rest of the floor, an arrangement that had worked very satisfactorily since her parents had opened the hotel. Now, with the middle two floors turned into accommodation for convalescing Officers, the arrangement still suited, giving the family the necessary privacy. Offices on the ground floor enabled Violet to manage the running of the hotel owned by her father-in-law. Today, it being Christmas and the patients sent home, the rooms were empty and the children could enjoy greater freedom.

The kitchen ran beneath the ground floor restaurant, bar and lounge area. Before the war it had boasted a first-class chef and twenty kitchen staff, but now they relied on Martha and several girls from town, who were also at home for Christmas.

Warmth enveloped Rose as she walked into the large, well-equipped kitchen. The smell of the bacon Martha was tipping onto a plate to go into the already lit oven filled Rose's nostrils, perking her hunger. Steam billowed from the boiling kettle on the huge range that took up one end of the room.

Cupboards and shelves lined the walls and a long table in the centre of the room had been laid with cups, saucers and plates. A large brown teapot stood in the middle of the table with a jug of milk and bowl of sugar.

Violet and her younger children arrived at the same time as Rose. "Good morning and Merry Christmas," Violet said. She kissed Rose's cheek. "And happy birthday."

The children too shouted, "Merry Christmas and happy birthday," before running into Rose's arms for a hug.

"And a Merry Christmas to you all," Martha said, ruffling Joshua's hair.

Florence pulled a doll out of the bag she was holding. "Look what Father Christmas brought me," she said, her face shining with delight.

"I got some soldiers and a rifle," Joshua said. He was two years older than Florence and, Rose thought, prone to seriousness. "Just like a real one. Now I can be a proper soldier." He held it up for Rose to see.

"Lovely," Rose said, although the thought of her youngest brother going to war horrified her. Thanks goodness he wouldn't have to. The war would be over long before he was old enough.

Martha glanced at Violet. "Breakfast is ready. It's keeping warm and I've done the vegetables for your dinner. The pheasants are prepared. All you 'ave to do it pop them in the oven. I've left instructions. I 'opes you all have a lovely day."

Rose, who guessed she'd be the one doing the cooking in Martha's absence, saw the said vegetables in bowls set out on the long worktop and the large roasting pan covered with a clean cloth.

"And the same to you, Martha," Violet said, going to one of the cupboards in the tall dresser that ran the length of the wall. She took out an envelope and two parcels, one obviously a bottle, which she handed to Martha. "Just a little something to keep you going. Please give our best wishes to your family."

Martha took them. The envelope contained a nice bonus and the heavier package a joint of meat. The bottle would be her husband's favourite whisky. "You're very generous, Mrs Stone. So kind."

Once Martha had gone Rose helped Violet set out the children's breakfast. "What time did William get in?" Violet asked.

Rose shrugged. "Not sure. After I went to bed."

"I hope he's okay for today and hasn't started celebrating too soon."

"I'll go up and fetch him," Rose said. "Don't want his birthday breakfast spoiled."

Upstairs Rose banged on William's door before opening it and barging in. She went over to the bed and shook him awake. "Come on, sleepyhead. Big day today."

William groaned and rolled over. He struggled to open his eyes and gaze up at her. "Whattimeisit?" he mumbled.

The smell of alcohol laced his breath. "Oh no, William. Don't tell me you've been drinking. Ma will be mad as a cat." Rose was pretty mad herself. How could he be so selfish?

"I only had a couple."

Rose didn't miss the slight slur in his speech.

"Never again," he said, rolling away from her. "It's that chap Barney. Devil incarnate he is. I should have known better. Oh God, I feel sick."

"Serves you right." Rose threw the covers back over him and strode to the window. She drew open the curtains flooding the room with light. He groaned again.

"You'd better get up right now," she said. "If Ma catches you you'll be for it."

"Aw, sorry, Sis." He grinned and her anger ebbed away. "Give me ten minutes I'll be down bright-eyed and bushy-tailed."

"You'd better be." Rose sighed but she could never stay cross with him for long. She only hoped Ma never found out.

Downstairs the kitchen glowed with warmth and the chatter of her younger brother and sister who were tucking into the breakfast Martha had prepared.

"Is he all right?" Violet asked as she buttered another piece of bread for Joshua.

"Yes. He'll be down directly. That bacon looks good. I didn't know we had any left."

Violet smiled. "Food parcel from Grandma and Gramps," she said. "They sent the pheasant and fresh vegetables too."

"How lovely," Rose said, glad she'd managed to steer the conversation away from the state of William's health or the likelihood of his joining them any time soon.

They'd almost finished their breakfast by the time William ambled into the kitchen.

"Ah. At last," Violet said. Rose noticed the edge to her voice.

"Any coffee?" he asked, turning away to avoid Rose or Violet's eyes. He poured himself a cup from the china coffee pot on the side.

"I've saved you some bacon," Violet said. "Do you want your eggs fried or scrambled?"

"Er. Not very hungry," he muttered.

"What?"

"Scrambled please. Yes. Scrambled. Thanks." He sat at the table with his coffee. Florence and Joshua were eager to show him their toys. From the look on his face Rose wouldn't be surprised to see whatever he ate making a second appearance within short time of him eating it. She had no sympathy for his self-inflicted condition, but it was their birthday and she didn't want it spoiled.

"William and I can take the little ones to church this morning if you like," she said. "Give you some time to yourself to get everything ready for later."

"Thank you, that would be a help," Violet said and smiled. It seemed that she too was prepared to forgive William his inconsiderate behaviour, given that it was his birthday.

Violet placed a plate of bacon and scrambled egg on the table in front of William. "There you are," she said. She turned to Joshua and Florence. "Come on then. Upstairs and get ready. Rose and William are taking you to church this morning. Won't that be lovely?"

She ushered them away.

"Thanks," William said, pushing the plate of food away.

"Shame to waste it," Rose said, noticing that Ma had given him three rashers of bacon whereas she'd only been given one. She sat down beside him and finished it off.

Rose's offer to take the children to church with William gave him a chance to recover in the fresh air away from Violet's further scrutiny. Outside he revived a little. A stiff breeze blew in from the sea and the air was sharp and diamond hard. Florence walked sedately, her springy curls bouncing around her head, holding Rose's hand, while Joshua, tall for his age and slender like Gabriel, skipped ahead. By the time they arrived at church all their cheeks were glowing.

The Christmas Day service at the church in town was a tradition, one of the small things that, since the outbreak of war, had become even more important. A way to maintain perspective and pretend everything was normal. Most times, with the choir singing and organ music rising to the rafters, you could almost be forgiven for forgetting that there was a war on at all, even if only momentarily.

It wasn't so easy to forget it today, with half the men from the town missing and the congregation being made up mostly of women.

Rose could burst with pride at the thought of Pa fighting for his country, but she still wished he hadn't gone. Although she was lucky. At least her family were around her. Several people in town had lost loved ones. Fathers and husbands who'd never return to see their children grow up. Mothers who'd never see their sons again. All lost in a war that was supposed to be over by

Christmas but was still going on. She'd been humbled in the spring when she saw the parade of men in uniform, proudly marching through the town, singing their rousing songs, their boots thundering on the road. Brave heroes ready to take up arms to protect their country and their families. People watching had cheered and waved flags. She wondered where they were now, the men, and what sort of Christmas they'd be having.

She enjoyed the Christmas service, the sharp smell of the pine decorating the church mixing with the warm aroma of wax from candles that flickered in the dim light. She took pleasure in the solemnity of the service, the organ music and the joyous outburst of voices rising in song with the uplifting promise of hope. Her heart swelled with the music.

After the service she nodded and chatted to as many of the people as she could before they left to walk home. William on the other hand sat surly and quiet throughout the service. Outside he stood, head bowed, hands in his pockets shuffling his feet and hardly spoke to the people Rose chatted to. On the way back he stopped by the railings along the Promenade.

"Are you feeling all right?" Rose asked, worried in case the sickness of the morning had returned and would spoil the day.

"Barney's signed up," William said. "That's what the celebration was about last night. He's got a place on a merchant ship and he wants me to go with him."

"Go with him? Where? Why?" Rose felt as though the earth had shifted beneath her feet. She was no longer on solid grounds. Of course she knew of William's frustration at staying at home and his love of the sea, but, like Ma, thought it a passing fad that would soon be replaced by something else.

"To see the world, Rose. There's a big wide world out there and the merchant ships are just as important to the war effort as the naval ones." He paused. "And it's just as dangerous."

"But you can't, William. Ma will never allow it. She'll never agree to your going."

He shrugged. "We'll see," he said.

Rose's heart fell into her boots. If William went away…

"Come on," she called to Joshua and Florence who'd taken the opportunity while they were distracted to dash down to the strip of beach left by the turning tide and throw stones into the water.

If William left she'd be more determined than ever to go and train as a nurse. All the men at the hotel talked glowingly of the doctors and nurses who'd saved their lives and Rose wanted to do the same. She wasn't a man so couldn't go to war, but she could still do her bit and make a difference to people's lives. That at least would be useful.

Chapter Three

Back at the hotel William said he had some errands to run and the children went upstairs to play with their new toys. Rose went to the restaurant to make sure everything was ready for when their guests arrived. She had happy memories of staying with her Aunt Hope and Uncle Silas when she was growing up and of their regular summer visits. Ma always seemed happier when she could show her sister how well she was doing, although Rose pushed that thought to the back of her mind. With Pa away things would be very different this year, but seeing Hope, Silas and the children meant a break from the hard work and the feeling of isolation the war had thrust upon them. Ma would put on her very best show and they would all benefit.

She glanced around the restaurant which, with the help of the staff, had been decorated with streamers and paper-chains. A large tree adorned with baubles and candles stood in one corner with gaily wrapped packages spread around its base. Several tables had been pushed together in the centre of the room, covered with starched white linen and decorated with bunches of holly and trailing ivy tied with red ribbons. The best dinner service and cutlery had been brought out for the occasion.

She counted the chairs. Ma would sit at one end of the table with, she had hoped, Pa at the other. But Pa hadn't arrived. She sighed. It had been so long since he'd gone away and the lively, happy atmosphere of the hotel had gone with him. The Officers who came to the hotel to recover from their injuries brought with them a sense of great relief and gratitude, but the character of the place had changed from one of bubbly excitement to one of sombre reflection.

She kept telling herself that he'd have come home if he could. Only a war could keep him from them. She understood that he felt duty bound to fight for the country that had given them so much and its future, but that didn't stop her wishing he could come home so they could be a family again.

She hadn't had a letter from him either. Not for weeks now. He wrote to each of them every week, although often the letters came all together, weeks apart. Always chirpy and upbeat. Never mentioning anything to give them any cause for concern. Ma read some of her letter to them and they did the same. It seemed to bring him closer. She kept telling herself it was because of postal delays. He was all right. He had to be all right. She couldn't bear it if he wasn't. He wasn't here because he'd missed the boat, or perhaps he couldn't get the promised leave. He'd have written she was sure, especially if he couldn't get leave. He'd have let them know.

She took a deep breath and, satisfied that everything was in order, looking elegant and refined, just as Ma would want it, she went upstairs to get William's birthday present.

Upstairs Violet glanced at her reflection in the long mirror in the bedroom she shared with Gabriel. Pale winter sunlight barely lit the room, peeking in through the brocade curtains. She tidied the bed, smoothing the bedspread over the rumpled disarray caused by the early morning visit of her children. The elegance and style of the room never failed to delight her. It was the room wherein she'd spent most of her honeymoon.

She sighed. She wished Gabriel could be here to see his children enjoying the gifts he'd had sent. It was over six months since his last leave and she missed him every day with every fibre of her body. Every day she awoke wishing he was lying beside her. Every day during their marriage she'd marvelled at her good fortune in marrying him, a man who clearly adored her. His wealthy family was an added bonus. If only he was here now…

She'd made herself a new dress, hoping he'd be home to see it. The velvet cross-over top, edged with white lace, hugged her bosom, buttoning at the side. The nipped-in waist flowed into a sleek but simple skirt that swished around her ankles. The style flattered her, and it had turned out quite well, but she worried about the colour. Red wasn't always a good choice with her mass of unruly auburn curls. She sighed and clipped a crystal tipped ornament into her hair. It would have to do.

She smiled at the thought of the day ahead. Her twins would be sixteen today. She remembered the day they were born and the wonder she'd felt holding them in her arms. The memory brought a warm glow of pleasure. Could it really be sixteen years ago?

She'd been sixteen when she'd run away with their father, that no-good Bert Shadwick the magician, who'd promised her the world. How long ago that seemed now.

The sound of a car drawing up outside drew her to the window. She beamed with pleasure when she saw her brother-in-law's car parked at the hotel entrance.

"They're here," she called to the children as she dashed past their doors and down the stairs.

She gathered the children, buzzing with excitement, in the hotel lobby. Silas, six foot tall and almost as wide, pushed the door open and Hope walked in. "You made it," Violet said, rushing to embrace her sister.

"Yes, and look who we've brought with us," Silas said, moving to one side.

Violet stopped short. Her jaw dropped as Gabriel stepped out from behind Silas. She gasped. Her heart leapt in her chest and she whooped with joy.

The children jumped up and down with delight. She ran to him and threw her arms around his neck. "Oh you came after all. I'm so glad. Why didn't you write? Why didn't you let me know? I was so afraid you wouldn't …"

She didn't get any further. Gabriel's lips on hers stopped any more chatter as he swept her off her feet. Everyone laughed and cheered. Joshua and Florence grabbed their father's legs, making it impossible for him to move. Rose and William stood beaming like two Cheshire cats.

Laughing, Gabriel put Violet down, gave Rose and William each a hug, picked up both his younger children and carried them into the bar where the lounge had been decorated with bunting and tinsel. A fire burned in the grate filling the room with its warmth. When he'd put his children down he wished William and Rose the best birthday ever.

"Now you're here I'm sure it will be," Rose said, her eyes shining.

"I wouldn't have missed your birthdays for anything," Gabriel said. "Certainly not a silly old war."

He sat in one of the overstuffed armchairs placed around the room. Low tables stood at convenient distances and pictures on the walls, depicting seascapes and summer beaches, gave the room a homely feel. Florence climbed onto his lap.

Hope kissed Rose and William on both cheeks while Violet greeted Hope's children. Rose took everyone's coat and then set about making coffee and tea. Violet perched on the arm of Gabriel's chair, wishing she could have him all to herself.

William went with Silas to bring in the luggage and the huge box of presents to go under the tree.

"Why didn't you let me know you were coming?" Violet said to Gabriel. "And how come you've arrived with Hope and Silas?"

He chuckled. "I only just managed to catch the boat," he said. "Then the train from Dover, but it was quite late last night and I knew I'd never get a train on Christmas Day so I telephoned Silas and he graciously came and picked me up from the station."

"I'm very grateful that he did," Violet said. She kissed him again, despite being in company. "Welcome home."

Over hot drinks and biscuits the conversation turned, as it usually did these days, to the war, how long it would last and how it was going. Gabriel didn't want to be drawn on the subject and Hope, Silas and the children were tired from the early start and the long journey. William helped them with their luggage and showed them to their rooms so they could settle in before lunch.

Gabriel, left with Violet and the children, wanted to know how they'd been getting on in his absence.

"I'm learning to knit," Florence said, her little voice filled with pride. "Mummy's teaching me. She knits socks for soldiers." She said it as though knitting socks for soldiers required an unimaginable level of skill, one she could only aspire to.

Gabriel smiled at Violet. "Socks for soldiers," he said. "You obviously have a hidden talent."

Violet giggled. With Gabriel at home her world had suddenly became bearable.

"I collected conkers," Joshua said, not wanting to be left out. "Hundreds and thousands of conkers." His eyes and arms spread wide to show Gabriel the enormity of his collection.

"Conkers?" Gabriel said. "I expect the munitions works were very grateful."

"Yes," Joshua said, warming to his theme. "They're going to use them to make...cord something." His brow furrowed.

"Cordite," Gabriel said. "Excellent. Well I'm happy to hear you've all been doing your bit while I've been away."

"You won't go away again will you, Daddy?" Florence asked.

"I'm afraid I have to," Gabriel said. "But not for long I hope. Then we'll all be together again in a safer, better world."

Violet forced a smile onto her face as her heart dropped. She knew how committed Gabriel was to the war effort. But if it took him away again she wasn't so sure she felt the same.

"And what about you, Rose?" he said. "How are you getting on?" He paused. "Sixteen. Quite the young lady these days I'll warrant."

"Rose helps me in the hotel," Violet said. "I don't know what I'd do without her." She knew Rose wanted to do more than help change beds and serve meals to the convalescing Officers in the hotel, but again the

24

thought of losing her wasn't one Violet was ready to contemplate.

Rose shrugged but her tight-lipped expression said more than words ever could.

"Come on now," Violet said, suddenly brightening. "Let's get you upstairs and freshened-up for the Christmas festivities. Plenty of time for the rest when you've settled in."

When Violet got Gabriel upstairs it wasn't just freshening-up she had in mind. Her heart raced with anticipation as she said, "I've missed you so." She melted into his arms under the fierce heat of his kisses.

"I've waited so long," he said.

"Me too."

"What about dinner? Our guests?" he said between kisses.

Violet gave a throaty laugh. "Rose can manage dinner and I'm sure our guests will find plenty to entertain them."

"I expect you're right," Gabriel said as he watched her unbutton her dress.

Chapter Four

It didn't take long for the guests to settle in and they were soon downstairs again. Rose put the pheasant in to roast, with the vegetable to cook slowly, following Martha's instructions. The weather being dry and bright, William persuaded Silas to take him for a short drive in his new motor car. Hope and her children, having been in the car for the long drive from London, welcomed a chance to stretch their legs when Rose suggested a walk on the beach while the dinner cooked.

"I can take my football," Joshua said. "Sean can play with me with it." Rose wasn't sure how much of an opponent Hope's six-year-old son would be for Joshua, but agreed to the ball being taken.

Stepping out into the cold, sharp air Rose breathed it in, finding it bracing after the snug stuffiness of the hotel. Traces of frost iced the branches of the trees, but the sky was clear and bright. The children ran, helter-skelter down to the beach. They didn't seem to feel the cold. Rose and Hope stood watching from above. Several couples, well wrapped up against the wind, walked arm in arm along the Promenade. They nodded to Rose as they passed.

Olivia, who Rose thought quite mature for her nine years, was happy to play with Florence and help her collect shells while the boys ran about, shouting and laughing, lost in their game.

They stood watching for a while, Rose shouting encouragement to the boys when the breeze took their ball out of reach, then Hope said, "It's very peaceful here. You're very lucky. In London the streets seem to be filled with soldiers, there are shortages and everyone's afraid of the bombings."

Rose gazed across the water, the summer blue turned winter grey. She sighed. "It's only quiet because all the men have gone," she said. "The town feels empty and deserted now, as though it's holding its breath, waiting to see what happens next."

Hope brushed a curl of blonde hair that had escaped from under her hat across her forehead. "And you, Rose. Are you holding your breath to see what happens next?"

Rose laughed. "I suppose I am," she said. "I'm glad Pa's back, even if it's only for a little while. It will be like old times again."

"Yes. I can see how happy you all are to see him," Hope said.

"We're happy to see you too," Rose said. "It's a shame Peter couldn't get leave and come too. I would have loved to see him."

"Me too," Hope said. "I miss him every day. I console myself with the thought that he's doing his duty as he sees it. It's what he wanted." She shivered. "Come on, it's getting a little chilly out here and I expect you need to get on with the dinner."

They were about to head back when a man and his dog came onto the beach. The dog started barking and ran after Joshua's ball, trying to catch it in his mouth but only succeeding in sending it bouncing further away.

The man ran after him. "Brutus, come here," he called but the dog took no notice, continuing to run after the bouncing ball.

Joshua caught up with him just as the ball bounced into the sea. He caught the dog by the collar and the man, breathing heavily as he reached him, clipped the lead onto it. "I'm sorry," he said. "He doesn't usually run away."

Sean came up. "Can we pet him?" he asked, holding out his hand to stroke the dog.

The man smiled. "Yes, of course."

Sean stroked the dog's head and ruffled his ears. "We had a dog once," he said. "But he died."

By this time Rose and Hope had joined them on the beach.

"Peter's dog, Patch?" Rose asked, remembering the puppy Silas bought for Peter shortly after they'd taken him in. It had been his constant companion and meant the world to him.

"Yes," Hope said. "Very sad. He pined terribly when Peter left. Wouldn't eat or anything, just sat by the door waiting for him to come home. One day he escaped and ran out into the road. A car hit him. We buried him in the garden."

"Does Peter know?" She knew he'd be devastated.

"Yes. The most difficult letter I've ever had to write." Hope shivered in the cold.

Rose would have loved to talk more and hear about Peter and how he was getting on, but Hope was right. A stiff breeze off the sea brought an icy chill. "Come on, children," she called. "Best get back or dinner will be ruined."

Joshua collected his ball and the children came scampering back. Rose wished everything in life could be as easy.

By the time they returned to the hotel Violet and Gabriel were downstairs, so Rose went to the kitchen to see to the meal while Violet poured everyone a pre-dinner drink.

Rose had timed the cooking to perfection, which, as Hope pointed out was something Violet had been singularly unable to master when they shared a home.

"Pheasant?" Hope said. "I didn't know you could still get game birds. This is a real treat."

"Gabriel's father sent them," Violet said. "Together with all the vegetables you see on the table."

"Really? How kind of him," Silas said.

After the meal and a dessert of plum pudding, brandy sauce and mince pies prepared by Martha, they retired to the lounge for coffee and brandy.

William gathered up the gifts from under the tree and took them in. It being Rose and William's birthday they were first to receive their presents.

"Should I make a speech?" William asked.

Everyone laughed.

"Better not," Violet said. "Not until you've opened your presents."

"Well, it's a truly momentous occasion," he said. "Not every day that you turn sixteen."

"That's true," Gabriel said. "I think that calls for champagne." He went behind the bar and returned with two bottles of champagne in a cooler with ice. "I guessed we might be needing these," he said.

"Wow! I don't know how you managed it," William said. "But it's most welcome."

"Silas helped," Gabriel admitted. He poured everyone, except the young children, a glass.

Rose was first to open her gifts. She could hardly breathe when she saw the delicate silver locket engraved with a rosebud from Violet and Gabriel. It was the loveliest thing she'd ever seen. "Oh, it's beautiful," she said, opening it. Inside there were pictures of Violet and Gabriel taken on their fifth wedding anniversary. "Thank you. I'll cherish it always." William stood and fastened it around her neck.

William gave her a brooch made of rose-quartz in the shape of a rose. "I hope you like it," he said.

"I love it," she said, as she pinned it onto her dress. "It's just the thing. You must have gone to a great deal of trouble to find it." William blushed. She leaned over and planted a kiss on his cheek and he blushed even more. "It's wonderful," she said. "How clever of you."

Hope and Silas had bought her pearl earrings and Florence and Joshua gave her a writing set with paper, envelopes and a pen.

"No excuse for not writing now," Gabriel said.

Rose laughed. "I'll write twice a week from now on," she said.

Then William opened his gift from Rose. He looked a little puzzled at first, until he realised what it was. "It's a dummy," he said. "A ventriloquist's dummy." His eyes shone with delight. "Oh Rose, it's amazing. Where on earth did you get it?"

Rose's heart swelled with happiness seeing William with the gift she'd chosen. "I had him made specially," she said. "He's called Amos Little. I thought you might like him."

"Like him? I love him." He looked like a ten-year-old kid again as he put his hand up under the dummy's jumper and worked his mouth. "Thank you, Aunty Rose," the dummy said.

Everyone, except Violet, laughed.

William leaned over and kissed Rose's cheek. "Thank you. Now I'll be able to entertain the troops."

"You'll need a lot more practice," Violet said. "I saw your lips move." She was the only one in the room who didn't appear to be enjoying William's enthusiasm.

Violet and Gabriel gave him a model of their boat, the *Violet Rose*, which was moored in the harbour.

"It's a beauty," William said. "You've gone to a lot of trouble."

"Well, we know you love the boat," Gabriel said. "I thought you'd like it."

"I do," William said holding it up to admire it. "It's just like her. Look, it's even got the propellers that go round." He flicked them to show how they moved. "Thank you, I'll treasure it." A broad grin stretched across his face.

Hope and Silas gave him a compendium of games and Joshua and Florence a copy of *King Solomon's Mines*.

Florence got a china tea-set from Hope and Silas and Joshua a wind-up truck. They'd bought Violet some expensive soaps and Gabriel a silver lighter engraved with his regimental crest.

Violet had bought gifts from the local craftsmen; an amethyst brooch for Hope and a pearl tie pin for Silas. She gave Olivia a bead bracelet and Sean a wooden truck.

"Oh, and Peter sent these." Hope handed packages to William and Rose. When they tore off the paper they found each had a sketch in a silver frame. "I had them framed," Hope said.

Rose's showed a young girl sitting on a swing. She had a delicate face framed by a mass of dark auburn curls. William's showed a young boy with blonde hair and blue eyes, dressed in a sailor suit sailing a boat on a pond.

Rose laughed. "They're delightful," she said. "So clever of him. He must have drawn them from memory."

"I doubt his memory is that good," William said, "although the boy does look familiar."

"He always enjoyed the holidays he spent with you and Rose," Hope said. "Things like that stick in your mind. Pleasant things."

"I must write and thank him," Rose said and felt a flush of pleasure at the thought.

The afternoon sped by in a flurry of wrapping paper and gasps of delight. Dusk fell, the blinds had to be drawn and the lights put on before the gift giving and coffee and brandy were finished and they were onto the champagne. Hope offered to help Violet clear up. "It won't take long if we both do it," she said.

"I'll help," Rose said jumping up to start collecting up the dirty crockery.

"You should be excused duties," Hope said. "It's your birthday."

Rose laughed. "I don't mind," she said. "Happy to help," and she was. It wouldn't have felt right, sitting upstairs with the men while her mother and aunt did the dishes.

Chapter Five

Rose hummed to herself as she collected the dishes in the restaurant and sent them down in the dumb waiter to be unloaded and washed up. It had been a good meal, everyone said so and she was pleased for Ma who'd gone to so much trouble.

She'd been overwhelmed with the generosity of the gifts she'd received too. She touched the locket that hung around her neck and the brooch William gave her. She was so lucky to have such a lovely, generous family.

Downstairs in the kitchen she found Hope unloading the dirty crockery while Violet watched.

"I'm sorry I gave the staff the day off," Violet said when she saw the pile of washing-up. Hope laughed. "Don't worry, we'll soon make short work of it between us," she said.

Rose filled the sink with hot water and plunged the dishes in. Reluctantly Violet picked up a drying cloth and handed another one to Hope.

"It was a lovely dinner, Rose," Hope said. "You're a very good cook."

"Martha prepared it all," Violet said. "Rose only had to put it in the oven."

Rose forced a smile to her lips. What would Ma know about what she'd had to do? The kitchen was the least likely place she'd ever be found. "It was no trouble," she said, placing a dripping plate on the draining board.

Her ears pricked up when she heard Violet ask, "How's Peter? Have you heard from him lately?"

"He's well, I think," Hope said. "He writes. Not as often as I'd like of course." She picked up the wet plate and started to dry it. "He seems to have settled down and made friends. His letters are chatty, but then they would be wouldn't they. They're all censored so I don't suppose we're getting the true story."

"No. I think you're right," Violet said, picking up the next wet plate. "From what we hear from the Officers who come here it's hardly a picnic."

"Do you get many seriously wounded?"

"No. The ones who come here are well on the road to recovery. Mostly injuries to arms, legs, feet and fingers. They only stay until the Medical Board decide whether they're fit enough to send back or should be invalided out and sent home." She handed the plate back to Rose. "You missed a bit."

Rose took the plate and washed it again.

They continued with the washing and drying up, Hope and Violet stacking the plates on the side to be put away later. The only sounds the swishing of the water and clinking of the crockery.

"William's turned into a fine young man," Hope said after a while. "You must be very proud of him."

Violet shrugged. "Of course I am, but I'm afraid he may be falling into bad company. I swear I've smelt drink on his breath when he's come in from patrol. It's his friend Barney Braithwaite. I think he's a bad influence."

"Barney's joined a merchant ship. He wants William to go with him," Rose said and then immediately wished she hadn't.

"What!" Violet's voice rose several octaves. "A merchant ship? But he can't. He's far too young."

Rose shrugged. "They're taking them young these days," she said, plunging another pile of plates into the water. "William told me himself."

Violet threw her tea towel down. "We'll see about that," she said and stormed out.

"Oh Lord. What have I done?" Rose said, pulling her hands out of the water.

"Quick, go after her," Hope said, handing Rose a towel. "Catch her before she confronts William in front of everyone."

Rose ran out after Violet, drying her hands as she went. Upstairs everyone had moved to the ballroom, which was used for Saturday concerts for the Officers. Rose caught up with Violet just as she was about to open the door and rush in. She grabbed her arm. "Don't, Ma. It's his birthday. Don't spoil it for him."

Violet glared at her.

Rose looked through the round glass window in the door and saw William sitting on a stool in front of the stage with Amos on his knee. The children sat on the floor in a semicircle in front of him. Silas and Gabriel were at each end of the half-circle, sitting on chairs and obviously joining in with the performance. A burst of laughter and clapping reached her ears as he worked the dummy making it speak to the audience. Violet must have seen it too.

Rose watched Violet's anger being held in check and replaced by narrowed eyes and clenched jaw determination.

"I'm sorry. I shouldn't have told you," Rose said. She felt terrible. Although William hadn't said it was a secret she felt sure he'd be mad at her for telling Ma.

Violet took a deep breath. "I'm glad you did," she said. "There's no way he's going to join the merchant navy. I won't have it. I won't." Rose could almost feel her stamping her foot with rage.

Rose felt more in control now. "Perhaps Pa can have a word with him?" she said. "He'll listen to Pa."

"Well he certainly won't listen to me," Violet said, but she backed away from the door. She looked torn between going in to confront William and leaving it, as Rose suggested, to Gabriel.

She glanced again at Rose. "Thank you for telling me. Perhaps you're right. Now is not the time. I'll get Pa to talk to him. Get that silly idea out of his head." She glanced through the window into the hall. "You might as well go in and watch. After all you bought him the damned dummy thing."

"Amos. That's what he's called. Amos Little."

Violet shrugged and walked away.

Downstairs in the kitchen Hope was finishing the dishes. Violet picked up the tea towel.

"Everything all right?" Hope asked.

"Not really."

Hope sighed, her shoulders slumped. "He's sixteen, Violet. You can't keep him home forever. Not these days."

"I know, but I worry about him." She picked a plate off the draining board but made no attempt to dry it. "Do you know what he was doing up there? He's in the hall with that ventriloquist's dummy entertaining the children."

Hope looked bemused. "So?"

"Seeing him there…" she drew a breath, "Suddenly I saw his father, Bert Shadwick. I can tell you, my stomach turned over."

The twins had never met their father. The family never spoke of him. It had all happened so long ago she'd put it behind her, but, memories, like bad dreams, often return to haunt you. To Violet, seeing William turning into Bert would be her worst nightmare coming true. She half-wiped the plate but didn't let it go. "He's so like him, same flop of blonde hair, same innocent blue eyes and devastating charm." She slammed the plate onto the side table, almost breaking it. "And with starting to drink… Oh Hope! Supposing he turns out like Bert? I couldn't bear it. I really couldn't."

Hope shook her head. "William's nothing like Bert," she said. "Bert Shadwick was a charlatan. A conman, a seedy little man with even seedier ideas. William's nothing like that. He's honest and open, with a lovely nature. A touch of stubbornness perhaps, which I expect he gets from you, and a suggestion of dash, but he's not like Bert at all." She put another plate on the draining board.

"Honest and open? So that's why Rose had to tell me about him joining the merchant navy?"

"She didn't exactly say that, did she?" Hope said. "She merely said his friend had joined up and wanted William to go with him. Not the same thing is it?"

Violet huffed. She hadn't always got on well with her sister, but since they'd both married and had children she'd come to appreciate Hope's down-to-earth good sense and practicality; a virtue she freely admitted she may sometimes lack. Still, why did she always have to be so infuriatingly right.

Hope stopped what she was doing. "They're his children but you and Gabriel brought them up and they're a credit to you. You should be proud of them both."

Violet smiled, her bad temper evaporated. Hope was right. William could be a little reckless and Rose too timid for Violet's liking, but they were nothing like Bert. She was proud of them both.

"And as for joining the merchant navy, how old were you when you ran off with Bert?"

Violet blushed. "Sixteen," she said, "but that was different. I was in love." She could almost hear Hope's unspoken response 'yes, and look how that turned out'.

"Perhaps the twins are more like you than you think," Hope said.

Violet put her tea towel down. "Leave the rest," she said. "We might as well go and join them upstairs."

As they went up the stairs she realised Hope had seen something she'd failed to see, or at least failed to acknowledge. Her twins were growing up with minds of their own.

Things didn't get any better later that evening when they were sitting in the lounge after the children had gone to bed. William produced a pack of cards and started showing them some tricks to entertain them.

"Where did you learn to do that?" Violet snapped, trying but failing to keep the ice out of her voice.

A sudden silence filled the room. Everyone stared at her.

Baffled, William said, "I found a book of magic tricks in the local bookshop. I've been practising. It's just a bit of fun. Not doing any harm am I?"

Violet drew a deep breath.

"He's quite good for an amateur," Hope said. "But he's got a long way to go to be as good as Silas's sister, Dexi."

Everyone laughed. Silas's sister Esmé, got her nickname Dexi due her dexterity with cards. Playing poker with Dexi had been a big part of the attraction in

Silas's gentlemen's club. Now she ran her own casino in Paris. "As he says, Violet. Just a bit of fun."

Violet let out her breath. "He obviously has too much time on his hands," she said.

Chapter Six

Rose was glad to have Pa home. If anyone could talk Ma into letting her go to London to train as a nurse it was Pa. With him already serving he was bound to be on her side. At breakfast the next morning she was down in the kitchen early and had already made a start on setting the table when Gabriel came down.

"You're an early bird too," he said when he saw her. "I thought I'd get out and take a walk along the front. You have no idea how much I've missed it. Seeing the sea every morning, hearing the screech of gulls and feeling the wind in my face."

"I'll come with you," Rose said seizing the opportunity to talk to him alone. "Is Ma not up yet?"

Gabriel laughed. "No. I fear she may be some time." He glanced at her. "You'll need a coat."

She ran and got her coat and hat, then linked her arm through his. It gave her a warm, comfortable feeling to be walking along with him. A stiff breeze whipped the waves into breakers that crashed on the shore. She tied the scarf holding her hat tighter under her chin and breathed in the bracing air. They walked for a while in silence, each lost in their own thoughts, until he stopped and leaned on the railings.

"I've missed this," he said. "From here the war seems so far away you could almost forget it's happening. It's a different world, Rose. A very different world."

"But one I want to be part of," she said. "I expect Ma's told you about me wanting to train as a nurse."

He turned around, still leaning on the rail. "No. She hasn't mentioned it."

Rose sighed. Ma had obviously decided to ignore her wishes, just as she ignored anything she didn't agree with. "I'm sixteen now," she said. "Old enough to leave home. I've been working with the VADs – Voluntary Aid Detachment – but I want to do more. If I trained as a nurse I could do something really useful."

"And you want me to persuade your mother that it would be a good thing?"

"Yes. She'll listen to you. Please, Pa."

Gabriel turned to gaze out over the water. He took a deep breath. "It's a big thing, leaving home at your age. You're still very young. Ma loves you deeply. She wants the very best for you. I'm not sure being a nurse…"

"Nurses are needed. You must know that. Please think about it, Pa. I want to do something useful with my life not…" her voice faded away. She couldn't say 'not spend it, changing sheets and serving dinners'. That would negate everything he'd aimed for in life. Running the luxury hotel owned by his father on the seafront had been his ambition and he'd excelled at it. She couldn't pour scorn on that. "Please think about it, Pa," she said.

He stood up and started to walk on. She skipped to catch up and put her arm back through his.

"I'm not sure you've thought it through," he said. "But I will think on it. I'll want to hear what your mother has to say. We have to abide by her wishes."

Rose nodded. She couldn't see why they always had to 'abide by her wishes', but she loved Pa, trusted him and had a feeling that he possibly did know the best way to get round Ma.

Walking along with him, watching his face as he took in all the sights, the salty smell of the restless sea and sound of the waves on the shore, she came to appreciate how attached he was to the place he'd made their home. It was as though they were all part of it. He'd come back to a place and people that represented everything he held dear and a way of life he was prepared to go to war to preserve. Perhaps he didn't want it to change, or couldn't understand why she'd want to leave it.

"This will always be my home," she said gazing around. "No matter how far I travel I'll always come back to it." Her glance embraced the sea and the sky. "Perhaps going away will make it feel even dearer to me."

Gabriel stopped to stare at her. He smiled and pride filled his eyes. "You've a lot more going on in that head of yours than meets the eye," he said. "I wonder if your mother realises that."

Back at the hotel by the time Violet made it down to breakfast Hope had seen to all the children. They'd breakfasted and been sent up the top floor playroom.

"You shouldn't have to do that," Violet said. "Where's Rose?"

"She's gone out with Gabriel," Hope said. "Anyway, I don't mind. I enjoy seeing the children eat well. Can I get you something?"

"Just tea please," Violet said. "I don't expect we'll see William any time soon. I believe he was quite late last night."

William and Rose had invited friends to join them in the bar for birthday drinks last evening. It was almost three in the morning when Violet heard the party break up and the guests depart.

"Have you said anything to Gabriel about William wanting to go to sea?" Hope asked.

Violet shook her head. "Not yet." A wide grin filled her face. "We were far too busy last night making up for lost time." She sipped the tea Hope handed her. "I'll speak to him today," she said, putting the cup down and glancing at her sister. "You think I'm wrong to stop him?"

Hope shrugged and poured herself a cup of tea from the big brown pot. "Not wrong to try I suppose, I just remember trying to stop you running away when you were sixteen. It didn't work did it?"

Violet sighed. "But a merchant ship, Hope. He could be away for years." Then she recalled that Hope's adopted son, Peter, was away fighting a war from which he may never return and she felt a stab of guilt so fierce it tied her stomach in knots.

"Did you try to stop Peter joining up?" she asked.

Hope sighed. "I didn't want him to go, but he's eighteen. I think he saw it as his duty, and with all his friends volunteering I didn't want him to stand out as being any different." She put her teacup on its saucer. "It was his choice."

"And you're proud of him, I mean, glad he went?"

"I'd have been proud of him whatever he did."

They were interrupted by the return of Rose and Gabriel who were both ready for a hearty breakfast.

"I'll leave you to it," Hope said, "and see if I can tempt Silas to a walk along the Promenade now the sun's come up."

"I'll go and see if any of the children want to go with you," Violet said. "The wind's blowing up and there may be rain later so now would be the best time to go." She wanted to talk to Gabriel before

43

confronting William. She hoped he'd support her and together they'd have a better chance of keeping him at home.

Rose and Gabriel had finished breakfast when William appeared looking the worse for wear. Rose went and poured him a cup of coffee from the pot keeping warm on the stove.

"Good night?" Gabriel asked.

William grinned. "The best ever," he said. Rose handed him the coffee. "I don't know how you do it, Rose. You were as late as me and yet you're up at crack of dawn looking as fresh as a daisy."

"I didn't overdo the celebration," she said. "What you need is a good old fashioned fry-up."

He blanched. "Just coffee's fine."

Gabriel laughed and slapped William on the back. "I'll leave you in Rose's capable hands," he said and chuckled as he went out.

Rose poured herself a cup of tea and sat next to her brother. "I expect Ma will want to have a word with you later," she said.

He groaned. "Can't a chap have a little too much on his birthday without an inquest afterwards?"

"It's not that," she said. "I'm sorry. I let slip about Barney joining the merchant navy and wanting you to go with him. Ma didn't take it too well."

William frowned. "If Ma had her way we'd both be here forever. She still thinks we're five years old. She had to know sooner or later. Now's as good a time as any."

"You're not cross then?"

"How can I be cross with you, Rose? You're the dearest, sweetest thing. No. I was going to tell her myself so you did me a favour. And with Pa home it'll come easier. At least he'll understand."

Upstairs Violet was sorting through some magazines for Hope to take home when Gabriel walked in. She greeted him with a kiss. He slipped his arm around her waist and pulled her close for another kiss, holding her as though he never wanted to let her go. It was a good feeling to be held so close.

"I want to talk to you about William," she whispered in his ear. "Rose tells me he's thinking of joining a merchant ship. I want you to talk him out of it." She brushed her lips against his cheek.

He let her go and led her to the settee. They both sat. "It's not just William we need to talk about," he said. "Rose has been telling me she wants to train as a nurse."

Violet said nothing but thoughts raced through her brain like wild hares. Her children were growing up and she didn't want to lose them. In her heart she knew she was being unreasonable. She vividly remembered her determination when she was sixteen to follow her dream of being on the stage. It hadn't turned out well for her, but she wouldn't have missed those days, bad as they were, for anything. She'd made mistakes and learned from them. They'd made her the person she'd become. William and Rose would make mistakes too, she couldn't protect them forever, or live their lives for them. "You think I should let them go?" she said.

"I think it would be foolish to try to stop them. Better they go with your blessing than without."

"But a merchant ship, dearest? We're losing cargos every day."

"William is an excellent sailor. He understands the sea and all its moods. It's all he's ever wanted."

Violet recalled William's enthusiasm for the sea while he was growing up. Messing about on boats was his favourite pastime. "That's no reason to allow him to sign his life away on a merchant ship," she said.

Gabriel took her hand and kissed it. "I know you only want what's best for him, but he's grown up. We live in uncertain times. Keeping him here when all his friends are joining up. He may come to resent it."

Violet hesitated. She didn't want William or Rose to go away at all, but she wasn't stupid. With everyone else, all their friends' children going to war it was inevitable.

"Would you be happier if it was a Naval ship?" Gabriel asked.

Hope blossomed in her heart. "Infinitely," she said. "Then at least he'd be with people who'd be responsible for him. He'd have proper training, get leave and we'd know where he was. I could be proud of him then."

Gabriel smiled. "The discipline wouldn't do him any harm either," he said. "I have a friend in the Admiralty. We were at Eton together. I'll see what I can do."

"Will they take him so young?"

"I understand they're not too fussy about checking a recruit's age these days. Lots of boys younger than William have been taken on."

"But he's only just sixteen. Can't it wait? Ask if he'll take him when he's eighteen. Then we'll be able to promise something in the future which may keep him home. Do you think?"

Gabriel pouted. "I'll try," he said. "But if William's adamant…"

"Then a career in the Navy is better than the alternative." She had to smile at the thought of William as a dashing Naval Officer. He'd certainly set the ladies' hearts aflutter.

"What about Rose?" Gabriel asked.

Violet sighed. "Rose is capable of so much more than she's doing now. She's bright and hard-working. In a few years' time she could be running this hotel, or one like it. Nursing would be a waste of her talents."

"It's what she wants, my love. Nursing is a noble profession, especially now. I've been there. I've seen the difference those nurses make. They can't cure the wounded, or save their lives, no one can. But they can comfort them, hold their hands and give them some peace. I've nothing but the greatest admiration for anyone who can do that and I'd hope, God forbid, if it happened to me there'd be someone like Rose there to help me through it."

Violet sat silent. The idea of anything bad happening to Gabriel haunted her. She clung on to the one thought that helped her through this terrible time. "The war won't last forever. What will she do then?"

"As you've seen for yourself, men coming back from the war will have life-changing injuries. They'll always need people like Rose to care for them."

"I was hoping to introduce her to some eligible young man who'd give her a home and provide a comfortable living. Making a good marriage is still the best way for a young girl to secure her future."

"I don't think Rose sees marriage and children as her salvation. She wants to see the world before she settles down," Gabriel said.

"But bed baths and slop pans? It's not what I envisioned for her."

"It's what she wants."

"I don't know," Violet said. "It's such a big step and to lose them both…" She couldn't contemplate the loss but even then, at the back of her mind she knew there were families who'd lost so much more. "Am I being selfish wanting to keep them here? Keep them safe?"

"No, my darling. You're being like every mother in the universe. You could keep them here and they'd be safe, but what sort of fenced-in life would that be? And they wouldn't thank you for it."

Violet took a deep breath. Gabriel was right. They'd go sooner or later. They were old enough now and had minds of their own. As he said, better to go with her blessing than without.

Chapter Seven

Later that morning Gabriel helped Violet do a stock-take in the bar.

"I'm impressed you manage to keep the bar so well stocked," he said. "Especially with supplies being so difficult."

Violet beamed. "I grew up in a pub," she said. "It's second nature to me." Her smile told him she was pleased he'd noticed.

They'd almost finished when Hope and Silas arrived back from their walk. Despite the sun the day was cold. A light rain blew in from the sea and clouds were gathering along the horizon. "How was your walk?" Violet asked, seeing them windblown with rosy cheeks.

"Bracing," Silas said. "Any hot coffee?"

Violet laughed. "Coming up," she said.

The children had declined the offer of a walk, preferring to play with their new toys and Violet was glad she didn't have wet clothes and chilly children to deal with. Coffee was served in the bar area with warm-from-the-oven scones Rose had made.

William and Rose joined them.

"We saw the fishing boats out at sea," Silas said. "I wouldn't fancy that job in this weather."

"That'll be the crabbers," William said. "They'll be out lifting their pots. They won't be out far."

"Even so I'll stick to summer sailing," Silas said. "I expect your boat's laid-up for winter."

"No, not at all," William said. "This time of year the fishing's even better. Talking of which, can I take Uncle Silas to see *Violet Rose*? He hasn't seen her yet. She's just like the model Ma and Pa gave me."

"A new boat?" Silas said.

"Yes. A forty-footer with an inboard engine. Pa bought her last summer but he's hardly had a chance to go out in her."

"Yes. She's my pride and joy," Gabriel said. "I wish I'd been around more instead of leaving her to William who's managed to make the most of her."

"She goes like a dream," William said. "I wish I could show you."

"I'm not sure that's such a good idea," Violet said. "It's a bit blowy and I do believe it's starting to rain again. Won't be much fun getting soaked. Anyway it'll be too rough."

"We'd only be in the harbour, Ma. We won't be taking her out," he paused, "unless…" he looked questioningly at Gabriel.

Gabriel chuckled. "Ma's right. The weather's not certain. It wouldn't be much fun if a storm does blow up. Perhaps we'll go out another day. We could go to the harbour, just for a look though. I wouldn't mind seeing her again and we might even be able to pick up a few lobsters for tea if the crabbers have been out."

"I'll drive us up there in the car if you like," Silas said putting his coffee cup down.

"It's almost time for lunch," Violet said. "Perhaps this afternoon then."

Over a lunch of cold cuts of ham, various cheeses, pickles, herring paste and wedges of bread and butter they talked about boats, escapades, people they knew and memories of shared holidays and jaunts. Gabriel noticed how Violet blossomed in company. Seeing everyone sitting around the table, he felt more at ease and happier than he had in a long time.

After lunch Gabriel, Silas and William set off in Silas's car for the harbour. "Don't be out too long," Violet said.

Gabriel kissed her. "Don't worry, we won't be."

After a short drive they arrived at the harbour. The earlier rain had eased off although the wind had picked up, rattling the lanyards against masts and swelling the rolling waves. Silas parked by the harbour master's office. Seeing them the harbour master came out. He looked delighted to see Gabriel and shook his hand. "How long are you home for?" he asked.

"Only until the end of the week," Gabriel said.

"Are you going out today?"

"No. Maybe tomorrow if the wind drops. It's a bit breezy today. Just want to have a look over the boat and make sure William's been taking good care of her."

The harbour master laughed. "Oh he's done that all right. Never seen anyone so fussed about a vessel," he said. "Good to see you any rate." He went back into his office.

Gabriel, Silas and William walked to where *Violet Rose* was moored.

"She's a beauty," Silas said, as Gabriel helped him aboard. The three of them managed to sit comfortably in the cabin. "Very nice," Silas said, gazing around.

"Come and see the motor," William said, which to him was the most interesting thing about the boat.

They were admiring the motor set below deck and the shaft that turned the propeller when the sound of a loud siren filled the air.

"Air raid? In daylight?" Silas said. Glancing up at the sky.

"No that's for the lifeboat," Gabriel said. He jumped out of the boat and ran along the harbour wall, searching the horizon. The dying embers of a flare dropped into the sea about five miles north of the harbour. An elderly man in oilskins came running along the jetty. Gabriel recognised him as the coxswain of the lifeboat. He hurried back to the boat.

"There's a yawl gone aground on the rocks up by the point," the coxswain shouted, his wind-burnt face creased with concern. "Can you get us there?"

"Erm." Gabriel only hesitated for a second. Living by the sea for the last ten years he knew the drill. Anyone in trouble you helped out, no matter who or what. He'd volunteered with the lifeboats in his early days. Now, since the war, with the young men all gone, the lifeboat depended on the few elderly fishermen left and today there were none of them about. To launch the lifeboat would take at least an hour. They were in the boat. They could be round the point in less than half that time. "Can you show us where?"

"Aye."

"Cast us off then."

The coxswain released the ropes holding the boat and by the time he jumped aboard a grinning William had the motor running. As the boat moved away from the jetty Gabriel fetched oilskins from the cabin. He gave some to Silas. "You'll be needing these," he said as he pulled his own on.

Outside the harbour waves crashed against the side of the boat, the sea a wind-whipped winter grey. Gabriel felt a stomach churning stab of fear as they were hit by a wave or thrown around in a swirling surge of water, but William skilfully guided them through it. Distant thunder rolled in the sky and sudden slews of sleeting rain, carried on the wind, lashed against the cabin walls.

They'd been going about fifteen minutes, the coxswain scanning the sea through his binoculars and Gabriel, braced against the rail, gripping it and trying to hold back the nausea that threatened to rise up in his throat, doing the same, when the coxswain called out, "Over there!"

He pointed to where the upturned hull of a yacht lay, banging against the outcrop of rocks. "Can you get in nearer, lad?" he yelled at William.

"Tides coming in and there's a fierce current runs from above the point," William called back. "We'll be battling against it. Best to go further up and let the current bring us down."

"Oh aye," the coxswain said.

So they motored on past the rock, riding the waves, until William turned the boat about. As he turned a wave crashed against the side of the boat sending up a drenching shower of spray. The next wave crested and carried them back towards the wreck crashing against the rocks. Flotsam from the wreck floated around them. William cut the motor and they drifted closer until he dropped the anchor to stop them going further in.

The coxswain and Gabriel stood on deck by the rail, braced against the roll of the boat, scanning the sea until Gabriel saw a man in yellow oilskins clinging to a lump of wood with one arm while holding onto a boy with the other.

"There," he yelled, pointing them out.

Silas, standing next to him, lifted the lifebuoy from its fastenings and picked up the coil of throw line which he tied to the boat's rail. Gabriel kept his binoculars trained on the man and boy.

Silas braced himself, weighing the lifeline in his hand until he stood steady against the rail. The boat rolled and he almost lost his footing. He steadied himself again and waited until the boat rose on the swell, then, taking a breath, swung his arm back and threw the rope. The buoy on the end of the rope landed to the left of the man clinging to the wood and the sea took it further away carried on the backwash of a spent breaker.

The coxswain yelled something but his words were lost in the wind and crashing of the waves against the rocks. Gabriel heard Silas swear as he hauled the line back in and threw again. This time it went to the right and the sea took it close enough for the man to grab it.

Not for the first time in his life Gabriel was glad of Silas's size and strength. He could think of no one else who could have managed that throw. Together they hauled the line towards the boat with the man clinging on, dragging the boy with him. They'd come about halfway when the boy slipped from the man's grasp and floated away from him.

"Noooo!" Gabriel yelled.

The next thing he saw was William strip off his jacket and boots and dive into the sea. He watched in horror as William swam towards the boy who drifted further and further away. Gabriel stood, frozen to the spot, his heart in his mouth.

"We've got 'im," the coxswain called as he helped Silas pull the man onto the deck in the descending darkness, the rain lashing their faces.

Gabriel stood transfixed, his gaze on William's back as he swam towards the boy. His heart pounded and sickness swirled in his stomach. Twice he lost sight of him in the rolling waves and his heart faltered. He could hardly breathe.

Silas appeared next to him, resolute determination engraved on his face, his eyes narrowed in concentration. Intense but calm, he stood, braced against the rail, watching until William reached the boy and grabbed him, turning to swim back to the boat.

Gabriel held his breath as Silas waited for what seemed to him an agonising, frozen in time moment, until the boat rose again on the swell. He threw the line, perfectly timed and stunningly accurate. William grabbed the lifebuoy. Together they pulled him back to the boat. William handed the boy up first into their arms.

"I'll take 'im," the coxswain said. Gabriel and Silas pulled William onto the boat, where he lay shivering on the deck.

They helped William into the wheelhouse where the rescued man sat, wrapped in blankets, out of the wind and rain. The coxswain was rubbing life back into the boy's body. Silas helped William out of his wet clothes. Gabriel threw off his oilskins, wrenched off his jumper and wrestled William into it, rubbing his arms and body to bring back the circulation as he did so. He swaddled him in the blanket Silas handed him. "Damn fool," he said as he wrapped him up.

"Yes. But a brave one," Silas said.

Gabriel shook his head. His stomach churned. What if anything had happened to William? What if he'd been lost to the sea? How could he face his mother again? His heart still pounding from the shock, he lifted the anchor, started the motor and steered them all back to the harbour.

The man and boy were taken away in the ambulance the harbour master had called. The coxswain went with them. "You best come an' all," he said to William.

"I just want to go home and have a hot bath," William said. Rivulets of water ran down his face which was turning blue. He looked exhausted but the tots of medicinal rum kept on board for emergencies had revived him a little. In the freezing cold air Gabriel thought it best to get him indoors and dry as soon as possible. Silas drove a shivering William and a silent, thoughtful Gabriel, still in shock, back to the hotel.

Chapter Eight

Rose, who'd gone to her room to fetch her writing pad and pen for the thank you letters she had yet to write, saw the car draw up outside the hotel. "They're back," she called to Violet and Hope who were in the sitting room going over patterns for a possible new spring wardrobe.

"Better start dinner then," Violet said putting the patterns to one side. "We'll have time for a drink while it's cooking." They all went downstairs, arriving just as Gabriel and Silas walked in with a sorry looking William, still wrapped in the blanket.

Gasping with alarm, Violet rushed forward to help him. "What on earth…"

"William's just pulled a boy from the sea," Gabriel said. "Saved his life."

Violet stared at him. Shock had drained the colour from his face. Only Silas looked pleased with himself. "Bravest thing I've ever seen," he said. "You can be proud of him."

Violet looked from one to the other. They all looked bedraggled, but William worst of all. "Oh my darling boy," she said, going to hug him.

"I'm alright," William said brushing her off. "Just need to get dry and warm."

"I'll run you a bath," Rose said. She could see from her mother's face that Gabriel had some explaining to do and it wouldn't be easy. She'd blame him. She always did.

"Thanks." William said and went with Rose, leaving Gabriel and Silas to tell Violet and Hope what had happened.

Upstairs Rose started the bath, and went to fetch some clean clothes while William sat on the bathroom stool, still shivering. Rose brought him some fresh towels.

"Water's good and hot," she said. "You can tell me what happened afterwards." She turned the tap off. "Give me a call if you need anything. I'll just be next door."

"Thanks, Rose," William said. "Honest, I don't know what got into me. I just couldn't let that boy drown."

"You did the right thing," Rose said. "I'm proud of you and I'm sure Ma and Pa will be too, once they get over the shock."

"Aye, the shock. That water was a shock. Cold as a hoar frost it was. Still, all done now. I hope the lad's all right."

"If he is it'll be thanks to you," she said and left him to get on with his bath.

Downstairs Gabriel and Silas told Violet and Hope all about the rescue while sipping her best brandy. Violet could see they had no choice but to help out, it's what anyone would have done, but it didn't put her mind at rest regarding William's part in it.

"How could you let him?" she said. "He could have been drowned." Sickness fell over her at the thought.

"It all happened so quickly," Gabriel said. "I couldn't stop him."

She couldn't speak. She just stared at him, feeling utterly wretched.

He took her in his arms to comfort her. "William's been swimming in the sea since he was six," he said.

"He's the strongest swimmer I've ever known. And he saved that boy's life. That should count for something."

"You should be proud of him," Silas said.

"Oh I am," Violet said. "Of course I am." But she feared for his future. Being part of something like that would only reinforce his desire to go to sea and negate her argument that he was too young.

Over dinner with the children they talked some more about the rescue. "It was nothing." William chuckled with glee. "Just thought I'd go for a swim." Everyone laughed, except Violet who shuddered at the thought of what might have happened and his cavalier attitude towards it. It was just the sort of flippant, offhand remark Bert might have made when he'd successfully executed a particularly difficult trick.

"I couldn't have done what William did," Gabriel said. "I raise my glass to him."

Everyone raised their glasses. "To William," they all said.

By the time dinner was finished everyone was treating William like a real hero.

"He deserves it," Silas said.

Rose glowed with pleasure. In her eyes William had always been a hero.

Later, when Hope and Violet were alone Hope said, "You need have no worries about William turning into Bert. Bert would never have dived in the sea to save anyone. He'd be too busy taking bets on who would survive."

Violet laughed.

"He's headstrong and impulsive like you," Hope said. "But perhaps that's a good thing. From what I hear from the men fighting this dreadful war you're either quick or your dead. Quick's better."

Violet couldn't agree more.

The next morning Hope and Silas and their children were packing up ready for the journey home. They wanted to be back in London before the New Year. Rose was helping Olivia with her luggage when the doorbell rang. She opened the door and found the lifeboat coxswain and the Chief Coastguard Officer standing on the doorstep.

She showed them into the bar as Violet and Gabriel came down the stairs.

"How's the lad?" the coxswain asked. "Is he recovered?"

"Yes, thank you," Gabriel said. "Well, you can see for yourself." He sent Rose to fetch William while Violet offered their guests refreshments.

When William arrived he asked about the boy. "Is he going to be all right?"

"Yes, thanks to you," the coxswain said. "He's making a good recovery. The hospital are keeping him and his grandfather in for a day or two, else they'd be here themselves. They owe you a debt of gratitude."

"I'm just glad that they're all right and it wasn't a waste of effort."

"You're a brave lad," the Chief Officer said. "We could do with a few like you in the Service which brings me to the point of this call."

"So it wasn't to see how I was?"

"Not entirely, although we're both glad to see you looking so well. No. You may have heard that we've lost our Ward Officer and two Extramen. They're on minesweepers now. We're desperately short-handed.

I'm looking for replacements and, if you're interested, I'd be happy to sponsor you."

"What? Join the Coastguard?"

"If you've a mind to. It can provide a good career for someone like yourself." He paused. "You'd have to apply to the Admiralty, of course and there'd be an exam to pass…"

"I doubt that'll be a problem," Gabriel said, recalling his earlier conversation with Violet.

"He's only sixteen," Violet said.

The Chief Officer smiled. "So are a lot of lads, on ships and at the Front."

Violet looked chastened. "Would he be able to live at home?"

"At the beginning. There'll be training, he'll go away for that, but I'd be requesting a local posting at least at first. Until he got his sea legs."

"Would he have to go to sea?" Violet sounded worried.

"He'd be in the Naval Reserve. Could be called up at any time. That's not a problem is it?"

"We'll have to think about it," Violet said. "It's a big thing…"

"Aw, Ma," William said. "I'm going to leave home sooner or later."

"We don't have to decide today, do we?" Gabriel said. "We'll give it some thought and let you know."

The Chief Officer smiled. "That's fine. I'll just leave the papers here until you make up your mind." He took a large brown envelope out of his inside pocket and laid it on the table. "You'd be made very welcome, lad," he said to William.

Rose showed them out and when she returned she saw William had gone and so had the large brown envelope.

A few days later a letter arrived from Mr A. J. Davenport, the owner of the yawl. It read:

Dear Messrs Stone and Quirk and Master William Stone,

It is with heartfelt gratitude and humility that I write to you to express my undying thanks for so bravely rescuing myself and my grandson, following our ill-advised Boxing Day outing. My deepest and most sincere thanks and admiration go to you all, especially the lad who saved my grandson's life.

It's a debt I can never repay and one that will never be forgotten. If there's ever anything I can do for you, please don't hesitate to ask.

I hope you will accept these small tokens of my appreciation, although nothing will be enough to satisfactorily demonstrate the depth of my gratitude to you.

With my deepest regards and thanks,
Anthony J. Davenport.

Together with the letter there was a case of Scotch whisky '*for the gentlemen*', a bouquet of flowers '*for their wives*' and an engraved silver cigarette case, '*for the lad*'. The engraving said: '*Forever in your debt, AJD*'.

Gabriel immediately opened the whisky and William, grinning widely, shrugged as he put the cigarette case in his pocket. Rose could see how pleased he was.

By the time Gabriel returned to his regiment three days later he'd spoken to his chum at the Admiralty and William had been assured of a place on a training course in Portsmouth. He'd also persuaded Violet to allow Rose to apply for nursing training in London, provided she stayed with Hope and Silas and wrote home every week.

With a fresh intake of recovering Officers in the hotel Violet was kept busy fighting her own battles with the domineering Director of Voluntary Organisations, in charge of assigning VADs, and a Medical Officer whose sole aim was to return as many men as possible to the Western Front. Rose felt life returning to normal, at least for a little while.

William was the first to leave.

"Are you taking Amos?" Rose asked, seeing him being shoved into his rucksack.

"Of course," William said. "He's my mate. Can't leave him behind."

Rose laughed. William had been practising with the dummy most days and she could see him using it to entertain the other recruits. He'd never had any trouble making friends and she could see why.

"Promise you'll take care," she said.

"It's only a training course," he said. "No danger – yet."

It may be only a training course, Rose thought, but to her it was the beginning of something much bigger. They'd never been apart. "I'll miss you," she said.

His face shone with excitement, his blue eyes sparkled like a summer sky. She saw again the small inquisitive, chatterbox boy he used to be, always leading her into mischief. Now he was almost a man.

"I'll miss you too," he said. "Miss you hanging on to my coat tails stopping me doing anything foolish. You were always the sensible one."

She laughed. "I don't know about that," she said.

"I do." He kissed her cheek. She blushed with the sheer pleasure of it.

"You'll do," she said.

"You too." It was what they always said to each other whenever they went anywhere. Her heart almost burst.

"Well, can't hang around here," he said. "Come on."

Together they walked down the stairs, Rose trying to swallow the lump rising in her throat.

Downstairs he slung his rucksack on his back. He didn't want any fuss and he insisted on making his own way to the station. Rose knew that when he went part of her would go with him. He was her hero. She couldn't begrudge him the chance to do what he's always wanted and she was happy for him, but it didn't make the parting any easier.

He kissed Violet goodbye and hugged Rose. "I'll write as soon as I get there," he said. It was clear he was looking forward to the adventure and both Rose and Violet stood on the hotel steps watching him until he turned a corner out of sight.

Everything was changing. With Pa gone and now William the hotel would seem empty of joy, the best parts of her life gone with them.

Violet sighed. Rose wasn't the only one who'd just seen a huge part of her life walking away. She looked at Rose. "Tea and cake?" she said.

Rose smiled. "Tea and cake."

A few days later Rose received confirmation of her place on a training course at St Thomas' Hospital. A new excitement churned within her. This was her chance to do what she'd always wanted, make her own decisions and stand on her own two feet. She couldn't wait.

"Be careful, don't speak to anyone on the train and ask Aunty Hope to ring me as soon as you arrive," Violet said as she helped Rose pack the small suitcase she would take. She'd ordered a taxi to take her to the station.

Rose hugged her ma. "Don't worry, Ma," she said. "I can take care of myself."

"Yes. I'm sure you can." Violet hugged her again. Rose saw something in her eyes she'd never seen before. "You're a good girl, Rose," she said. "I don't think I've ever told you how proud I am of you."

"Thanks, Ma. I won't let you down."

"I know you won't. Now, hurry along. You don't want to miss that train."

Rose wasn't sure, but as she got into the taxi and turned back to wave, she could swear she saw her mother wipe away a tear.

Chapter Nine

When Rose arrived at Kings Cross the station thronged with military men either going to the Front or returning on leave with their clothes and boots still caked with Flanders' mud. She recalled what Hope had said about the streets being filled with soldiers. She made her way out through the crowds of women seeing them off or greeting them on their return. Her heart lifted when she saw Silas had come to meet her.

Driving through the constricted roads the honking of car horns added to the rattle of wheels and shouts of the carriage drivers vying for space on the crowded, narrow cobbles. Rose had forgotten how difficult it was to move through the busy, noisy, packed streets of London. The buildings looked different too; their windows boarded up and blacked out, several showed signs of bomb damage. It was very different from the peace and quiet of Great Yarmouth.

"Here we are," Silas said helping her out of the car and retrieving her luggage. "I know Hope is looking forward to seeing you."

Walking into Hope's house brought a flood of memories of holidays, outings and happy times. With their growing family Hope and Silas had moved into a four-storey town house in the city between Southwark and Blackfriars Bridges. It all seemed a long time ago.

Hope greeted her warmly. "I've put you in one of the front bedrooms," she said. "You'll have a view of the river."

"I'll take your luggage up," Silas said.

"We have to pretty much fend for ourselves these days," Hope said. "Daisy's working as a VAD at the Stepney Supply Depot. She mans the phones and even

Mrs H, the cook, does two days a week at the Seamen's Mission. Still, we manage well enough."

"Thank you. Ma said to telephone when I arrived."

"Of course. I'll ring her now. If you want to go and make yourself at home I'll put the kettle on. I expect you could do with a cup of tea after your journey."

Rose went up to the second floor room overlooking the river. She unpacked her case, putting the dresses she had brought into the wardrobe and the rest of her clothes into a chest of drawers next to an ottoman under a tall sash window. She glanced out. Hope was right it did give a good view of the river, but seeing it Rose couldn't help but compare it to the view of the sea and open sky from the hotel at home. Compared to the vast expanse of ocean the river looked overcast and grey, Its muddy brown water was crowded with boats going about their business. She could see the bridges and hear the noise of the traffic below. An atmosphere of urgency and importance permeated the air, a marked contrast to the peaceful slow pace of life at home.

She arranged her hair brushes, combs, pins and a perfume spray Violet had given her as a going away gift on the dressing table. Tables at either side of the double bed held electric lamps. She put her writing case and jewellery box in one of the dressing table drawers and gazed at her reflection in the centre of the three hinged mirrors.

She sighed. Hope had left fresh towels on the bed for her, so, before going downstairs she popped into the bathroom, splashed her face with water and washed her hands.

Downstairs Hope had tea with sandwiches and cakes spread out in the first floor drawing room also overlooking the river. Silas had gone back to work at his club, which had been turned into a retreat for officers on leave; somewhere they could enjoy a bit of rest and recreation before going back to the Front.

"Alice has taken Olivia and Sean to the pantomime with her children, but I'm sure they'll be back soon," Hope said, pouring Rose's tea. "Please help yourself to whatever you want."

Rose took several sandwiches. "So, how are Aunt Alice and Uncle John?" she asked. "I must call in and visit them while I'm in London. How are the children?"

Hope's brother John ran the Hope and Anchor pub, where the family grew up. Married to Alice they had four children.

"Oh you know Uncle John. Since the restriction on opening hours, the watering down of drinks and the ban on buying drinks for anyone else, takings are down. It's his livelihood so of course he's worried about it. Alice and the children are doing well."

"I expect the cousins are quite close," Rose said remembering how well Alice and John's children got on with Olivia and Sean.

"Oh yes. Well, they're all about the same age so have a lot in common," Hope said. "Like you, William and Peter." She handed Rose a cup of tea. "I expect you'll miss William won't you."

"I will," Rose said. "But he's doing what he always wanted and so am I. I'm sure he'll write, when he remembers."

Hope laughed. "Yes."

Later that evening Olivia and Sean returned home full of the pantomime. Dinner was a lively affair and Rose soon relaxed and felt at home in the convivial atmosphere. Any nerves she had about reporting to St Thomas' Hospital in the morning disappeared.

The next morning Rose arrived on Westminster Bridge just before nine. She stood for some time, just staring at the building that seemed to intimidate even the river it stood beside. Had she done the right thing, coming here? Was her mother right trying to stop her? She took a breath, pushed all her fears and doubts aside, straightened her back, squared her shoulders and strode across the road to the hospital.

Inside the distinctive hospital smell of cabbages and carbolic lingered in the air. She gave her name at the reception desk. She was directed to a room along the corridor to wait with the other trainees. Her nerves jangled as her footsteps echoed on the wooden floor.

She opened the door of the designated room and glanced around. Most of the other candidates appeared to be a lot older than her and brimming with confidence. She swallowed, stepped in and went to sit next to a blonde girl who looked to be one of the youngest.

"Hello," the girl said. "My name's Cissie." She offered her hand. Rose shook it.

"Rose," she said.

"Good to meet you, Rose," Cissie said. "Where are you from?"

"Norfolk," Rose said. "You?"

"Originally from Wales, but I've been living in London best part of two years now. Are you staying at the hostel?"

"The hostel? No. I have family nearby. I'm staying with them."

"Ooo lucky you."

"Are you in the hostel then? What's it like?"

"Cold as a stepmother's heart. Honest, you'd think a bit of coal wouldn't go amiss. Like gold-dust it is."

Rose thought of the blazing fire in her bedroom the previous evening, still glowing with embers this morning. She was about to sympathise when a large woman, crackling with starched linen, bustled into the room. She consulted the clipboard in her hand.

"Miss Addison Stone," she called.

As she stood up Rose heard Cissie whisper, "Blimey. Double-barrelled."

Five more names, including Cissie's, were called and the small group left the room to collect their uniforms and begin learning all about the Nightingale Training School for Nurses.

Cissie told Rose she was nineteen and came from a large family. She'd grown up with five brothers. It was the eldest being killed at Ypres that had decided Cissie to train as a nurse. She'd been a VAD but wanted to do more than make up trays, serve food and change library books. Two of her brothers were currently serving in Egypt. By the end of the first day Rose and Cissie were firm friends.

Over the next weeks Rose worked tirelessly stripping and remaking beds, washing patients and serving meals. They started in the general wards and Rose's heart went out to the people lying helplessly in bed. After three weeks she and Cissie were assigned to one of the wards designated for wounded soldiers sent to the hospital for specialist surgery. The first time she visited the wards her heart leapt into her mouth at the raw reality of blood and bone. Nothing had prepared her for the brutality of the injuries she saw there. She'd seen men on convalescence before, but the horror of the fresh wounds brought the devastating consequences the men had to face home to her.

"Remember you are professionals," the matron told them. "Nothing shocks you, nothing unnerves you. You are always cheerful. You are the face of hope and a return to health. Don't let me down." And she didn't.

On the ward she was allocated an experienced nurse to shadow, a woman in her early forties named Nurse Potter. A stickler for 'the right way to do things' Nurse Potter stood over her while she washed and shaved men, changed dressings checked temperatures and learned about medications. She admonished Rose if she took too long to do a job or didn't do it correctly. "We haven't got all day," she'd say and hurry her on to the next patient.

"Aw, leave her be," the older men would say. "It's nice to see a pretty face," but Nurse Potter wasn't moved.

Some of the younger patients were embarrassed being bathed by such a young nurse and said they'd prefer to do it themselves but again Nurse Potter insisted as 'they wouldn't do it right' so Rose washed them as gently as she could and tried to spare their blushes. Most days she was run off her feet fetching and carrying, there always seemed to be so much to do.

The men themselves weren't above playing jokes on her either to relieve the boredom of long days being immobile.

They'd ask her to come and look at something in the bed, or feel something under the covers, saying they'd lost something could she find it, or could she look at a non-existent rash in a particular spot, usually somewhere young ladies weren't supposed to look. Rose took it all in her stride, always offering to fetch Nurse Potter and they gradually desisted. Some days she worried that she'd never learn, she made mistakes and Nurse Potter rescued her on several occasions when she got something wrong.

"No, no, no," she'd say and step in to take over while Rose burned with embarrassment. If she didn't pass Nurse Potter's assessment she'd be sent home to be a chambermaid for the rest of her life.

The worse days were when she helped out with the patients who arrived daily on stretchers. They arrived fresh from the Auxiliary Hospital in Dover after assessment, their clothes still spattered with Flanders' mud and still carrying the stench of the trench on them. They had lost limbs or been horribly disfigured and some were barely breathing. It was Rose's job to wash the dirt, disease and smell of death off of them, but the sight of them brought swirling nausea and fierce anger to her stomach. It was all she could do to stop herself being physically sick and several times she had to excuse herself and take time to fight back the tears and recover. The close connection to men who had been through so much was something else she had to get used to.

Over time her admiration for the men in the wards grew. Young men whose lives had been turned upside down but who told her they were the lucky ones. They were alive and back in Blighty and would never be sent back to the Front. Their fortitude and extraordinary courage astounded and humbled her. She took every one into her heart.

Every day brought new reminders of the men fighting at the Front. She thought of men and boys she knew who'd signed up without a moment's hesitation. Friends she'd grown up with who would see the wounds at first hand, the freshness making them even more alarming.

By the end of each day she felt heart-sick, bone weary and emotionally drained. Her legs and feet ached from walking.

One day she got lost in the multi-floored building with its long corridors and numerous offices. Sister had sent her to the pharmacy to collect some supplies and she'd been so tired and distracted she hadn't noticed where she was going. She was saved by a white coated junior doctor who took pity on her and escorted her back to the ward. After that she made sure to take note of the places she passed so she could get back safely. She thought she'd never find her way around but eventually she did.

Every evening she avidly read Florence Nightingale's *Notes on Nursing*, devouring all seventy-six pages until she knew them by heart.

She was glad to be working on the same ward as Cissie and same shifts so they could spend their breaks together in the canteen. Cissie told her all about life in the hostel, which usually consisted of several anecdotes about the oddities of the other residents, and they'd both end up laughing.

In the evenings they'd walk together to the end of the bridge before saying goodbye. As the evenings lightened they began going out together. Rose's favourite place was a small cafe in the Strand where soldiers on leave met up for a sing song. There was a piano player and often one of the lads would give them a song. It reminded Rose of home and the Saturday night concert parties Ma held for the convalescing Officers.

Cissie's favourite was the cinema and she'd drag Rose to the Gaumont whenever there was a Charlie Chaplin or Mary Pickford film on. "It's therapy," she said. And it was. Then there were walks in the park, theatres and galleries to visit. There was no shortage of things to do to take their minds off the horror of the wards.

Cissie was the person Rose turned to whenever she felt the loss of a patient, or saw a particularly bitter mutilation to a man who'd had a promising career before the war. "How do you cope?" she asked while they were having tea in the canteen. "With so much badness in the world?"

Cissie sighed. "You have to push it to some small part of your mind and not think about it," she said. "The thing is not to think. I never think. You can't afford to give a piece of your heart to every handsome face with a hard luck story, no matter how much you want to."

She finished her tea and glanced around as though trying to avoid the subject. Then she smiled. "It's not all bad. This war won't last forever. One day soon it will be over and we can all put it behind us and go back to our families."

What's left of them, Rose thought.

"Come on," Cissie said, jumping up. "Let's get another cup of tea. I'm having one of those buns." She turned and went to the counter. Her sudden rush of forced gaiety didn't fool Rose. She knew Cissie's feelings ran as deep as her own.

Chapter Ten

April brought the first breath of spring. Trees and flowers came into bud. Primroses and crocus appeared in the churchyard and the evenings began to lighten. The days were warmer with sudden showers. Rose wrote regularly to her mother and to William, who'd finished training and, much to Ma's disgust had signed up on a Cruiser rather than go home and join the Coastguard.

'*They promised a home posting*,' Violet wrote, but it was to no avail. The Navy needed people like William and he jumped at the chance to join up, just as Rose knew he would. His letters were full of enthusiasm and she could see him working alongside the other men, making friends and enjoying every minute of it.

Violet wrote about the people in the town, food supplies and the difficulties of running the hotel when there were shortages of everything, including staff, but she always hoped Rose was doing well and looked forward to her finishing her training so she could work in a hospital nearer home.

Rose got used to being woken by the sound of guns and looking out to see the after-glow of bombs exploding around the docks. Several times she'd had to run for shelter when the air-raid warning went. Luckily most of the strikes were well away, but one bomb had fallen quite close and in the morning the streets were littered with the debris of shattered buildings. That night they'd woken the children and run with them to the shelter in Hope's garden, glad of it to keep them safe.

One night she watched from a window to see a Zepp shot down on the other side of the city. She wrote telling William about it. She wanted him to know he wasn't the only one facing daily danger. She told him she'd heard the guns, the sound carried on the still night air. Then streams of ack-ack fire criss-crossed the sky followed by huge flashes and bangs. She watched as a ball of falling flames dropped towards earth and disappeared behind the skyline. *'Even at a distance it was impressive.'* she wrote.

She didn't mind the early starts, twelve-hour days and late finishes. Walking across Westminster Bridge to the hospital each morning the air felt fresh and cool, as though the horrors of yesterday had been washed away and she stood in the centre of a city battered but still breathing. At least she thought she was helping in some small way.

One day she was with Sister checking in the new arrivals, helping them off the stretcher onto beds so they could be cleaned up and assessed.

She thought she saw someone she recognised. She couldn't be sure. He looked very different now. He'd lost some skin on his face, his hair was singed and charred, wound dressings covered his arms and chest and a blanket covered his legs. He lay there, silent, sullen with soulless eyes staring up at her, not seeing. She wondered what was going on in his mind.

Later, in her break, she went and sat by his bed, just watching. She was sure it was him. His name was Joe, he was nineteen and he'd been a boat builder in the yard at home. He hadn't moved since they brought him into the ward.

The next morning she went to see how he was getting on. There was no change. She dropped by after her shift but he just lay there, staring at the ceiling.

She was used to men who came in wounded being uncommunicative and withdrawn. She knew that once the doctors had seen him, his wounds had been dressed, given time, he'd rally and they could talk. Two days later she was proved right.

"I know you," he said, when she came and stood by his bed. "You're Rose. Your ma and pa run the hotel. Have I died and gone to heaven?"

She laughed, glad to see him getting better. "No such luck I'm afraid," she said. "I'm a probationary nurse and I'm working here. You've been wounded and you'll just have to get on with it."

He seemed grateful. "I understand I've lost a foot," he said, "among other things. They're going to get me a new one. Better than the old one. I don't have to worry about getting bunions or cutting the toenails."

She looked at his chart. He was due for surgery that afternoon. "You'll be fine," she said. "The doctors here are amazing."

"And the nurses?"

She smiled. "Yes, they're pretty amazing too," she said.

He looked suddenly serious and reached out and took her hand. "If I come through will you come and see me?"

"Of course," she said. "You're on my round."

"No. I mean after. When I get sent home."

By home he meant Norfolk. What could she say? She withdrew her hand. "If I get a chance to visit home I'll come and see you," she said. "But it's not likely to be anytime soon, the way things are."

"Sorry," he said. "I just thought…hoped…a man can dream…"

Her heart turned over for this lad, his life changed forever, like so many others.

It wasn't unusual for the nurses to be chatted up by the patients. It was part of their recovery and she wasn't the only one to set the men's heart beating and their blood pressure up a bit. Cissie too got her share of compliments and offers. With her blue eyes and blonde hair they thought she was an angel sent from heaven just for them. She always laughed it off, telling them to behave themselves. "You're not in the trenches now," she'd say.

"Thank God," they'd reply and they'd laugh and feel a little better.

The next day when Rose went to see Joe in her break, she learned they'd taken his leg off below the knee, but at least he was alive. After that she went and sat with him whenever she could. They talked about the people at home they both knew.

"You remember old Garvey at the grocery store?" he asked her one day.

"Yes, I knew him and his wife."

"He was out there with us. His wife sent him a tin of biscuits for Christmas," Joe said. He laughed. "By the time we'd passed 'em along the line they were all gone. 'E wrote and asked her to send another box."

Another day he told her about the music. "Funny thing was, we 'ad a gramophone an' all," he said. "In the officer's dugout. You could hear it all along the line. Strange hearing music in that place. Miles and miles of nothing but mud and muck and music. Jazz it was, playing in the evenings." He chuckled. "As if we could dance."

He shook his head "One place even had a piano and a chap who could play it. Trouble was 'e only knew one tune. Played it night and day."

He told her about the card games, the gambling, the concerts and the practical jokes they played on each other. He told her of the different characters from all walks of life. He never mentioned the shelling, the bullets or the casualties. He knew Lenny at the boatyard and even about the dummy he'd made for William.

"Did he like it?" he asked.

"He loved it," Rose said.

"How is William?"

"He's fine. He's joined the Navy and is doing something he's always wanted to do."

"The Navy? That's what I should have done," Joe said. "No mud and it would have been a lot cleaner."

Rose wrote to Violet telling her about seeing Joe and Violet sent one of the convalescing officers round to his mother with some flowers and a note wishing him well and hoping he'd soon be home.

A few days later Joe was moved to a hospital in Kings Lynn where his wound could heal and his mother could visit. Then he'd be fitted with a new limb and sent home.

"I'll write," he said when Rose came to say goodbye and wish him well. "If that's all right?"

Rose didn't have the heart to say no.

Chapter Eleven

One evening when Rose arrived home she was surprised to see Hope laying the table for guests.

"Alfie's coming," Hope said. "He said he's bringing someone he wants us to meet." She grinned at Rose. "Do you think there's a romance on the horizon?"

Rose laughed. She remembered Hope's younger brother, her Uncle Alfie, but hadn't seen much of him as he was often away when they visited. She recalled that he had a crippled leg and that he'd been kind, funny and clever. It would be good to see him again.

"I'd love to see him settle down with the right person," Hope said.

"Will he be staying here? I could help get his room ready."

"No," Hope said. "He said he's staying in town as he has to leave early in the morning."

Rose knew that his work sourcing supplies for the troops took him all over the country. "I'll go and get changed then I'll give you a hand," she said.

That evening as she prepared the meal Hope thought about Alfie, who'd been nine when Ma and Pa died. He'd lived with them and Silas had been like a father to him. Whatever he planned to do he'd want Silas's approval. If he was bringing someone to meet them it could only mean that's what he wanted.

She remembered when he was little he'd brought them heartaches and joy in equal measure. Even though he'd been bullied at school and affected by the loss of their parents, he never complained. She knew of his struggles and hoped he'd found someone who could be to him what Silas was to her; a tower of strength and her reason for living.

When he arrived she noticed he still wore a leg brace and walked with a slight limp, but she thought he looked fitter than she'd ever seen him. He'd filled out and his shoulders broadened. The fresh air and country living obviously agreed with him. He handed her the box he carried which contained a ham and a selection of vegetables. "Fresh from the farm," he said.

"And much appreciated," Hope said, surprised and delighted with the gift. She took the box to the kitchen then welcomed him with a hug.

A girl with brunette hair plaited neatly around her head and cheeks with a healthy country glow, followed them in. Shorter than Alfie but plumper, the word buxom sprang to Hope's mind.

"This is Jenny," he said, beaming all over his face.

"Pleased to meet you," Jenny said almost dropping a curtsy.

"Come on up and meet the family," Hope said, taking Jenny's arm. "You must tell me all about how you met Alfie and how long you've known him."

Jenny glanced at Alfie.

Alfie laughed. "Be prepared to be interrogated," he said.

Upstairs Silas was in the drawing room with Rose and the children. When Alfie introduced Jenny approval shone in Silas's eyes and Hope saw Alfie relax.

Rose kissed Jenny's cheek. "Any friend of Uncle Alfie's is welcome," she said. "I hope we'll be friends."

The children too were excited to see their uncle. Alfie picked Sean up and swung him around. "How are you, champ?" he said.

Sean grinned. "Better than you," he said, laughing.

Alfie smiled at Olivia. "I swear you've grown six inches since I saw you last," he said. "You're going to be tall like your dad."

Silas beamed with pleasure at his remark. Olivia chuckled and kissed Alfie's cheek. "Good to see you, Uncle Alfie," she said. "And to meet you," she said to Jenny who shook both their hands.

"Where have you been?" Sean asked, so Alfie told them about his travels around the West Country, the beautiful scenery, the rolling hills, the trees and the meadows.

"It's wonderful," he said. "The space, the enormous sky and to breathe clean fresh air after the dust and dirt of London. You should try it, Hope."

Hope laughed. "I think I'm too settled to want to move anywhere, but you seem happy. Now, tell us, where did you two meet?"

"Jenny's a land girl," Alfie said. "She works on one of the farms I visit. As soon as I saw her I knew I wanted to get to know her better."

"He kept coming back to the farm," Jenny said. "The farmer was fair mazzed about it." Her voice had a soft Devon burr.

"Couldn't keep away," Alfie said. Hope noticed he'd caught some of her accent. "That was six months ago and we've been seeing each other ever since." He took Jenny's hand. "We want to get married as soon as possible."

Hope saw the love in their eyes as they looked at each other. She was glad.

"And you want our approval?" Silas said.

"That would be nice, but I'd marry her anyway," Alfie said.

"And what about your family, Jenny? What do they think about it?"

Alfie answered. "Her mother died when she was young. We have that in common." Hope detected the bond between them and the way his fact lit up when he talked about her. He was more alive and animated than she'd ever seen him. "Jenny's pa is serving overseas but I met him and asked his permission. He approves."

"Well, you have our approval too," Silas said. "This calls for a drink. I think we have a bottle of something suitable left in the cold store from before the war."

"Whoo hoo, a wedding," Sean said.

"Congratulations," Hope said getting up and hugging them both. Rose and Olivia added their best wishes before Silas shooed the younger children off to bed while he went to the cold store to get the champagne. They'd eaten earlier as they both had school the next morning.

Over dinner Alfie asked Rose about working at the hospital.

"It's very rewarding, she said, and went on to tell him about the patients and the other nurses. "I feel I'm in the right place and I'm grateful for Aunt Hope for putting me up."

"What about William and your pa. I expect you miss them terribly."

"I do," Rose said. "William's joined the Navy and Pa's doing his bit overseas. I'm very proud of both of them."

"Yes, I'm sure you are, and rightly so," he said. Then he told them of his own plans. "We can't do anything until this war is over," he said, "but there's a place I've got my eye on. It's an old coaching inn on the Taunton road. Two bars and ten rooms. It's run down now but I've put a reserve on it. I'll be an innkeeper in the family tradition and with the rooms we can do bed and breakfast."

Hope gasped with surprise. "You'll be running a pub? Just like Ma and Pa?"

Alfie grinned. "Yes, that's the plan."

After dinner Rose cleared the dishes and Jenny offered to help with the washing-up.

Alfie winked. "All ready trained," he said.

When Rose and Jenny had gone Alfie said, "Well, what do you think? Isn't she marvellous?"

"She's very attractive," Silas said. "I can see why you like her."

"Like her? I love her and she's more than attractive. She's beautiful, inside and out. She's warm-hearted and kind, honest and clever. Hard working too and just…just…wonderful."

He sipped the champagne Silas poured into his glass. "I've never felt so right about anything or as at home as I do with Jenny. I want to provide a home for her and any children we may have."

Silas smiled. "You've always been a good judge of character," he said, "and I can see you've thought this through. You have our blessing."

"I can see she makes you happy," Hope said "That's all I care about."

"She does," Alfie said.

Hope hugged him again and Silas shook his hand.

Later that night when they went to bed Hope told Silas she was feeling old. "Little Alfie getting married. It hardly seems possible," she said.

He took her in his arms. "I know, my darling. Eventually all our chicks will fly the nest and we'll be left old, crotchety and alone."

Hope laughed. "You'll never be old and crotchety to me," she said. "You'll always be the solid, dashing, handsome man who stole my heart."

"And you'll always be the only one in the world whose heart I'd want to steal," he said.

In Silas's arms that night Hope had never felt happier and more loved. She hoped Alfie would one day feel this way too.

Alfie and Jenny were married in Jenny's home town on a bright sunny day in late June. Jenny's father managed to get leave to give his daughter away. Only Silas, Hope, their children and Rose were able to attend from the family, although Violet and John sent their best wishes and promised to have a 'proper do' when the war was over.

George, Hope's friend Margaret's son and Alfie's best friend from school was best man. Harold and Margaret hadn't been able to make it to the wedding but sent their best regards. George still walked with sticks and Hope saw the special bond between the two boys who'd both had difficulties to overcome.

A few of Jenny's friends made up the remaining congregation.

Watching her little brother waiting for his bride brought a tear to Hope's eye. In her mind she saw again the tow-headed boy in short trousers with an engaging curiosity about the world around him he used to be. Where did the years go? She puffed up with pride seeing the man he had become. Ma would be proud of him too, she thought. She'd always had a soft spot for her youngest child, the after-thought, who, she said, had been blessed with the gift of perception that the others lacked.

Every head in the congregation turned as Jenny walked down the aisle. Dressed in a simple summer frock, with wild roses entwined in her plaited hair and carrying a bouquet of meadow flowers, she looked serene and beautiful.

Hope wiped a tear from her cheek as they exchanged vows. The service felt evocative and deeply meaningful. Hope remembered her own wedding day and hoped that Alfie and Jenny would be as happy as her and Silas.

She breathed again as the organ music swelled to the rafters and Alfie and Jenny walked down the aisle together as man and wife.

Alfie had arranged for drinks and light refreshment to be served in the local pub after the service.

"I'm so glad you came," he said to Hope. "I don't mind about the others, but it wouldn't be right getting married without you being here."

Hope's heart stuttered as she realised how much her and Silas had come to mean to him. "I wouldn't have missed it for the world," she said.

Later, watching him greet his guests, she said to Rose, "He's grown into a fine young man. I'm so proud of him."

"He's a credit to you," Rose said and again Hope's heart fluttered.

Hope and Silas had given them a large cheque in lieu of a present. The smile on Alfie's face when they gave it to him was all the thanks Hope needed.

That evening, after the drinks the bride and groom climbed into Alfie's car to travel to the hotel by the coast Alfie had booked for their honeymoon. They only had two days, as they both had to be back to work after that.

"She looked so beautiful," Olivia said on the drive home. "I didn't expect her to look so lovely."

"Well, they are in love," Rose said. "Everyone in love looks beautiful."

"Will they be coming to live with us?" Sean asked.

"No," Hope said. "They'll be setting up home on their own."

"So will we see Uncle Alfie again?" Sean persisted.

"I'm sure they'll visit," Hope said and realised she wasn't the only one who'd miss Alfie.

"I thought they both looked splendid," Rose said. "And so happy."

"Yes," Hope said. "I think they'll both be very happy for a very long time."

"Like forever?" Sean asked.

"Yes, like forever," Hope said and the certainty of it filled heart and she was glad.

Chapter Twelve

July turned hotter, the sun blazed in a clear blue summer sky. The walk to work alongside the river was pleasant enough, but in the hospital the wards became stuffy and airless. Even with the windows open the ward felt hot and the smell of sickness lingered.

Once a week, Rose had an afternoon off, when she'd change into her best blue afternoon dress, roll her hair up around her head and look a good deal older than her sixteen years. Then, with Cissie, she'd go to the afternoon tea dances held in some of the hotels catering for recovering soldiers. Their favourite was the Addison hotel owned by Gabriel's father just off the Strand which, like his other hotels, now catered for convalescing soldiers. The restaurant had been turned into a canteen and the bar/lounge area a make-shift dance hall. Here a three-piece band played and tea was set out by frilly-aproned servers at a long, white-clothed table. It was a touch of civilised opulence in what Rose considered had become a dreary, worry-ridden world.

Part of her thought dancing in the afternoon somehow wicked, a bit too risqué for a well brought up girl like her, but Cissie laughed when she told her how she felt.

When they arrived she glanced around at the couples on the floor to see if there was anyone she recognised. The men were barely older than her, nineteen at most, and far too young to be so damaged. Some injuries were visible, others not so obvious but they all wore the look of men who'd faced their worst fears and were wearied by it.

The girls were more spirited. Although mostly Voluntary Aid Detachment workers or shop girls, Rose had met some who drove buses, worked on the railway or delivered post. Women who weren't content to sit at home waiting for their men to return. She'd even spoken to one who worked as a police officer.

They collected their cups of tea and found a table. Cissie was soon up and dancing to the music in the arms of a young man who looked as though he should still be at school. Rose, happy to see her friend enjoying herself, sat at the table watching. After a while a man approached her. He walked with a limp. Older than most of the other soldiers, head-turningly handsome with dark-hair, piercing blue eyes and rugged features unmarked by scars, Rose thought him the most striking man in the room. He bowed. "Would you do me the honour?" he said, indicating the dance floor.

Rose's heart fluttered. Why not, she thought. She stood and he took her in his arms.

"I'm afraid it's more like a shuffle than a dance," he said, his accent betraying his Irish upbringing. "Bullet wound in the leg, but you looked a bit lonely sitting there. I thought I'd rescue you."

"That's very kind of you," Rose said. "But I assure you I wasn't in need of rescuing."

"No? Pity." He grinned. "My friends call me Ferdie. I hope we can be friends. What do people call you?"

"Rose," she said.

"Rose? A beautiful name for a beautiful girl."

"I don't know about that," she said.

"Come now, don't be modest. You're easily the prettiest girl in the room." His hold on her tightened as they moved around the floor. She felt his breath on her cheek and breathed in the musky aroma of him. They drew the attention of the others dancers too. She felt as though she'd been especially chosen and a bubble of happiness blossomed inside her.

As the music faded he walked her back to the table. "Can I get you a cup of tea, or something else?" He raised his eyebrow suggestively as he said 'something else'.

Rose laughed. "Thank you, but no," she said. "I'm with my friend and not a bit lonely."

"Well, that's a shame so it is," he said just as Cissie arrived back at the table, breathless from her exertions on the floor.

"Well, Ferdie," she said. "I see you've wasted no time." She turned to Rose. "I need to warn you about this one. Has the cheek of the devil in him and is not to be trusted."

"Oh, Cissie," he said, clutching his chest. "It's me heart you're breaking. Won't you allow me to join you?"

"No," Cissie said. "Ignore him, Rose. He'll soon get fed up and go away."

He gave an exaggerated gasp. "That's hard, Cissie. And I thought we were friends." He picked up Rose's hand and kissed it. "I'll leave you in peace with this harridan," he said. "But I'm sure we'll meet again." He shook his head sadly at Cissie and limped away.

Rose laughed. "Who was that and what was it all about?"

"Oh," Cissie said. "Don't mind him. He always tries it on with the new girls. You're better off keeping clear."

Rose shrugged. She wasn't so sure she wanted to keep clear, or to have Cissie decide what was good for her. He was the most exciting thing that had happened to her in a long while. Wasn't she entitled to a bit of excitement too?

The following week, at a different hotel, Rose saw him standing by the tea table chatting to a girl in VAD uniform. He turned and saw her, she smiled, his gaze moved to Cissie, walking in next to her, and he turned back to the VAD.

Rose felt slighted. He'd seen her, she was certain of it. After their last meeting she felt sure he'd been attracted to her. She'd smiled. Had Cissie's presence put him off?

"You get the tea and I'll find a table," Cissie said.

Rose joined the queue for tea. She stood close enough to smell the scent of him and feel his presence. If he was interested in her, now would be the perfect opportunity to speak to her. He didn't. He glanced at her, smiled and walked away. Rose's hopes and her heart fell to the floor. She was surprised no one heard the crash.

She danced with several other young men. Every time she moved around the floor she found herself distracted, looking for him, wondering if he was still there, who he was dancing with, or if he was watching her. He wasn't. Was Cissie right? Was he a man who tried it on with the new girls, playing fast and loose with their affections, or had she built up the encounter in her mind, made more of it than it really was?

After the dance, on the way home Cissie noticed her sullen mood. "What's the matter, cariad? Didn't you enjoy it?" she said

"I enjoyed it well enough," Rose said. "Just a bit tired. It's been a long day."

The following week they went back to the Addison hotel for the afternoon tea dance. Again Rose found herself looking round, wishing she could see him again. She danced with several young men, but her heart wasn't in it. She began to wonder why she'd come. He wasn't there. Once more she felt the disappointment as they walked home, and it started to rain.

A few days later, after a particularly harrowing day at work, she left Cissie at the end of Westminster Bridge to go their separate ways. Slate grey clouds gathered for a summer storm and rain had darkened the sky. A light drizzle made walking uncomfortable and Rose shivered in her light coat. She wished she'd remembered her umbrella. She hadn't gone far along Victoria Embankment when she saw a man lurking in the shadows smoking a cigarette. When she got closer he stepped out in front of her, lifted his cap and bowed.

"Good evening, Nurse Stone," Ferdie said.

Taken aback Rose gasped. "You? How do you know my name?"

"Ah, Nurse Stone, I made it my business to find out. Now don't tell me Nurse Stone has a heart of stone. You surely won't be cross with a poor chap wanting to know more about you when he's heading to the front line to risk life and limb?"

"Heading to the front line?" Her heart skipped a beat.

"Yes. MO's passed me fit. Apparently a bullet in the leg is no reason not to fight. I ship out tomorrow."

"Tomorrow? And you thought you'd waylay me tonight?"

"Indeed. Who else would I choose to spend my last few hours in this country with?" He raised his hand and touched her cheek. A distant longing shone in his eyes. "So beautiful," he said.

Rose couldn't make up her mind whether he was kidding her, chatting her up or if he really did want to spend time with her before…"

"Take pity on me. Come and have a drink before I depart. We may never get the chance again."

Rose didn't know what to say. She could hardly refuse to have a drink with him and anyway she wasn't sure she wanted to. "Well," she said her heart a flutter of indecision.

"Unless you prefer to stand here in the rain," he said.

Rose laughed. He took her arm and they ran across the road and up a side street where they found a pub.

Warmth enveloped them as they stepped into the bar. A fire burned in the grate and lights around the room gave it a cosy feel. Ferdie shook the rain off his cap and went up to the bar. Rose found an empty table and took off her coat. He ordered a beer for himself and a gin and tonic for Rose. He hadn't asked what she wanted.

"Here we go," he said, putting the drinks on the table. He slipped his coat off and put it on the chair. "Let's drink to a rosy future."

Rose giggled and sipped the drink. It tasted fine so she had some more. She didn't usually drink but gin was her mother's tipple so she thought it must be all right.

"So, my sweet Rose of Tralee, did you know the rose is the flower of love and passion," he said. "It's associated with Venus, the Goddess of love."

"Is that right," she said taking another sip of gin.

"Yes," he said. "But roses have thorns. Thorns that can tear a man's heart to shreds. Do you have thorns, Rose?"

Rose considered this. It felt new and exciting being chatted up by a handsome man in uniform and tomorrow he'd be gone overseas. He may never come back and she'd never see him again. "No," she said. "No thorns."

He slipped his arm around her waist and planted a gentle kiss on her cheek. "Good," he said. "Then we'll get along fine."

They chatted for a while, he bought more drinks, the evening wore on. Everyone in the pub seemed so merry. Ferdie chatted to some of the other soldiers. The bar hummed with conversation and laughter. Rose only started to worry when she realised how dark it had become outside. She felt a bit strange too, so she said she wanted to go home.

"Then home you shall go," he said. He helped her up and into her coat. He put his coat on and together they made their way out of the bar. Outside, in the fresh air, her legs turned to jelly.

"Steady now," he said, holding her up, almost carrying her. Fuzziness filled her head, she felt light-headed and started to giggle. He led her into an alleyway where she leaned against the wall. His breath warmed her face, his lips found hers. She responded to his kisses as warmth flowed through her like melting butter. His hands explored her body, running all over her.

Suddenly, the intensity of her feelings scared her. She tried to move. His kisses became rougher, more urgent. He pressed harder against her. She felt his hand on her skin, touching her breast. As his body moved against hers another feeling rose up inside her, a sensation she'd never experienced before. She felt powerless to stop him even if she wanted to. Was this what everyone warned her about? It wasn't unpleasant, far from it.

"Oh, Rose," he whispered.

The sound of his voice, hoarse with emotion, broke the spell.

"What the—"

If it hadn't been for the fire warden passing by just then and moving them on she knew it would have gone much further.

Back at the side of the road he hailed a cab and helped her into it. She noticed the top of her blue serge dress was open and her lacy camisole clearly on display beneath it. She pulled her coat around her.

"Write to me, Rose," he said, pushing a piece of paper between her breasts. He closed the cab door, gave the cabby her address and half-a-crown and disappeared into the gloom.

When she got to Hope's house it was past midnight. She let herself in, not wanting to disturb anyone. Up in her room she pulled the paper out from between her breasts. She smoothed it out and read *'Cpl. F. Giggs, 7th Irish Fulisiers'* then a BEF Post Office Number. She folded it in half and put it in her writing case, then lay on her bed replaying the events of the evening over and over in her mind.

She was late getting downstairs the next morning. Hope hovered over the breakfast things which were laid out on the table. Silas had already had his and gone out. "You were late last night," Hope said. "I didn't hear you come in. You missed dinner. I worried."

"Sorry," Rose said. "I ran into a friend and we went for a drink. I didn't think."

Hope frowned. "You look a bit peaky. Is it just the late night or is there something else?"

Rose's heart turned over. Was it so obvious? She hadn't slept. Hope was right. When she'd looked in the mirror this morning she'd seen dark shadows under her eyes, her face pale as moonlight. She'd pinched her cheeks to bring some colour and wondered if she should buy some rouge. All the other girls wore it, and lipstick. She'd never bothered. Perhaps it was time she did. "I'm just tired," she said.

"Well, you have been out every night this week," Hope said. "You don't want to make yourself ill."

"I won't," she said. "Anyway, I'll be staying in tonight. I have some letters to write."

She had a quick breakfast of tea and toast as she didn't want to be interrogated about her night out.

When she arrived at the hospital an early train from Dover brought an influx of wounded soldiers and a Zeppelin raid the night before brought another hundred casualties, which kept her busy all morning. She hardly had time to think, but when she did it was Ferdie she thought about. He'd be on his way to France now. One man among the thousands who'd be there, going because they had to. Because they had no choice. Visions of his face when she left, the raindrops sparkling in his hair, memories of his body pressed into hers, the musky woody smell of him, all buzzed around in her brain. Every mud spattered soldier who came into the ward reminded her of the dangers ahead of him. It was almost more than she could bear.

Chapter Thirteen

When Rose heard that her Uncle John had been called up she went to see him at the Hope and Anchor, the pub where her ma had grown up and where she and William had been born. Cissie went with her.

"Come and meet the family," she said.

Her Uncle John's eyes lit up when they walked in. Several men standing around the bar also perked up. John finished serving an old man who shuffled off, then came out from behind the bar to greet her.

"Rose, what a lovely surprise," he said. "Hope told me you were staying with her but I didn't expect to see you in this neck of the woods." He kissed her cheek and held her by the shoulders to look at her. "My goodness, you look all grown up. The last time I saw you…"

"I know, I was a nipper. This is my friend, Cissie. We work together."

"You're both very welcome. Alice will be delighted to see you. She's upstairs with the children." He lifted the flap and ushered them through the bar into the back hall where he called up the stairs, "Alice. You'll never guess who's come to see us." He turned to Rose. "Sorry I can't come up. Can't leave the bar until the relief barman comes in. I'll see you later though."

Rose and Cissie made their way upstairs. "A pub in the family?" Cissie said, laughing. "I knew there was a good reason I chose you to be my friend."

Upstairs Alice showed them into the parlour where two boys were on the floor playing with some lead soldiers, a young girl played with a doll and an older girl sat in a chair reading a book.

"Hello, Amy," Rose said. Her mind filled with memories of playing with Amy when she was little. The girl stood up.

"You must let me get you both a drink," Alice said.

"I'd love a cup of tea," Rose said.

"Me too," Cissie said.

"I'll make it," Amy offered and disappeared into the kitchen.

"She's a bit shy," Alice said and Rose remembered how she'd been a quiet little thing when she was small.

"I've never been upstairs in a pub before," Cissie said. "It's quite charming."

"Thank you," Alice said. She turned to Rose. "You remember Alexander, John Junior and Emily. They should be in bed by now."

"Aw, Ma," the boys said in unison.

Alice smiled. "School tomorrow," she said and the boys reluctantly put their toys away. Emily, who was six, took her doll with her.

"I'll be in to tuck you up shortly," Alice said.

Amy came back with the tray of tea and some cake she'd found in the larder.

"I hear Uncle John's been called up," Rose said. "Will he go? I would have thought that, running a business, he could defer or be excused."

"He could," Alice said. "But he won't. He's seen so many of his friends go and feels it's his duty."

"How will you manage with the pub and everything?" Rose said.

Alice shrugged. "We have one barman left. Ma helps out and Amy. With the reduced opening hours I'll manage. Trade's slower now. Most of the local men have gone and when they're home on leave they want to live it up and go to the West End." She poured the tea Amy had brought in and handed Rose and Cissie each a cup. She sighed. "John says we'll be looked after. They'll pay extra when he goes overseas and he reckons he'll be home soon and we'll all be better off."

Rose could tell from the look on her face that she wasn't happy, but, like everyone else, there wasn't much she could do about it.

"I'll just go and tuck Emily in," Alice said. "Then Amy can read her a story."

Amy smiled and asked Rose about her work at the hospital.

Rose and Cissie chatted to Amy until Alice returned, then John joined them. He got them all a drink. "Something a bit stronger than tea," he said.

"I hear you've been called up," Rose said when he handed her a glass of light ale. "When do you go?"

"Next week," he said. He touched Alice's hand and leaned over and kissed her cheek. "I can't stay home and expect other men to go and fight to protect my family and not join them. The more of us who go the sooner it'll all be over and we can get back to living our normal lives."

Rose was glad she'd called to see him before he went. She felt the family bond strengthen. They were family. They looked after each other.

"It's good to see you, Rose, what have you been up to?"

Rose told them all about Alfie and Jenny's wedding. "She's lovely," Rose said. "Just right for him. Very nurturing, she'll look after him and he'll look after her. They'll do well together."

John chuckled. "Hope told me he's thinking of going into the business," he said. "Going to run a country pub."

Rose laughed "Yes, that's right. It seems the trade is in his blood too."

John beamed. "Good for him," he said. "What about you, Rose? Any plans to go into the hospitality business?"

"No fear. I know Ma and Pa have that in mind for me, but it's not what I want. I'm going to be a trained nurse. I think that's where my future lies."

"She's very dedicated," Cissie said. "We both are."

John nodded. "Women are doctors now and fulfilling all sorts of jobs they couldn't do before the war. The world is changing and the opportunities for women with it. I wish you well."

"Thanks." Rose smiled.

They chatted some more about the effect the war was having on the world as they knew it.

"John worries about the pub takings being down," Alice said, "but we are better off than a lot of people. I can't imagine what your ma goes through with Gabriel and William both away fighting the war, never knowing if …Oh, sorry…" She put her hand to her mouth as though trying to recapture the words and pull them back.

"It's all right," Rose said. "Pa and William are doing what they think is right. They couldn't live with themselves if they didn't. We all know the risks…" Her voice faded and tears sprang to her eyes at the thought of the risks.

"I for one think we should all make the best of what we've got," Cissie said gaily, coming to Rose's rescue. "Lots of men in uniform looking for a little excitement or a diversion from the war."

Rose immediately thought of Ferdie and a blush rose to her cheek. She hoped no one noticed.

"Yes," Alice said a little too brightly. "I'm thinking of opening up the hall on Saturday nights like we used to. Put on a concert or something. You remember, Rose. When your ma used to sing."

Actually Rose had been too young to recall those days but saw Alice's embarrassment. "She still does," she said. "In the hotel. She puts on a concert for the officers. A few of the locals come along and join in. We think it helps."

"I'm sure it does," Alice said and smiled.

By the time they left Cissie told Rose she'd gone up in her estimation. "Having a pub in the family. Can't do better than that," she said laughing.

"It's been in the family for generations," Rose said. "My grandparents ran it before Uncle John took over. They died before I was born, but William and I are named after them. Ma told me that my Aunt Hope was named Hope after the pub because my grandparents got the licence when she was born."

"There's worse things than being named after a pub and called Hope," Cissie said. "I'm named after St Cecilia, a martyred virgin. Try living up to that." They both laughed.

By August the hospital was busy with casualties from the Somme. Rose worked extra shifts when she should have had days off. She felt as though she was running on the spot, no matter how hard she worked, or the hours she put in, nothing changed. Patients well enough to be moved on were quickly replaced by others, their bodies just as mutilated and their lives and prospects just as shattered.

Every evening she wondered at the futility of patching men up just to send them back to war. Every morning she was first downstairs to catch the post. Thoughts of the evening with Ferdie filled her mind. She'd written to him but, as yet had received no reply. She put it down to the vagaries of the post from abroad, but this morning her hopes had flown high. This morning she carried a letter from Ferdie in her pocket. She opened it as soon as she got in, before she went up to the ward.

He'd arrived safely in France and missed her already. He hoped she was '*keeping herself pure for him.*' That made her laugh. He told her they were '*moving up the line*' and he'd write again when he could. Then he asked for a photograph, '*so I can carry your image with me to cheer me through the difficult times and remind me that there's something worth coming home for.*' That made her glow with pleasure. He must like her very much, she thought, if he wanted her picture to carry with him. She felt special. Then she read '*You know what I like.*' Her brow furrowed when she read that. She had photos of course, old ones, and one of her wearing her uniform taken when she started nursing training. She'd sent that to her mother. What did he mean 'you know what I like'? She couldn't ask Cissie as she hadn't told her she was writing to Ferdie, fearing her disapproval.

She thought about it all day, and the next day. In the end she went to a small photographic studio in Aldgate who advertised '*Photographs to send to the Troops*'. She rolled her hair around her head to show off her slender neck, one of her best features. Then she applied some rouge and lipstick. She wore a white blouse with a deep frilled collar and the pearl earrings Hope and Silas gave her for her birthday.

It cost nearly a week's wages but she was pleased with the result when she went back two days later to collect it. In the head and shoulders photograph the photographer had caught the wistful, almost dreamy, look in her eye. She appeared elegant, serene and, she thought, almost beautiful. She hoped Ferdie would think the same. She worried in case he didn't like it.

She wrote a short note and posted it before she could change her mind.

At the end of a month that had seen sultry weather and humid, heat filled days, Rose had a spare afternoon off. Being at a loose end because Cissie was working an extra shift, she offered to take Olivia and Sean to the park. It would give her a chance to walk in the sun, clear her head and forget for a few hours the horrors of the hospital. The children were on Harvest Holiday and Hope was glad to have some time to herself to get on with the voluntary work she did with Margaret.

"Are you sure you don't mind?" Hope said. "It's your time off after all."

"And I can't think of a better way to spend it," Rose said.

Olivia and Sean didn't need to be asked twice.

"The park, hooray," Sean said, rushing to get his ball. Olivia took a book.

They caught a cab to Hyde Park. Rose found a spot where afternoon sun sparkled on water beneath a cloudless blue summer sky. A light breeze rustled through the trees. People were out walking their dogs or sitting quietly on benches reading or simply enjoying the warmth of the afternoon. She found an empty bench near the playground. Sean ran to the swings and shouted for Olivia to push him. Rose sat watching children jumping on and off the roundabout laughing and pushing each other. The sun warmed her face. How could this be so peaceful and idyllic, she thought, when so much carnage is going on across the sea? It didn't make sense.

That night she dreamed she was on a carousel with gaily painted horses going up and down and round and round. Men in uniform jumped on, went round and round and then fell off while the music played, round and round in her head. She clung helplessly to one of the gilded poles going round and round unable to stop.

Chapter Fourteen

September brought cooler days but there was no let up in the number of casualties coming in. There seemed to be no end to the stream of stretchers arriving every day. Rose spent her time with Sister, booking them in, assessing their wounds and dressing as many as possible. Every ward was busy and Rose found the time away from them more precious than ever.

"You'd think I'd be used to it by now," she said to Cissie. "There was one young chap today…" her eyes filled with tears.

"I know," Cissie said, "but your pity will do more harm than good. Remember what Matron said. We are professionals. It's our job to persuade them that there can be a worthwhile future ahead of them. You have to harden your heart."

Rose was on the ward finishing a particularly difficult dressing when Sister came bustling in. "Nurse Stone," she said, her face flushed either from anger or rushing, Rose wasn't sure which. "I wouldn't normally allow such a breach of Hospital rules, but on this occasion…" She puffed up even more than usual. "You have a visitor. Downstairs. A man in Naval uniform. It appears that it may be urgent—"

Rose gasped. A man in Naval uniform. Who on earth…It was bound to be bad news…William… "May I?" she said.

Sister nodded. "Two minutes, just this once. I expect you back…" The last words faded from her ears as she rushed out and down the stairs.

Breathless she arrived in the lobby to see William standing staring out of the window.

"William! You're all right, I was afraid..." She didn't get any further. He turned round, and laughing, swept her off her feet and hugged her.

"Good to see you, Sis," he said.

He put her down and she stood staring at him. He looked older in his uniform, dashing even. His blue eyes sparkled like crushed diamonds, his blonde hair had been cut regulation short but his face still oozed boyish charm. "What are you doing here?" she said, afraid it was some mischief he'd got himself into. You could never tell with William.

"The ship's in dock at Chatham. They're fitting some new equipment. I've been sent here to the Admiralty to collect new orders."

"Have you seen Aunt Hope? Where are you staying? How long have you got?" The questions came thick and fast to her brain, falling over themselves to get out.

William laughed. "I haven't seen Aunt Hope yet. I came here first to see you. I have to report to the Ministry of Shipping today. I expect I'll be sent back tomorrow. I was hoping to stay with Aunt Hope and thought perhaps we could hit the town tonight. You could show me all those places you've written about. They sound like fun."

"Oh William. I'm so glad to see you. Of course we'll go out on the town tonight, if you have time."

"Good. I'll see you back at Hope's." His smile widened. "And bring that girl you're always writing about. She sounds like fun too."

Then he was gone. Rose stood for several seconds to gather herself. William was here, although not for long, but life was always more exciting when William was around. He had a way of lighting up the shadows and coaxing a smile from the most sour-faced curmudgeon. Her heart lifted. She wasn't even surprised Sister, usually a strict keeper of rules, had broken them to let him in. He'd charm the devil himself if he wanted anything. He hadn't changed a bit.

The afternoon flew and as soon as they could get away Cissie went to the hostel to change and Rose rushed to meet William at Hope's house. When she arrived she found he wasn't alone. Another man in Naval uniform sat drinking a cup of tea. He stood up when Rose entered the room.

"This is Glyn." William said, indicating the sandy-haired young man. "Poor blighter's only got forty-eight hours before he has to report back to the ship. Aunt Hope says we can all stay tonight so I thought he could come out with us."

Rose grinned. So like William to arrange everything.

"Hello," Glyn said in a soft, melodic Welsh accent. "I hope I'm not intruding."

"Of course not. You're very welcome," Rose said taking in his gentle features. A smile lit up his hazel eyes.

"Where's your friend?" William asked.

"She went to change," Rose said. "She'll be here shortly. How long are you staying?"

"I've to report to Portsmouth tomorrow afternoon for training on the new radio telegraphy equipment. A couple of weeks in dry dock for me."

Rose felt a surge of relief. At least he'd be safe for a couple of weeks. Then Cissie arrived. She'd changed into a midnight blue afternoon dress that brushed her calf. Rose thought she looked quite classy. "This is Cissie," she said.

"Pleased to meet you." William shook her hand and gave her his brightest smile.

Cissie smiled back and Rose saw the flash of admiration in her eyes.

Glyn said hello too then Rose went up to change into something more suitable for the evening. She chose a jade green dress that reflected the emerald of her eyes. She fastened her silver locket around her neck and pinned the rose quartz brooch William had given her to the dress. She brushed her dark auburn hair up into a roll and pinched her cheeks to bring a little colour. Overall she was pleased with how she looked.

Hope insisted they eat something before going out. Silas joined them for dinner with Olivia and Sean. In the dining room Rose saw Amos Little propped up on one of the chairs.

"You've brought Amos along?" she said.

"I've been entertaining the children," William said.

"He's being modest," Glyn said. "He entertains us all on the ship. He does card tricks as well. He could go on the stage."

"I'm not sure his mother would approve of that," Hope said.

"Why not," Rose asked well aware of Ma's views on the subject. "She always hankered after a stage career herself. Why shouldn't William?"

Hope looked uncomfortable. "That's something it's best to ask her," she said. "Pass the gravy, Olivia," and the subject was dropped.

Sean asked about the ship. "How big is it? Are there many people on it?"

"Huge and lots," William said, indulging him.

"We read about Jutland in the paper," Silas said. "Put up a good show by all accounts."

"We certainly showed them," William said. "But I hear you're not entirely safe here. Rose told me about the Zepps."

"You'll have seen the damage yourself," Silas said.

"Yes. I can't believe how much London has changed," William said. "As well as the Zepps changing the landscape there are new buildings everywhere. They've even drained the lake in St James's Park where I used to sail my boat. They're putting up new buildings for the Admiralty I believe."

"The lake was drained as it was thought the night-time glow might direct the Zepps to Buckingham Palace. All the parks and open spaces are being used for government business these days," Silas said. "Hospitals, Ministries, even allotments. All temporary of course, but everyone is doing their bit for the war effort."

"Well, I for one can't wait until it's all over," Hope said, helping herself to some more potatoes.

Rose realised Hope didn't like the war being discussed over dinner so she asked Glyn about his home town and both he and Cissie each spoke about growing up in Wales and how they missed the green fields, the sheep and the constant wet weather. The rest of the meal passed pleasantly talking about their respective homes and families.

After dinner Rose, Cissie, Glyn and William set off for the West End where Cissie said all the action was.

"Don't be too late home," Hope said as they were leaving. "Don't forget you have an early start in the morning."

"Don't worry, I'll look after them." William grinned.

"Don't fuss, woman," Silas said. "You're not too old to remember what it was like being young enough to stay out all night and still make it into work the next morning."

"Oh yes," Hope said, laughing. "Those were the days."

Cissie took them to the Ritz Hotel first where a band played in the ball room and dancers filled the floor. Glyn ordered champagne which arrived in a bucket of ice. "Might as well push the boat out," he said. "You never know when you'll get another chance."

William whisked Cissie onto the floor.

"He doesn't waste much time, does he?" Glyn said, pouring Rose a glass of champagne.

Rose shrugged. It all looked so glamorous, the glittering chandeliers, the white and gold walls, the music and the men in uniform making the most of their leave to forget the war for a few hours in the company of beautiful young ladies. Rose recognised one of the nurses from the hospital in the arms of a soldier, spinning around the floor in time to the music. It was a different world compared to the horror of the wards.

"Have you known William long?" Rose asked.

"We trained together and luckily got assigned to the same ship. He's a good mate."

"More or less the same as me and Cissie," Rose said. "I don't know how I'd have coped without her."

"We have to grab our happiness where we can these days," Glyn said. "You never know how long it's going to last."

Rose began to think there was more to this young man than she'd originally thought.

"I'm glad William's found a good friend," she said.

Rose watched William and Cissie as they danced cheek to cheek, two blonde heads entwined as close as hair in a braid. It soon became clear that Cissie, who'd warned Rose about hardening her heart and not losing it, was completely bowled over.

"He's a charmer all right," Glyn said, watching Rose. "Still, I expect you're used to that."

"Oh yes," Rose said remembering how, even at school, William enchanted everyone from the oldest teacher to the youngest pupil, as though their adoration was his by right.

"Shall we?" Glyn asked nodding to the floor.

Rose smiled and they joined the others on the floor. Dancing with him brought fresh memories of Ferdie. She wished she was in his arms but that felt like some sort of betrayal. Glyn was lovely. It wasn't his fault he wasn't Ferdie.

She wasn't a particularly good dancer but Glyn guided her effortlessly around the floor. She wondered at the fresh clean smell of him and the ease of being in his arms. She found she was enjoying herself more than she had anticipated.

Glyn claimed Cissie for the next dance and Rose sat at a table with William. He took out his silver cigarette case and offered Rose a cigarette. She shook her head. He took one out of the case and lit it with a match from the book of matches on the table.

"Are you happy?" she asked him.

He thought for a few moments. "Yes," he said. "I am. I'm doing a job I enjoy with people I get on with. I'm making a difference and saving people's lives. You?"

Rose sighed. "Well, it's harder than I thought it would be, but I do feel I'm helping and I'm appreciated by the patients, if not by Sister."

"Does she give you a hard time?"

Rose chuckled. "No more than one would expect," she said. "No, they're all very good and I'm lucky to be where I am. But happy?" she pouted. "Not sure about that, but I'm content and that's enough."

He smiled. "You'll do," he said.

She laughed. "You too," she replied and knew that the bond between them would always be there as strong as ever.

"So you're not going home to live with Ma?"

"No," Rose grinned at him. "I don't think she's forgiven them for signing you up to a ship instead of basing you at home as promised."

He laughed. "They wanted to," he said, "but I persuaded them to let me sign onto a ship. It was my choice." He drew on his cigarette and blew the smoke out in circles that floated up to the ceiling. "The world's changing, Rose. This war, the men fighting it, it's turned everything upside down. The old order is being swept away. You can't put new ideas and freedoms back in the box. It won't work. We have to make the most of it."

Rose picked up her glass. William had changed, that was for sure. The mischievous, endearing, amiable boy had gone and in his place was a man who knew what he wanted and how to get it.

After the hotel they went to a cabaret club, then another bar and ended up in the early hours at the cafe in the Strand that Rose enjoyed most. It was crowded and noisy with the piano playing and men singing, but they managed to find a table.

Rose almost burst with pride and pleasure when Glyn got up and gave a heartfelt, rousing rendition of Cwm Rhondda (Bread of Heaven) in his deep baritone voice. Cissie joined in along with a group of Welsh Fusiliers sitting at another table.

"That reminded me of home," Cissie said, tears glistening in her eyes. "It's a long time since I heard it sung so beautifully."

Glyn blushed.

By the time they made it home, tired but uplifted and happy, the boys barely had time to wash, freshen up and pack before enjoying the bacon, eggs and fried potato Hope had prepared using her entire meat and egg ration for the week. After breakfast they all said their hurried goodbyes and promised to write, then Silas took William and Glyn to the station to catch their different trains. At least they'll both get a chance to sleep on the train, Rose thought.

They were walking to the hospital when Cissie told her she'd promised to write to William. "Do you mind?" she asked.

Rose wasn't surprised. "You don't need my permission," she said.

"No, but I wouldn't want anything to spoil our friendships. If you're not happy about it—"

"You'd write anyway."

Cissie laughed. "Yes, probably. He's quite something, your brother."

"I know a lot of girls who'd agree with you," Rose said. "I wouldn't want you to be hurt." She adored William beyond measure but wasn't blind to his faults. "You must realise William's not…not…how should I put it? Not a stayer."

"I'll take my chances," Cissie said. "It might not last, but it'll be fun while it does."

Rose knew there was nothing she could say or do. William had cast his spell and Cissie was caught up in it. I hope William will treat her kindly and let her down gently, she thought.

The next evening Rose wanted to know more about her mother's reluctance to sanction a career on the stage for William when she'd longed for one herself and, hearing about Cissie and Glyn's family had made her wonder more about her own. While they were clearing up after dinner she asked Hope, "What was my father like?"

Hope rattled the pans. "You should ask your mother."

"I have. She won't talk about him but you must have known him. I just want to know what he was like."

Hope shrugged. "He was a magician. He cast his spell over her. He was handsome." She wrinkled her nose. "No, not handsome – more disarming really. Witty and filled with boyish charm. Your ma fell for him in a big way. She loved him. He let her down. He caused her – all of us – a lot of trouble. I doubt she wants to be reminded of that."

"Was he so bad, if she loved him?"

"Not at first. No. Then he was all magnetism and charisma, but people change. Circumstances, life…

Don't judge her too harshly. It hasn't always been easy for her."

"Is that why she's so against William going on the stage?"

"That, and the fact that it's a highly unstable, not to say disreputable, profession. Unpredictable and often short lived. It's a hand to mouth existence that can be ruthless, soul destroying and relentlessly cruel. I think Violet learned that the hard way."

"She's afraid William may turn out like him?"

Hope sighed. "Yes, but she's wrong. Oh, he has his father's looks and charm, but he also has strength of purpose, integrity, courage and passion. He knows right from wrong and has a gentleman's understanding of life's obligations. We can thank Gabriel for that. He's been more of a father to you and William than Bert Shadwick ever could." She smiled at Rose. "William can do far better than a life on stage," she said.

Rose thought she understood her mother better now. "Thank you for telling me," she said.

Chapter Fifteen

The last of summer faded into autumn. Rose noticed the changing of the seasons as she walked to work. Flowers and trees turned golden and russet brown, the air dampened and chilled, a morning mist hung over the river. The summer sounds of music, chatting and laughter were replaced by the honking and hooting of boats as they made their way to and from the docks. Some days were so wet and muggy she'd arrive at work spattered with mud from the road. A quiet despondency seemed to hang over the city.

That morning the postwoman handed her a bunch of letters, she glanced through them and found three addressed to her;. one from William, one from Gabriel and one from Violet. Nothing from Ferdie. She sighed and put them in her pocket to open during her break at work. She put the rest on the sideboard for Hope.

She didn't get a chance to open her letters until lunch time when she sat in the canteen while Cissie queued for their tea and sandwiches. She opened Ma's letter first.

Violet had written about the people she knew in the town, all the news and gossip. She'd been to see Joe's mother who'd visited him in the hospital in Kings Lynn. They all hoped he'd be home soon. She said Nesta, her friend who ran a B & B had turned it into a hostel for VADs. She mentioned a couple of Officers they'd had in. Slightly wounded, she said. That made Rose chuckle. Her mother obviously saw them as good matrimonial prospects. Then she told Rose about Florence's latest efforts at knitting and Joshua's collecting horse chestnuts just as he had a year ago. Could it really be year since last October? She remembered Joshua's excitement then and wondered if he was as excited this time. The sudden stab of memory made her realise how much she missed them, Florence and Joshua. They'd be growing up in her absence. She sighed at the thought. Great Yarmouth felt a long way away.

Finally Violet wrote about her preparations for Christmas and said how much she was looking forward to Rose coming home for the festivities. A dull ache of dread formed in Rose's stomach as she saw the battle ahead. Ma wanted her home for Christmas. She wasn't even sure if it would be possible. Of course some staff could have leave, but she was a probationary nurse, the bottom of the pile. Even if she could get leave she wasn't sure she wanted it. They were already making Christmas preparations at the hospital; services in the wards, decorations, a choir, musical entertainment and she wanted to be part of it, doing her bit. Someone had to work over Christmas, why not her?

She sighed, folded the letter and put it in her pocket.

She opened Gabriel's letter next. It was dated a few weeks ago. He thanked her for the chocolates she'd sent which he'd shared with his troops. He told her the weather had turned colder, the mornings misty and half-dark. The men appreciated the socks and other home comforts her ma had sent. They were moving up the line.

She pictured him, his gentle sweetness and unhurried charm, struggling through the mud. He'd taken a Commission with his old Cavalry Regiment and he'd be with the horses pulling supplies through the mire to the lines at the Front, where the heavier trucks and lorries got bogged down, or the terrain was too difficult for them to get through. At least if he was there, she thought, he'd make sure the horses requisitioned from estates like his father's weren't ill-treated.

She read on. He said he'd managed a few days respite near a market town where the streets were lined with gabled cottages and the square buzzed with life. He said it reminded him of market day in Swaffham. The people there were very much the same as people at home. They were billeted at a farmhouse and had eaten well for the first time in weeks. There was an orchard with apples and the horses were able to run out in the field and graze green grass. There was beauty too. The nights were bitter but the sky drenched with stars and the moon a luminous glow of ghostly white. If it wasn't for the constant booming of guns and the star-bursts of exploding shrapnel it would be idyllic.

He hoped she was keeping well and not finding the work too onerous as he knew she must be dealing with sights and realities beyond anything she could have imagined. He told her he and Ma were proud of her. He reassured her, as he did in every letter, that though things were difficult now they'd get through it and be together again soon in happier times.

She smiled when she read that he hoped to get some leave soon and see her in person. Meanwhile, he sent his love.

She folded the letter and put it in her pocket. She'd write back to him tonight.

William's letter was shorter. That made Rose smile. He wasn't the world's greatest letter writer so she appreciated the effort he'd made. It had been posted from Chatham shortly before he rejoined his ship, so she had no idea where in the world he was now.

He said that the training course had been worthwhile, he was glad to be back aboard and looked forward to setting sail again.

Reading his words brought him sharply into focus. She could almost see him writing it, his wide, mischievous smile, his blue eyes shining with excitement at what lay ahead. The thought of him brought a warm glow to her heart and a stab of sorrow at not being near him. She missed him more than ever.

He wrote that Glyn had said he hoped to see her again. *'(You could do worse)'* he'd put which made her laugh. At the end he told her to behave herself and beware of falling for wounded soldiers. He wrote *'Amos sends love'* and finished with kisses.

Cissie arrived at the table with a tray of tea and sandwiches. "Ooo, letters. Anything interesting?" she said.

"It's from William," Rose said.

"I got one too," Cissie said.

"He says Glyn hopes to see me again. He says, quote, 'You could do worse'. Honestly, he's as bad as my mother. She wants to introduce me to some 'eligible officers'."

"Yes, he said the same about Glyn in my letter. Said he'd taken a shine to you."

"What? After just one dance?" As she said it the memory of 'just one dance' with Ferdie and what she felt about him entered her mind.

"Well," Cissie said, pouring the tea, "according to the girls in the hostel it might not be such a bad idea to bag a husband now. With all the young men being killed or injured there's going to be a shortage after the war. They reckon we should get in quick if you don't want to end up an old maid."

Rose laughed. "I'll take my chances," she said.

Rose was transferred to a medical ward to complete her training. Here she accompanied the doctor on his rounds, supervised medication, gave injections and took blood. She learned about the various diseases, how they were to be treated and that the doctor's word was law.

In marked contrast to the previous ward, the patients were elderly and their conditions long-term or terminal. Many were resigned to their fate and felt no need to socialise with each other. They only talked about their ailments, or complaints. She missed the camaraderie and good humour of the soldiers, who were always joshing each other and competing for the attention of the nurses.

She compared notes with Cissie during their break and found she felt the same.

"When we're qualified we'll have more choice," Cissie said. "I think I might go for paediatrics. Definitely not geriatrics."

Rose laughed. "I don't mind the old folk," she said. "They're sometime funny and they have tales to tell. The thought of children being ill tears my heart out. I think I'm best suited to surgery. At least there you have people who are getting better."

Chapter Sixteen

November brought the first frost, icing the streets with white. A bitter chill blew in from the river and Rose was glad of her thick coat, hat, gloves and scarf. Her breath vaporised in the morning air as she walked to work. She stopped on Westminster Bridge to gaze out at the river. Watching the boats and the never-ending changes the seasons brought always lifted her heart and made her realise how lucky she was to be in such a place. It looked so normal and, at this hour, so peaceful she never failed to be heartened by it.

At least she arrived at work in a good mood ready for the trials of the day. Usually, by the end of it she felt very different. She worried about the patients, her ability to help them and their futures. If it hadn't been for the nights out with Cissie and seeing life going on as usual in town the work could easily have distressed her more. It felt like a constant battle that they were nowhere near winning.

All her doubts, fears and worries evaporated when she arrived home one evening. Hope greeted her in the hallway, catching her before she could disappear into her room as she usually did after a hard day's work.

"We have a visitor," she said. The smile on Hope's face made her rush into the drawing room where Gabriel sat having a cup of tea with Silas.

As soon as she walked in Gabriel jumped up and she ran into his arms.

"Why didn't you let me know you were coming?" she said. "I'd have come home earlier."

"I've only just got here myself," Gabriel said. "I'm on my way back from Norfolk. Ma sends her love. She's looking forward to having you home for Christmas."

"I know," Rose said. "She wrote, but I'm not sure I can…"

He smiled. "We'll talk about that later," he said. "First I want to hear all about what you've been up to. Silas tells me you have a pretty busy social life."

"I've been lucky," she said. "Thanks to Uncle Silas and Aunt Hope putting me up."

"I hope you haven't been too much trouble."

"No trouble at all," Silas said. "We've been happy to have her here."

Hope called them into dinner. Gabriel put his arm around Rose's shoulders as they walked through to the dining room.

"It's good to see you," she said and kissed his cheek.

"This looks lovely," Gabriel said as Hope served the meal.

"Luckily you've arrived on one of Mrs B's days," Hope said. "I can assure you my efforts wouldn't produce anything half as grand."

Only once everyone had been served did Hope sit down and fill her own plate. "We had a letter from Dexi," she said. "She told us she saw you."

"Yes," Gabriel said. "She was driving an ambulance towards Etaples. There was a tractor blocking the way ahead and Dexi stood in the road haranguing the driver in fluent French. She didn't hold back either. I've never heard a lady swear so well in French before."

Silas chuckled. "I'm not surprised given how long she's lived in Paris. That sounds like my sister. How did she look? She tells us she's well, but we do worry."

Gabriel thought for a moment. "She looked thinner…older…not so exuberant as when I last saw her and definitely not so well dressed." He became serious. "There was something about her – a look – a sort of quiet satisfaction, I think, as though she'd found something she cherished, a sense of purpose." He sighed. "It was a terrible place. Cold, muddy, dirty and the road almost impassable, but she seemed – well – happy to be there if you know what I mean. Fulfilled. She's doing a wonderful job, her and the other VADs."

"I should be there," Silas said suddenly putting down his cutlery. "Not here, warming my back-side on a chair while others are out there fighting to keep us all safe."

Hope saw the anger in his eyes. She knew of his frustration with the men in Whitehall who didn't seem to have any idea what was going on across the Channel. Her stomach clenched. It was the thing she'd been dreading since summer when married men up to forty-one were added to the list for conscription. "But you do your bit," she said. "Your work at the War Office—"

"It's not enough. I may be forty-four but I'm not over the hill. I'm a good deal fitter than men half my age. I bet there are men older than me over there, doing their bit, aren't there, Gabriel?"

Gabriel glanced at Hope and then at Silas. "Yes," he said. "Men in their fifties working on transport and supplies. We couldn't manage without them."

"I'm sorry, Hope. But I've waited long enough hoping it would all be over and the men coming home victorious. I can no longer sit here pretending everything is all right when we know damned well it isn't."

Hope forced her lips into a smile. She recalled that it was Silas who saved her brother Alfie from the fire that took her parents and she'd heard how he saved Dexi when her husband was killed in America. Silas didn't lack courage. He would always do what he thought right. She knew when she married him that he wasn't the sort of man to sit by and do nothing if there was something he could do to make things better. He had a conscience and she loved him all the more for it. "You want to enlist?" she said.

"I have to. There's no other choice."

Hope nodded. "So be it then. All we can do is pray that it'll be over soon."

"Thank you," he said, the softness in his voice letting her know how much her acceptance of his intention meant to him.

A great bubble of love rose up inside her for this man who had become her whole world.

After dinner Hope cleared away the dishes, Silas went to his office to see what arrangement he'd have to make for his business before he joined up. Rose and Gabriel sat in the drawing room having coffee.

"So, about Christmas," Gabriel said. "You know Ma's expecting you home."

Rose's heart dropped. "I know, but I have to work. She must realise that I can't just take time off when I want. It doesn't work like that."

Gabriel shrugged. "With William away as well it'll be a very different Christmas for her this year," he said. "I just thought – if you could manage it."

Rose sighed. "Well I can't," she said. She felt awful. She didn't want to disappoint anyone but she had her own life to lead. She had plans. "I'll write. I may be able to visit early in the New Year. I'll do the best I can."

Gabriel sipped his coffee. "You'll be finishing your training soon," he said. "Getting your Certificate."

She smiled. "Yes. In January."

"Ma's thinking you might transfer to a hospital in Norfolk where you could live at home." Gabriel said. "Even work at the hotel?"

Rose's jaw clenched. She'd spoken to Cissie about transferring to another hospital after they qualified. They'd both decided that London, as well as providing the best nursing training in England, also afforded the best opportunities for entertainment. "I don't think that's a very good idea," she said, desperately trying to think of a good reason why not. "I mean, the training I'm getting here is second to none."

Gabriel smiled. "And you're having so much fun you don't want to go home and live under your mother's wing."

Rose laughed. "As long as Aunt Hope and Uncle Silas will have me," she said, having a sudden second thought, "and with Uncle Silas going away I think I can be more help here."

It was Gabriel's turn to laugh. "Well, best wait until you see your ma to tell her. It'll be better coming face to face."

Rose leaned over and kissed him. "I knew you'd understand," she said and thought again how lucky she was having Gabriel as her pa.

Later Rose left Gabriel with Silas to talk about the war. She went to help Hope prepare the next morning's breakfast. "Will Uncle Silas really go?" she asked.

"Oh yes. I'm surprised I've managed to keep him home this long."

"Don't you mind?"

"It's no use minding," Hope said. "Silas will always follow his heart and his conscience He'll always do the right thing. I wouldn't want him any other way."

"How will you manage without him?"

Hope laughed. "The same way your ma manages without Gabriel and Alice manages without John. The same way every wife in the country manages. We'll rely on each other and just get on with it."

The next morning Gabriel was leaving to go to the station to catch the early train, Rose was on her way out to go to work when the post arrived. The postwoman handed the letters to Rose without her usual cheery 'good morning'.

Rose soon saw the reason why. On top of the pile of letters was a card from Etaples. Cpl. P Quirk was in hospital there suffering from slight/serious wounds.

Chapter Seventeen

Gabriel picked up the card, his face stony. "I'll take it up," he said. He glanced at Rose. "You'd better come too."

Rose nodded, her stomach churned. She knew how Hope and Silas felt about the boy they'd adopted. Memories whirled around in her head. She saw his face, pale as moonlight, the knowing look in his dark, intelligent, eyes, his unexpectedly engaging smile and the tousle of coal black curls tumbling over his forehead. A few years older than her and William he'd become William's hero. He'd follow him around asking questions about his life on the street, questions Peter always answered with surprising frankness. Now he was lying in a hospital bed far from home.

A lump rose in her throat and tears sprang to her eyes.

"It's Hope who'll take it the worst," Gabriel said. "We must do all we can to…" he shrugged and Rose saw how deeply the news had affected him. It was something that could happen to anyone and he was at a loss as to how to deal with it.

Rose followed him up the stairs to the drawing room where Hope and Silas were having coffee. Silas smiled as they entered, but his expression changed when he saw the card in Gabriel's hand. He dropped the newspaper he was reading and stood up. Gabriel gave him the card.

Hope gasped, her hand flew to her mouth. "No," she said, fear clear in her eyes. "It can't be…no…"

"It may not be too bad," Gabriel said, trying to allay her fears. "It says slight wounds and he's in Etaples. If it was serious he'd be at a Clearing Station and on his way home. We have to hope and pray for the best."

Silence reverberated around the room. Silas's voice was gruff when he eventually spoke. "He's a bright lad, strong and resilient. He'll pull through," he said.

Hope sat silent, her hand covering her mouth, unstoppable tears streaming over her cheeks.

"If there's anything I can do," Rose said. Even to her the words sounded hollow.

Hope sniffed and turned to gaze out of the window, hiding her face and her feelings until she could compose them into some sort of response.

"We'll be all right," Silas said. "I'll take care of her. You must get off or you'll miss your train."

He shook Gabriel's hand. "Thank you for…" he shrugged, unable to continue.

Gabriel grinned, putting on a brave face. "I'm sure he'll be fine," he said. "He'll bounce back, he always does."

Silas nodded. "You're right," he said. "If it was serious he'd be coming home. He's not. We'll take heart from that."

Reluctantly Rose walked to work. Her footsteps dragged as her heart was back in the drawing room with Hope. She recalled the first time she'd seen Peter. He'd come into their lives when they were five, at a time when Ma was away on business and they were staying with Aunty Hope. She wasn't sure why Hope and Silas had taken him in and later adopted him. All she knew was that the family owed him a debt of gratitude for some deed he'd done which concerned her mother.

It was something that was never talked about which made it even more intriguing. Hope and Silas had come to love and care for the boy as though he were their own. News of his injury would be just as devastating as an injury to William would be to Ma and Pa and she was helpless to do anything to ease the pain of it.

The air of despondency followed her around all morning, until Cissie asked he what was the matter. When she told her she realised how deeply the news had affected her too.

"They said 'slight wounds'. What do you think they mean by slight wounds?" she asked Cissie.

"Not life threatening," Cissie said. "It means they'll patch him up and send him back."

Rose's heart sank to her boots as another abyss of horror opened up in front of her. Of course they'd send him back. She felt even worse than before. Perhaps the 'seriously wounded' she dealt with every day were right. They were the lucky ones. They'd come home, not all of them entirely, but at least they were alive.

After an agonising week of worry Rose arrived home to find Hope in a much better mood. "I've had a letter from Dexi," she said. "She's seen Peter in the hospital."

Rose gasped with delight. "How is he?"

"She says he's in good spirits. Apparently he has broken ribs, a broken collar bone and shrapnel wounds to his chest and arms, but he will heal. She said, he will heal and we mustn't worry about him as he's in good hands."

"Oh, that's a relief," Rose said as her heart lifted a little. "It was good of her to write."

"Yes. But I won't rest until I see him for myself. She says he'll be coming home on leave as soon as he's fit enough to travel, so we may look forward to seeing him in the New Year."

A broad smile spread across Rose's face. "I'm so very pleased to hear it," she said and was surprised to find how much she too looked forward to seeing him again.

Rose tried to make sure she was the one who collected the post in the mornings. It wasn't difficult as the post usually arrived as she left for the hospital and she often met the postwoman on the doorstep.

She'd written two letters to Ferdie since sending him the photograph but had received no reply. She couldn't help wondering why, especially after Cissie's warning. Was she right? Had it meant so little to him when it had meant so much to her? True it was only one brief evening, but the memory of it stayed lodged in her mind to be replayed each night in her dreams. Had he not felt the same?

She told herself it was because he was busy fighting the war, he was in a place where they'd be out of touch, his letters had gone astray, anything but face the other reasons: he'd forgotten her, or worse, something terrible had happened to him.

She was on the verge of giving up any hope of hearing from him or seeing him again when a package, a bit bulky but not big, arrived for her. Her heart rose like a bird taking flight when she saw the handwriting and the BEF postmark. He hadn't forgotten her.

Hope came into the hall just as she picked up the package. "Is that the post?" she asked.

Rose blushed. She didn't want Hope to know she was corresponding with a soldier. She didn't want anyone to know. It was a secret she wanted to hug to herself, not something to be discussed and pronounced upon by others. Hope would only write to Ma, then she'd want to know all about him, his family and his prospects. Even with a war on Ma would espouse the benefits of a proper introduction and knowledge of his pedigree as though he were a prize stallion she was thinking of buying.

"Erm." Rose tucked the package under her coat. "There are some letters for Silas," she said and handed them to Hope. She picked up her bag and opened the door.

"Thank you," Hope said. She glanced out. "It looks a bit frosty out. Mind how you go."

"I will," Rose said and shivered as she walked briskly out.

The package burned under her coat. She couldn't wait to open it. She slipped it into her bag until she got to the hospital.

Thankfully the cloakroom was empty. Her heart pounded as she ripped the bag open. Not only had he written to her, he'd sent her a present.

She peered inside. Something soft and white. She drew it out. At first she wasn't sure what it was, just a bundle of lace. When she shook it out and held it up she found she was holding the scantiest, lacy, fine as cobwebs, underwear she'd ever seen. Did people really wear things like this? It wasn't the sort of thing she'd usually contemplate wearing, especially in late November.

A giggle rose up inside her. Then she saw the note. '*I look forward to seeing you in these.*' She gasped at the thought. Cissie was right. He was a naughty boy but she couldn't deny the thrill that ran through her. She recalled what Glyn had said about grabbing your happiness while you can. Her hand trembled as she put the lacy underwear back in the packet. Dare she wear them? She wasn't sure and letting him see her in them? Well, that was something else entirely. She pushed the package into her bag.

All morning the thought of what was lying at the bottom of her bag haunted her. She caught herself smiling when there was no reason to. Sister even caught her daydreaming a couple of times and admonished her. Visions of the underwear and her wearing it kept intruding into her thoughts, along with Ferdie and what he would think and, more importantly do when he saw her.

That evening she wrote back to him, thanking him for the gift and asking when he'd be on leave again. She told him she might have a surprise for him.

Chapter Eighteen

December brought snow which quickly turned to slush making the roads and pavements slippery and wet. Rose bought herself some new boots and a scarf to go with her warm coat. The river sparkled in the frosty mornings and pale dawn sunlight touched the facades of the buildings as she passed. People hurried, their heads down against the chill.

As the days shortened Christmas seemed to draw near quicker than ever. The snow turned to sleet and Rose hurried along sheltering under her umbrella, battling the sudden squally gusts from the river and trying desperately to keep at least a little dry on her way to work. These days she travelled to work and home again in the dark, the only lights the dim glow from the lamps on the boats going to and from the docks.

The weeks before Christmas seemed busier than ever with casualties still arriving daily.

At the hospital she pitched in with decorating the wards, pleased that at last the patients had something to smile about. A deep sense of pleasure filled her every time a wounded soldier recovered well from his operations and a spark of life came back to a face that had been wracked with pain and foreboding.

A smile, a cheery greeting, even an extra few minutes spent with a patient brought its own reward. The gratitude and appreciation they showed often overwhelmed her. No one was more delighted than Rose when one of them transferred to convalesce nearer to their home.

Things were different at Hope's house. With the colder, darker evenings Rose and Cissie were tempted out less often. Apart from the weekly visit to the cinema and the afternoon tea dances, they spent most of their time at the hospital. When they did go out they returned earlier than in the long summer evenings when it seemed to stay light until midnight.

Rose sat with Hope most evenings. When Silas left to join a training camp in the country it was the first time in their fifteen year marriage that Hope and Silas had spent any time apart.

"I'll be fine," Hope said, when Rose asked her how she'd manage. "We all find the strength we need when we have to. My sacrifice is small compared to others and I don't want Silas to worry about me when he will have so much more to worry about."

Rose spent her time either writing letters or practising some of the intricate embroidery stitches Hope, an expert needlewoman, was teaching her. She was stitching a sampler for Ma and hoped to have it finished for Christmas.

"My grandmother taught me," Hope said. "I'm delighted to be able to pass on her expertise."

"Ma always said your stitching was far superior to hers," Rose said.

Hope laughed. "Yes, I think she envied me that."

Rose knew that wasn't the only thing her ma envied about Hope but said nothing.

When Hope heard from Silas that he'd be home for Christmas but would have to leave for France the next morning the house became a flurry of preparation. Hope wanted his last day to be one he'd remember with joy and that would put his mind at rest about her coping in his absence. As part of Hope's plans she'd arranged for Daisy to come in to help her get ready and Mrs B to see to the meals. She managed to get a goose from the market (a special favour as she'd been such a good customer), as well as chicken and fresh vegetables to help eke out the home-grown ones she'd managed to store. Mrs B made mince pies and plum pudding. Hope had decorated the rooms with paper chains and garlands of holly and yew. A tree stood in the corner of the drawing room by the window, its branches heavy with candles and glittering baubles.

She invited all the family. Violet said she'd have loved to have come with her children, but couldn't leave the hotel as she had people there and so needed to stay at home. She sent her love and best wishes.

Alice said John would be home on leave for a few days before his overseas posting and they'd come with the children for dinner. She sent a ham (a gift from the brewery) to help with the rations.

Alfie and Jenny arrived on Christmas Eve. They travelled by train, catching a cab from Paddington station. Hope gasped when she saw them. "Why didn't you tell me?" she said, embracing a heavily pregnant Jenny. "When's it due?"

Alfie laughed. "We wanted it to be a surprise," he said. He put his arm around his wife. "All being well it'll be making an appearance in March."

"Many congratulation," Hope said. "Come upstairs and tell me all about it. What are you hoping for? A boy or a girl?"

Alfie and Jenny followed her upstairs.

"Jenny wants a boy, but I'll be happy with either as long as it's healthy," Alfie said. A stab of memory hit Hope. She recalled that both Alfie and his best friend George had been born with disabilities. "I'm sure he or she will be," she said but she wondered if that was why Alfie hadn't said anything. In case it turned out to be bad news. She put on a brave face. "Well you must both come in. Jenny can put her feet up while you see to the luggage. I've put you in your old room." Alfie's room was on the first floor at the back so he didn't have to use the stairs any more than could be helped.

Hope showed Jenny into the drawing room and pulled out a footstool for her. "It'll be lovely having you both here, even if it is only for a few days," she said.

Silas arrived later on Christmas Eve, happy to be home, but eager to join the men in France and Belgium supporting the front line. Hope was delighted to see that he looked healthy and well. He'd even broadened out a bit.

"Fresh air and exercise," he said. "It's all that running up and down hills carrying more than your own body weight in kit. Feel those muscles." Hope wanted to feel more than his muscles.

After dinner with the children, who were all over Alfie and Jenny and kept asking them questions, they spent a pleasant evening around the fire. Alfie and Jenny told them all about their life in the country and their plans for the future.

Hope put through a long-distance telephone call to Violet so that Rose could speak to her mother. Christmas Day would be Rose and William's seventeenth birthdays, and Hope knew how much Violet would miss them. She'd always made their birthdays special, because they'd arrived on Christmas Day.

It felt like an age waiting to be connected but when Rose heard her mother's voice a great swell of homesickness washed over her. She almost choked.

She wondered if she'd done the right thing deciding to work through Christmas at the hospital. She missed her home and family so much she ached inside, but then reasoned that she'd miss her work and her independence just as much and with William and Gabriel away, well, it wouldn't be the same anyway.

The line crackled and she had difficulty hearing what Violet was saying. "Happy birthday for tomorrow! Did you get the gifts?"

"I'm working at the hospital in the morning," she said. "Aunty Hope said there's a parcel from you. I'll open it tomorrow."

"We all miss you. When are you coming home?"

That brought a lump to her throat. "I'll be home in January," she said. "As soon as I get my Certificate." She'd already written to her mother and told her that. "How are Joshua and Florence?" The sound of their names brought a vision of them to her mind. Joshua, serious and pensive, Florence full of chatter and smiles. Another stab of guilt and sorrow at not seeing them hit her heart.

"Full of excitement and missing you. Here."

She heard Joshua on the line. "Hello…hello…ooo it's all crackly. Hello."

"Hello, Joshua. Are you behaving yourself?" She heard his laughter.

She tried to speak to Florence but her tiny voice sounded as distant as a faint echo fading over rolling hills. Then Ma came back on the line. "Take care of yourself," she said. "We all miss you and can't wait to see you soon."

"I know," Rose said. "I miss you too."

Then they said their goodbyes and Rose felt terrible all over again. They seemed so far away. She had tears in her eyes when she thanked Hope. "It was lovely speaking to them," she said.

Christmas morning was made more magical by a heavy fall of snow that covered the landscape, turning the dirty slush filled streets to picture postcard prettiness. They breakfasted together then Silas went out to make a few calls before he left the country.

Hope laid the table with the best cutlery and lead crystal glasses. A centrepiece made of candles on a silver plate surrounded by holly and winter jasmine graced the white linen cloth. She put their last bottle of champagne to chill while Mrs B prepared and cooked the meal.

Daisy helped Hope dress in her midnight blue silk 'Sapphire' dress. The one she'd worn when she worked for Silas at The Grenadier all those years ago. She'd had it re-modelled into a more fashionable style and let out to fit her fuller figure. Around her neck she wore the sapphire necklace Silas had given her. His first gift to her. Daisy helped her put her blonde hair up in ringlets caught at the back of her head to fall on her bare shoulders with tendrils framing her face. When she saw her reflection in the mirror she though the years had been kind to her. She hoped Silas would approve.

Rose spent the morning at the hospital, glad to be inside where the cheery atmosphere warmed her. Everyone appeared relaxed and happy, the mood of the season having captured everyone in its thrall. It was as magical as she'd hoped it would be.

After the morning round of washing and changing dressings, breakfast and doctors' rounds anyone who could walk or be wheeled made their way to the canteen on the ground floor for the Christmas Day service, a joyous, uplifting celebration of the nativity.

After the service VADs served coffee with tots of rum, mince pies and plum pudding while a choir sang. Rose went back to the ward with her heart lighter and the sound of carols and jingle bells still ringing in her ears.

Back in the ward the patients enjoyed a special lunch of roast goose and duck, provided by a benefactor from the country. After lunch the patients were left to rest or receive visitors.

"Are you staying for the concert this evening?" Cissie asked.

"No," Rose said. "It's my uncle's last day so I want to see him and the family before he goes."

"Good idea," Cissie said. "You never know if…"

"Yes. Thanks," Rose said.

"Sorry. Didn't mean…"

"It's all right," Rose said, but she knew Cissie was right. There was no guarantee they'd see any of them again.

Cissie gave Rose some luxury perfumed soaps for Christmas and a book on nursing for her birthday. Rose had, with Hope's help, made Cissie a black velvet evening bag embroidered with sequins.

Walking home Rose thought of Ferdie and wondered what his Christmas would be like. She'd sent him some cigars, chocolate and a tin of biscuits. She'd had a couple of letters from him, full of warmth. He'd even included a short poem she kept in her writing case. He said he was thinking of her and hoped she was thinking of him. He looked forward to seeing her again and *'carrying on where we left off'*. That had thrilled her.

She pictured him in the fog, snow and ice doing his duty and her heart swelled. He'd be with other men making the most of what they had 'over there'. She couldn't wait to be in his arms again, imagining the time they'd spend together next time he came home. If there was one thing that threw a damper over Christmas it was thinking of Ferdie so far away. It didn't seem fair.

Hope was delighted to see John, Alice and the children when they arrived for dinner, especially as John brought two bottles of wine to go with the meal. She showed them into the drawing room where they all fussed over Jenny and congratulated Alfie.

"Well, you're a sly dog," John said as he shook Alfie's hand. "Never knew you had it in you."

Alfie blushed but Hope could see how pleased he was. "A bit of a way to go to catch you up," he said.

John slapped him on the back and Hope saw a deep affection between the brothers that she'd never seen when they were growing up. Alfie had come into his own at last.

She'd forgotten how noisy and exuberant the children could be. Amy, the oldest, was the quietest. She made a beeline for Rose and wanted to hear about nursing and working at the hospital. Alexander, and John Junior, aged seven and eight, were more boisterous and Hope sent them out into the garden to play in the snow with Sean.

Alfie went with them. "Come on, let's see if we can build a snowman," he said.

Hope thought it was more likely to be snowballs they'd be playing, but said nothing. Emily, who was six, was the spitting image of Violet's daughter Florence. She chatted and played in the corner with her doll.

Hope thought Alice looked tired but that wasn't surprising. She was running the pub, albeit for reduced hours, and looking after the family.

Dinner was a noisy cacophony of conversation, jokes and laughter. Everyone, pleased to see Silas, wished him well.

"I've had a letter from Esme," he said (everyone else called her Dexi). "She's in St Quintans. She says troops pass through every day and she'll look out for me. If we stop there she knows a great restaurant we can have dinner."

"It sounds quite civilised," Hope said.

"Yes. My sister always did have a knack for making the best of things." She caught the note of pride in his voice.

The more lavish than usual spread and the plentiful wine put everyone in party mood, the knowledge of the brief time they had to enjoy it making it more poignant. Hope was pleased to see Jenny joining in the conversation, her face shining with happiness. She was witty and clever as well as warm-hearted and kind. Hope could see why Alfie adored her.

It was the best family Christmas they'd had for long time, but she couldn't help wondering how long it would be before they could all be together again.

After the main course John helped Hope clear the dishes while Rose got the dessert. Downstairs in the kitchen they stacked the dishes to wash later. Rose took the mince pies and plum pudding upstairs.

John seemed troubled so Hope asked if everything was all right. "You seem preoccupied," she said. "It's not like you."

"I worry about what will happen to Alice and the children if anything happens to me," he said.

"We'll take care of them," Hope said without hesitation. "You don't need to ask."

"You think Silas will be all right?"

"Of course he will," she said with more conviction than she felt. "He's indestructible. You should know that."

John smiled. The first time she'd seen him smile all day. "I do believe he is," he said and Hope knew he was thinking of the many situations he'd survived that would have seen off lesser men.

"He told me he'd be behind the lines, supporting the Royal Engineers in Belgium," she said. "You don't think he was saying that to stop me worrying?"

"No. Don't worry, Hope," he said. "They don't put men his age on the front line."

That may be true now, she thought, but how long would it stay that way.

After dinner they played charades and Amy tried a few magic tricks which failed dismally. They all laughed, but Hope thought about William and his tricks and knew Rose missed him most of all, especially on their birthday.

"Have you heard from William at all?" she asked her.

"Yes," Rose said. "He's spending Christmas escorting convoys in the Med. They'll be having a fine old time."

Hope nodded. Then she thought of Peter, lying in a hospital bed in France. How different all their Christmases were this year.

That night, when Hope lay in Silas's arms for the last time before he went away, she couldn't help but worry about their future. Why did this war have to spoil everything? Then she thought about what they were fighting for and knew that Silas, as always, was doing the right thing for his country, and his family's future.

Chapter Nineteen

New Year's Eve Rose and Cissie planned to go to a nightclub the other girls had been talking about to see in the New Year. Snow had fallen lining the roads and frost iced the air. Darkness, unbroken by any light, engulfed them as they walked. The passing traffic threw up waves of muddy slush.

"It'll be slippery later," Cissie said, "if this freezes over."

Rose hung on to Cissie's arm. "It's a clear night," she said. "I wouldn't be surprised if it does."

They found the club and went in. Inside it thronged with people. A jazz band played and the mood was one of high-spirited revelry. Cissie got them drinks while Rose found a table. They weren't sitting for long. Soon they were up on the floor joining in the dancing. They swapped partners, and mixed with the other dancers in a ring. Cissie danced with a soldier. Rose danced with a shy young lad no more than seventeen who worked in munitions.

By midnight the floor was full of people dancing the old year away. They linked hands for Auld Lang Syne. Everyone wished the next year would bring better news than the last. By the end of the evening they were both laughing and holding each other up.

On the way home the air-raid warning went.

"Oh God it sounds close," Cissie said as searchlights lit up the sky.

People were rushing to the nearest Underground station for shelter. Rose and Cissie joined them, being jostled and pushed as they went down the stairs. They picked their way through the crowded platform where families had bedded down for the night and found a spot to settle. Rose had been warm from the walk when they arrived but sat on hard concrete with tiles at her back, the cold soon seeped into her bones. She shivered and a woman sitting near them passed her a blanket to share. Another couple squeezed in next to them. The close proximity of the bodies around them kept Rose warm, if uncomfortable. Despite the discomfort they both managed to nod off for a few hours. When they awoke they only had time to dash out into the frost and snow and run home to change before going to work.

"Welcome to 1917," Cissie said.

Hope's New Year was a quiet one. She did her best to make it jolly for the children, but with Silas away it felt pointless. Olivia stayed up to see in the New Year. Sean wanted to, but by eleven o'clock Hope saw him nodding off in the chair, so took him up to bed.

"I wonder what Pa's doing right now," Olivia said. "I miss him so."

"Me too," Hope said. She'd been wondering the same thing. "I expect he'll be having a high old time if I know your pa. A few drinks in the Mess and singing Auld Lang Syne with his pals. Like his sister he'll be making the best of things." Still she was sure he'd be thinking of them. "Here's to him, and all being together again soon," she said and raised her glass. They both drank and Hope missed him more than ever.

Olivia went to bed but Hope waited up for Rose until she almost fell asleep in the chair. She watched the hands on the clock going round. She'd heard the air-raid siren and hoped they'd found shelter. She decided worrying about them wouldn't help anybody, so went to bed. She hardly slept. She heard Rose come in so got up and went down to see her.

In the middle of making tea and Rose's breakfast the doorbell rang. Rose went to answer it. A boy handed her a telegram for Hope. Hope's heart almost stopped. She gasped as thoughts roared through head and a cauldron of fear swirled inside her. She was all fingers and thumbs as she opened it. She breathed a great sigh of relief when she read it. Peter was coming home on leave. He'd be there in a couple of days.

Snow covered the ground and frost hardened the air as Rose walked home from the hospital a couple of days later. She had the afternoon off and planned to study for her final exams. As she approached the house she saw a cab at the kerb. A tall man in an army great coat, his cap pulled down against the cold, stood beside it paying the driver. A kit bag sat on the pavement next to him.

A sliver of doubt troubled her. She pushed it back.

"Peter?" she called and hurried towards him.

He looked up and a smile creased his features. His dark eyes crinkled with pleasure. "Rose," he said. "Ma said you were staying."

Seeing him, the easy smile, the familiar face, sent a rush of warmth through her. Then she saw the scar still livid on his cheek. She'd seen enough shrapnel wounds to know the damage would be far more extensive than that. She wondered how many other wounds scarred his body. She reached on tiptoe and kissed his cheek. "Aunt Hope will be thrilled you're here," she said.

He grinned. "I had hoped she wouldn't be the only one," he said.

She laughed. Same old Peter, she thought.

Hope appeared at the door. The smile on her face lit up the whole street. "Peter," she said, dashing down the path. "You made it." She hugged him, he winced. "Oh, I'm sorry. Is it very bad?"

"No. I'm fine really."

"I'm so happy to see you," she said, her voice warm with relief.

"Happy to be home," he said.

"Let's get inside out of the cold. Have you eaten?"

"Yes. I had something on the train."

"What? A currant bun and cold tea if I know the sort of thing they serve on trains. There's cold meat, cheese and pickles," Hope said. "And Mrs B came in and baked some of your favourite scones."

"I'll get it," Rose said, "and make tea, I expect you could do with it."

"That sounds wonderful," he said.

When Rose took in the tray of tea Peter stood to help. Now twenty, in his uniform without his coat and cap he looked taller and broader than she remembered. His black as night curls were shorn to dark spikes and she saw the wound stripe on his sleeve. In that instant her perception of him shifted from friendly familiarity to something more akin to awe. His eyes, sharp as coal chips regarded her. She found it hard to breathe.

He smiled, towering over her, and took the tray, placing it on the table. She breathed again, although her heart raced. There'd always been a grittiness about him, the toughness and resilience won living on the street still lingered beneath the well-mannered facade. Seeing him now there was no doubting it.

Unexpected excitement stirred inside her. The cups rattled on the saucers as she put them out with trembling hands.

"Peter's been promoted," Hope said. "Second-Lieutenant." Her eyes shone with pride.

"Really?" Rose said. "Congratulations. So they've recognised your worth at last."

Peter shrugged. "I've managed to survive longer than most," he said. "The CO seems to like me. I went to the right school and say the right things in the right accent."

"He's being modest. The citation says 'for courage and discipline under fire'," Hope said. "I've no doubt it's richly deserved."

"Well, it does mean more pay, two leaves a year and I get to eat in the Officers' Mess," he said.

Rose poured the tea and handed it round. Then she went and fetched the plates of cheese, bread, butter and pickles.

"This looks delicious," Peter said.

Over lunch he told them about the food in the various camps and his journey home. He had five days' leave before he had to report for Officer Training.

"It's a pity Pa isn't here," Hope said. "He'd have loved to see you."

"And I him," Peter said. "But he writes regularly and tells me he's happy where he is. He felt so useless here."

"Yes," Hope said. "He's not the sort of man to sit by and do nothing when the country's at war. So, what do you want to do while you're here? Any plans?"

Peter took a breath. "I want to go dancing," he said. "Hit the town and do all the things I've missed not being here." He glanced at Rose. "I hoped Rose would show me the best places to go these days. Somewhere a million miles away from muddy fields, rumbling guns and constant shelling."

"I'd be delighted," Rose said and thrilled at the prospect.

After lunch Rose went up to change. Her heart fluttered. It had been so long since she'd seen Peter she couldn't wait to catch up with him.

"Don't keep her out too late," Hope said as they were leaving. "Remember she has work in the morning."

"What, on Sunday?"

"Yes, even on Sunday," Hope said and Peter recalled that the bombing didn't stop on Sundays either.

They left Hope and walked along the Embankment in the gathering dusk, their breath vaporising in the cold frost-filled air. They stopped several times so Peter could gaze across the river, watching the boats. "It's so peaceful," he said. "You wouldn't know there's a war waging across the Channel."

"Until the Zepps come over," she said.

"Do you get much bombing?"

"No. Mostly they're stopped coming over the coast or they're well off target. Usually to the north or south of the docks. We get away quite lightly considering. It must be very different for you," Rose said.

He shrugged and turned to look at her. "What about you, Rose? Ma told me you were working as a nurse. It must be very different for you too."

She raised her eyebrows. "Yes, I suppose it is, but it's hardly the same."

They walked on. "I dreamed of sitting by a roaring fire drinking cold beer," he said. "Anywhere I can get one this time of day?"

She laughed. "'Fraid not," she said. Pubs won't open until later this evening, but I do know a cafe where we can get a great cup of tea."

He pulled a face. "Tea it will be then," he said.

They walked to the Strand. As they walked she recalled the Peter she'd known growing up. He'd refused the Commission Silas offered to arrange for him, preferring to sign up for the Gunners with the local lads. Hope was right; any promotion he got would have been well earned. That had always been his way. Fiercely independent he'd never taken advantage of Hope and Silas's generosity. Not that he hadn't been grateful for it. Hope said he was the most appreciative boy she'd ever met, never taking his good fortune for granted, always wanting to pay his own way. Stubborn, but with a shattering directness of manner. She saw it now. There was no pretence about him.

"So, do you have a boyfriend?" he asked as they sat having tea.

"Hmm. Maybe," she said.

"A soldier?" The question shimmered in his eyes.

"Don't worry I won't tell," he said. She got the feeling he was laughing at her.

"Perhaps." She didn't want to tell him about Ferdie. She knew he wouldn't approve and she didn't want him to think poorly of her.

He took a gulp of tea and gazed away. "I thought you were the sensible one," he said.

She bristled. "You mean dull?"

He turned to look at her. "No, not dull – thoughtful. Unlike William who was so impulsive he'd rush into anything without a thought for his safety, or anyone else's."

She recalled how William had saved a boy from drowning. "That's not always a bad thing," she said.

Peter gazed at her, studying her face, until fire burned her cheeks. He glanced away. "Just be careful," he said. "A lot of men 'over there' know they're unlikely to come back. You'd be surprised what men will get up to when their lives don't matter anymore. They'll do things aware they won't have to face the consequences of their actions. I wouldn't want you to be hurt by it."

The fire on her cheeks grew fiercer. Was he reading her mind? She'd been thinking of Ferdie, the fine as cobwebs underwear and his last letter asking when he'd see her in it. But Ferdie wasn't like that. No. He was different. What she'd felt in that alley…his lips hot on hers, the tempest that raged inside her at his touch, it was real…he loved her, she was sure of it.

"When you've finished your tea we'll go dancing," she said. "I know a place."

Rose took him to a dance hall near the hospital. Most of the girls there were nurses and Rose knew quite a few of them. Some of the men worked in the hospital, others came from the nearby shops and offices, or were soldiers on leave or convalescence. It wasn't a large hall but nicely decorated with bunting and there was a table and two women serving tea, coffee and cold drinks. The band played well known dance numbers. Peter danced with Rose and some of the other girls. The floor wasn't too crowded but there were enough dancers having a good time to make it feel you were surrounded by warmth, happiness and laughter. By the time the dance ended and they were on their way home Peter was in high spirits. He would have willingly gone on to a nightclub but recalled that

Rose had to work in the morning so was happy to walk her home.

"Thanks for taking me," he said.

"Anytime." Rose smiled. "You seemed to enjoy it."

"I did. It was just what I needed, seeing people behaving normally and enjoying themselves. It's restored my faith in humanity."

"Had you lost it then?"

"Easy to lose it when you're 'over there'," he said.

Chapter Twenty

The next morning Peter awoke to the sound of church bells. He forgot where he was for a moment, it had been so long since he'd slept in his own bed. He stretched, luxuriating in the unaccustomed comfort and the smell of clean linen. He glanced at the corner where Patch used to sleep. All gone now. Patch had been his best friend and constant companion when he was growing up. He vividly recalled the day Silas had brought him home, a wriggling bundle of fur. It was the start of a new life for both of them.

A storm of grief had hit him when he got Hope's letter. His memory filled with Patch's panting face, the affection in his soft brown eyes and his willingness to follow him everywhere. Against the terrible toll of death among the men he worked with, the death of his dog may seem a small thing, but to him it was like losing a limb, a part of him gone forever, and never able to be brought back. Tears sprang to his eyes. Of course he missed him, but he knew Hope had done her best for him and he'd be at peace now. That was some comfort. Getting the news in the midst of gunfire and shelling he'd felt as though his childhood had been buried with his beloved dog.

He was pondering how much his life had changed since he last lay here in this bed when the appetising smell of frying bacon tempted him out of it to dress and go downstairs for breakfast.

Rose had already left for work so he sat with Hope, Olivia and Sean. Hope and the children were all due to help out in the Refugee Centre after church.

"Do you have any plans?" Hope asked.

"I want to visit my parents' grave and I thought I'd call on Major Fortescue this afternoon. I told Silas I'd look him up when I was home."

Major Fortescue was looking after Silas's club, The Grenadier, in his absence. He'd lost an eye fighting the Boers and was now retired. The men who frequented the club respected him and Silas trusted him. Peter knew he'd appreciate the visit.

"Good. So you'll be home for lunch?"

"Thank you, yes."

A cold biting wind brought a glow to Peter's face as he walked to the church. He stopped at a stall in the road and bought a wreath of holly and winter jasmine. Probably left over from Christmas, he thought, but his ma would like it. He smiled at the thought.

Pastor Brown saw him as he entered the churchyard. "Morning, Peter," he said. "Home on leave?"

"Yes, sir," Peter said.

The pastor smiled. He looked older, greyer and more care-worn, but so did a lot of people these days. He glanced at the wreath in Peter's hand. "I'll leave you to it, lad," he said and walked away. Peter sighed.

In the churchyard an ancient yew spread its branches shading the path worn thin by the passage of feet. At his parents' grave a pale shaft of winter sunlight bathed the headstone in a silver glow. The grass around the grave had been cut and a bunch of lilies lay across it. He guessed Hope had left them. He removed the faded flowers and placed the wreath next to the headstone. That had been Hope's doing too.

Although aware of his debt to Hope and Silas he still thought of his ma and pa. Gone from this life when he was only four, the memory of them was hard to capture in his mind. His mother's face, his father's voice, seemed to blur as he tried to recall them. At least he felt close to them when he came here. He hoped they were proud of him. He knew they'd sent him to Hope that day, the day that changed his life. They'd saved him from the shells that killed the two men standing next to him at the battery placement, too. They were still watching over him, just as the pastor said they would all those years ago. After all, weren't they the ones who loved him best?

Other memories filled his mind. Memories of his life on the street before Hope took him in when he was eight. Those memories never went away, but they stood him in good stead for life 'over there'. Among the fighting men the resilience and self-assurance learned on the street came back to him. He felt more at home there, alongside ordinary men from different walks of life from every part of the country, than he ever had at the posh school they'd sent him to, although he appreciated all it had taught him. He'd never felt comfortable there, always feeling as though they were better than him. Not cleverer, but they had the advantage of having been born into privilege. Among working men he had the edge, a better education, an ability to speak to the officers in their own language and a deep understanding of the difference between them.

A light breeze whispered through the conifers, fallen leaves skittered along the path. He stood for a while in quiet contemplation. A good place to stop and think and clear his mind of all the noise and confusion he'd left behind. He gazed out across the churchyard.

Rose's face drifted into his consciousness. Last time he'd seen her she'd been about thirteen. Tall and gawky, long limbed, awkward, like a new-born colt finding its feet. Now she was beautiful. No, more than that. Out from under William's shadow she'd blossomed. She was kind too. He'd seen that.

He recalled growing up and envying them their closeness. He'd wished he had a sister like Rose. Someone who'd care for him more than they cared for themselves. Someone to be the other part of him, the good, kind part that he thought might be missing.

Then he thought of her at the dance last night, her laughter, the sparkle in her eyes, the way she moved, her perfume, the warmth of her smile. A thought skittered across the surface of his mind. Perhaps it wasn't a sister he wanted after all. He sighed and smiled at the thought.

When he got home Hope had made a hotpot which she served with potatoes and bread. It was just what he needed after standing out in the cold so long. He thanked her for looking after the grave.

"It's the least I can do," she said. "I know how much it means to you."

He nodded. The children chatted about their morning. They were going out with friends in the afternoon.

On his way to The Grenadier, Peter bought a bottle of whisky. It was the Major's favourite tipple.

Major Fortescue greeted him warmly. He wanted to hear all about the conflict and Peter's part in it. He took him to Silas's office, opened the whisky and poured two glasses. They sat each side of the fire that roared in the hearth.

The Major congratulated him on his promotion. "Well done," he said. "I know Silas is proud as punch." He raised his glass and took a drink.

Peter raised his glass and drank too.

"So, how is it? Over there?" the Major asked, his eyes bright with anticipation.

Peter smiled. He knew the Major would want every detail, however insignificant. "Well, it's not like your war," he said. "No horses galloping into battle. For the first six months I dug trenches alongside infantry men and engineers." He chuckled. "I thought I'd get lost in the mazes. They were everywhere, but it's surprising. I soon found them as familiar to me as the London streets."

The Major nodded. "I've seen the pictures. It's hard to imagine living like that."

"The smell's the worst," Peter said, "but you soon get used to it. It's the men make it all bearable." He took a drink.

"Then I moved on to heavy artillery behind the front line but still close enough to suffer the bombardment from every direction. Good bunch of men there too. Ox, a farmer from Devon, pulled me out of the crater when we were bombed. He talks about green fields and deep valleys and cares more about the countryside being laid to waste than he does about anything else. Then there's Harry, a chirpy cockney who can get you anything your heart desires at minimum cost. He must be making a fortune," Peter said.

The Major nodded and poured them each another whisky. "There's always them as'll make profit out of other people's misery," he said. "Greed, cruelty, selfishness, cowardice or courage, intelligence, honour. No aspects of human behaviour remains hidden when men face their own mortality."

"It's a great leveller," Peter said.

"A great leveller?"

"Yes," Peter said. "Bullets don't discriminate, nor do lice, dysentery or trench foot. Doesn't matter if you're an officer or a bank clerk, enlisted or conscripted, we all get shot at or bombed the same. 'Over there' we all take the same risks and we're all just as likely to end up broken or dead."

"You take the same risks but don't get the same rewards," the Major said.

"You're right," Peter said. It was a sobering thought.

The Major took another drink. He told Peter some of his exploits in India and South Africa. They talked about the unique camaraderie between men who stand alongside and depend on each other against a common foe.

"There's nothing like it," the Major said. "I felt closer to my men than I did to my wife, God rest her soul." He took a swig of whisky. "Spent more time with 'em too." He chuckled and his face lit up at the memory.

He refilled their glasses. "Did I tell you about the time I..." then he launched into another amusing anecdote.

They spent a pleasant afternoon, sharing the whisky and reminiscing, each relating their own individual experiences. At the end of the afternoon, as dusk fell, the Major thanked him for coming. "Only get Officers in here," he said. "Hooray Henrys five minute out of the OTC. What do they know? They know nothing about the lads in the trenches, or the troops behind the lines. Nothing about their relentless courage and belief." He took another swig of whisky. "Lions led by donkeys. In my day..." He lapsed into reverie.

Peter thought about the lads he'd spent time with in the trenches and the officers in charge of them, all filled with an absolute conviction that they were going to taste victory against an enemy they'd been told had to be defeated. "They'll soon learn," he said, a wry smile on his face. He finished his drink and promised to keep in touch when he returned to France.

The Major shook his hand and grabbed his arm. "By God, lad," he said. "I wish I was your age. I'd be out there like a shot."

Peter, sufficiently mellow from the drink and conversation, had no doubt about the truth of it.

Chapter Twenty One

The next day Peter wanted to visit past haunts and look up old friends. He said he'd call on Alice and the children too.

It felt strange walking through familiar streets that no longer looked or felt the same. The town had taken a beating and its face was changed. He saw it everywhere, piles of rubble where buildings used to be, displaced people wandering the streets, men in uniform. Even the air felt full of dust. The boys he'd grown up with were all away, fighting the war, their families pleased to see him, but anxious for news of their loved ones. He couldn't give them comfort, he had none to give.

When he saw Alice he stopped for a beer and she insisted he have one of Elsie's pies for lunch. She gave him one to take back for Hope and the children. Amy and Alexander wanted to hear about his time in France, but Alice discouraged it.

"With John there, never knowing if or when he'd be back, I'd prefer it if we didn't talk about it," she said.

So they talked about the children's school, how they were getting on and what they intended to do when they left school.

"I want to run a pub, just like Pa," Alexander said.

John Junior wanted to drive a train and little Emily giggled when he asked her.

"How's trade?" he asked Alice. "How are you managing?"

"We're better off than a lot of people," she said. "The overseas payments help and John sends his pay. The pub brings in enough to get by."

When he left Alice he caught a bus to Holborn. He hadn't visited Harold Taylor's shop for years but he needed a new uniform and Harold supplied the Armed Services. He'd take his measurements and send them to the factory to be made up. They'd send the uniform to the Officers' Training Camp ready for when he arrived.

Walking into the shop brought a plethora of memories. The first time he'd been here was with Hope when she'd taken him to buy some decent clothes. A girl he didn't recognise worked in the shop now. Of course, the lad would have been conscripted. He asked for Harold and she nodded to the back. He went through. Harold greeted him.

"Second Lieutenant?" Harold said when he told him what he was there for. "Congratulations." He then set about measuring him.

"Is George about?" Peter asked. Harold and Margaret's son, George, had been his Uncle Alfie's best friend since their schooldays and Peter knew him well. George, who still walked with sticks, helped out in the shop when his health permitted.

"Not today," Harold said. "Not too good as it happens. He's at home with Mrs Taylor."

"Would it be all right if I called round, do you think?"

"I'm sure he'd be delighted to see you," Harold said. "Cheer him up no end."

After Harold had finished with the measuring and they'd swapped news about Hope and Silas and had a general discussion about the pros and cons of the war, Peter left to catch an omnibus to Mr and Mrs Taylor's home.

Margaret welcomed Peter when he arrived. "George is a bit off colour today, but I'm sure seeing you will perk him up. He doesn't get many visitors these days."

George was in the parlour reading a book when Peter arrived. He looked a little peaky. He put the book down and tried to get up to greet him.

"Don't get up on my account," Peter said.

"George sank back into the chair. "I'm all right really," he said. "It's just…" He rubbed his leg. Peter knew he'd suffered with his legs and bones since birth.

"I'll make tea," Margaret said. "I think there may be some seed cake left too."

"Lovely, thank you," Peter said taking a seat next to George. "I'm sorry I missed Alfie's wedding. You managed it though."

George brightened. "Best man," he said. "It was a grand day although they kept it small. Only close family and friends. Alfie's very lucky. She's lovely."

"So I hear."

"I have some photographs. My new hobby." He picked up his sticks and struggled to rise to get them.

"Can I—"

"No. I can manage."

Peter remembered how, like Alfie, he hated to be treated differently from anyone else.

Margaret came in with the tray of tea and cake. Peter stood to help her. He took the tray and put it on the table.

"Are you looking for the wedding photographs?" she said to George.

"It's all right. I've got them," George said. He made his way back to the chair carrying a fair sized bag.

"I have a few things to do," Margaret said, "so I'll leave you men to it." She smiled at Peter and he recognised the tactful withdrawal. George would speak more freely in his mother's absence.

Peter poured the tea while George sorted out the photographs. Apart from the bride and groom he had taken pictures of the guests. Jenny's father, puffed up with pride, Hope looking wistful and Silas staring adoringly at her. Peter smiled when he came to that one.

"Would you like it?" George said. "To keep? I can always make another print."

"Can I? Really?" Of course Peter had picture of Hope, Silas and the family he kept in his wallet, but this one caught something intimate between them. "They're all very good," he said.

George beamed. "Take as many as you like."

Peter saw one of Alfie and Jenny having a sly kiss as though they thought no one was looking. "Alfie would love this," he said, laughing.

"I could send it to him if you think…"

"I could take it. The Training Camp I have to report to is in Devon. I thought I'd leave a day or so early and stop off and see Alfie and his new wife."

"Excellent," George said. He sorted out a few more pictures for Peter to take. They drank tea and chatted about the things they'd shared growing up, the school they both went to and the people they knew. Peter told George some of the things the men in the trenches got up to, things designed to make him laugh and dispel any seriousness about the situation.

"How will you feel? Going back?" George asked.

Peter shrugged. "It's my job. It's what I'm trained to do. It's not as though I have a choice."

"But if you did have a choice?"

Peter thought for a minute or two. "I'd go back. I'd go back for the men there and the family. People who depend on me. I wouldn't want to let them down." He felt bad as he said it. He knew George wished he could do more for the war effort, but his extensive disability prevented it.

"I'm thinking of going back to school," George said suddenly.

"Back to school? Whatever for?"

"To teach. They're desperately short of teachers. I had a good education, as did you. I want to put it to some use. Seeing you has made up my mind for me."

"Will you be able to – manage it?" Peter asked.

"What? Sit in front of a class of eleven-year-olds spouting poetry and conjugating Latin verbs?"

Peter laughed. "Good for you," he said and the strained atmosphere of the afternoon lifted. Peter saw a new determination in George's face. He only hoped Harold and Margaret would approve.

Chapter Twenty Two

When Rose got home that evening she saw Peter's kit bag in the hall, packed ready for him to leave the next morning. She'd be sorry to see him go, but like so many others, she knew he had no choice.

Over a lively dinner with the family he said he'd like to take her out, somewhere of her choosing. "You've taken me everywhere I wanted to go," he said. "Now it's your turn to choose."

"There's an exhibition I'd like to see at the Burlington Gallery. Sketches. You do sketches don't you," she said, recalling the pictures he'd sent for her and William's birthdays.

"Peter's a brilliant artist," Hope said, her voice ladled with pride. "The Art Master at school said he'd go far."

"Yes, as far as Ypres at least," Peter said laughing. He glanced at Rose. "Do you really want to go to an exhibition or are you just saying that because of my interest?"

"No. I'd really like to go. You can tell me what's good about all the pictures. I'll appreciate them more then."

"If you're sure."

"I'm sure."

"Show her the picture you did of me," Olivia said. "In your book."

"Yes please," Rose said. "I'd like to see it."

"I'd like to see your drawings too, Peter," Hope said. "I haven't seen any of the recent ones. I'll clear these dishes while you get your sketchbook."

While Hope served the coffee Peter showed them the pictures in his sketchbook. As well as portraits of the men in trenches there were evocative drawings of the French landscape and cottages in villages where he'd stayed.

"I like the portraits best," Rose said, leaning over to see more clearly. "Who are they?"

"This is Ox," Peter said of one. "He's a good chap to have alongside you. A giant of a man who can carry ten times his weight in guns and ammunition." He turned the page. "Here's Harry and this is a chap we call Egg. Not sure why but everyone calls him Egg."

"What's that?" Sean said pointing to one of the barrel of a gun.

"That's an eighteen pounder," Peter said. "She's a beauty." Rose caught the affection in his voice.

Olivia grabbed the book. "Look here's one he did of me," she said flicking through the pages until she found it. She passed the book to Rose.

The drawing had caught Olivia perfectly. "It's very good," Rose said and turned the page. The picture on the next page couldn't be anyone but her. "Oh," she said. "It's me. When did you…I mean…how…but you've made me look…beautiful."

Peter took the book from her hand and stood up. "That wasn't me," he said. "It was God did that." He planted a kiss on her forehead. "Are we going out or what?"

Rose felt the blush rising up from her neck. "Yes, just coming," she called to his retreating back, her insides fluttering in confusion. They were still fluttering when he left the next morning.

After Peter left the routine of the hospital felt dull and lacking in excitement. She hadn't had a letter from Ferdie for a few weeks either and that played on her mind. Had anything happened to him? Or was he just bored with a girl who won't send a picture of herself in her underwear? Was she being too prudish, only sending him a formal photo? What did other girls do? Then the thought of him seeing other girls filled her mind and she began to panic. He'd be home on leave soon. She'd ask him then what he thought of her, if he was serious about her. She wanted to hear it from his lips, not on paper. Anyone can write anything on paper when they're in the trenches, fearing for their life.

Cissie noticed Rose's sullen mood. "You need cheering up," she said, so that evening they went out on the town and all Rose's fears and disappointments faded away with the music and dancing.

The following week all the Probationary Nurses were assembled in the canteen to receive their Nursing Certificates. Cissie said she was going home for a few days and Rose decided it was time she did the same. They both arranged to take some time off.

When she got home that evening there was a surprise waiting for her. William had stopped in to see her. He'd spent a couple of days leave in Norfolk and was on his way to meet his ship in Portsmouth. She rushed into his arms. He swung her off her feet in greeting. "I'm only here for one night," he said. "Off again in the morning, but I understand you have something to celebrate."

"Yes," she said, her voice marbled with pride. "As of today I'm a fully qualified nurse." She couldn't help the wide grin that stretched across her face.

"Proud of you," he said. "And Ma will be too. Let's go out and drink to your success."

Hope had prepared a celebratory meal from some haddock she'd managed to bag from the market and everyone toasted Rose's new status with the remains of the Christmas port.

"Will you be able to choose your next posting?" Hope asked. "Or will you stay where you are?"

"I'll stay," Rose said, "but I'll be asking to transfer back to the wards where they treat the wounded."

"Got your eyes on a soldier?" William chuckled.

"No," Rose said. "I just prefer the work and the satisfaction of being able to be part of it. You know – the war and everything. Everyone else in the family's helping. I want to too."

"You do your bit," Hope said, "and I'm sure they appreciate it."

After dinner William and Rose went to the Addison hotel bar where a pianist played the latest jazz numbers. They found a table and William ordered a beer for him and a glass of sherry for Rose. She didn't miss the envy on the faces of the other women in the bar when she walked in with William in his Naval uniform. Glancing around she wasn't surprised. He was quite the handsomest man in the room. The fact wasn't lost on William either.

"It's the uniform," he said as he brought the drinks to the table. "Gets 'em every time." He grinned.

"How was Ma?" she asked picking up her glass of sherry.

"The hotel keeps her busy," William said. "She misses Pa, but she's doing a great job keeping everyone in order. Far better at it than I ever expected. But you'll see for yourself."

"I'm going up tomorrow," Rose said. "First train."

"I know. Aunt Hope mentioned it. Ma said if I saw you to try to persuade you to move to a hospital nearer to home."

"Did she? Well, you've tried. Now can we get on and enjoy the evening?"

"Aunt Hope said you'd say that. She thinks you're just as stubborn and wilful as Ma was at your age."

Rose chuckled. "She's probably right then. After all, she should know."

William smiled but didn't pursue the matter. "So, no romance on the horizon?"

"No," Rose said. Ferdie's face flashed across her mind but she pushed it away. She still hadn't heard from him and didn't want to think about why. "You?"

"Not much chance at sea with three hundred men," he said and slurped his beer. "Cissie writes. She says you're the most studious girl she's ever met. Always at the books."

Rose laughed. "That makes me sound boring."

William shrugged. "You still both seem to be able to find ways of enjoying yourselves."

"We do," Rose said and sipped her sherry.

After the hotel they went to the cafe in the Strand for coffee and to join in the sing-songs there. William didn't want to be late home as they both had an early start in the morning.

The next morning Rose met William in the hall just as the postwoman arrived. There were some letters for Hope and one for Rose, from a BEF Post Office.

William grabbed it. "Ooo," he said. "What's this? A letter from a soldier. I don't recognise the handwriting. Who is he? Should I be worried?"

Rose blushed. She knew it was Ferdie's handwriting. "He's just a friend. Give it to me." She tried to snatch it back but William, sensing a game, held it up and danced away from her. "Perhaps I should open it? I'm your brother. I have to look out for you and I know what these soldiers are like."

Hot fury wound with fear grew inside Rose. "Give it to me," she said, anger sharpening her voice, but the more she tried to snatch it the more animated William became and kept moving away from her, waving the letter in the air.

"You beast," she said. "I hate you."

William stopped. "That's serious, Rose. What is it?"

The fear and fury leeched out of her. "Nothing. Just give it to me or I'll tell Ma about you asking to be put on a ship instead of taking the home posting you were offered."

"You wouldn't?"

"I would."

"Then she'd be more annoyed with me than she already is," he said. The sparkle in his ocean blue eyes dimmed with sadness. "Sometime I think she hates me too."

Rose immediately regretted what she'd said. "No, she doesn't. Neither do I. It's just that…" She didn't know what to say. It was true Ma was harder on William than any of her other children.

"I know. I remind her of our father, the no good scoundrel who got her pregnant then dumped her."

"How do you know that?"

"I asked Nesta Roberts. She's Ma's oldest friend. I knew Ma had something against me I just didn't know what. She told me all about him."

"So it's not your fault is it and you're not like him. Everyone says so. I think it's because Ma loves you best of all and it hurts to be reminded of the past."

"Do you think so?"

"I know so. You were always her favourite. Remember how she spoiled you growing up?"

A wide smile warmed his eyes again. "Yes. I was rather lovely then." He gave Rose the letter. "I may have his looks but, apart from being the handsomest man in the universe, I'm nothing like him."

Rose laughed. "Well, you certainly have his ego if the stories I've heard are anything to go by."

They left after breakfast, each to go their separate ways, William to Portsmouth and Rose to Norfolk. On the way to the station she missed him all over again, just as she had when he first went away. He's right, she thought. He's quite something in that uniform. Damn this war. Why can't it just end so we can all be together again?

She waited until she was on the train to open Ferdie's letter. He hands trembled as she did so. She quite expected a reference to the underwear but there was no mention of it. He said he liked her picture, very refined, he said which was not how he thought of her. Again the memory of his kisses in the alley assailed her. Yes, he was right, she thought. She hadn't been very refined then. Perhaps she should send him something a little more…what? Risqué? It was something to think about.

Chapter Twenty Three

An Infantry Captain on convalescence met her at Great Yarmouth station. "Your mother's a formidable woman," he said. "She's looking forward to having you home."

Rose smiled. "Glad to be home," she said, lugging her bag into the boot of the car. It was only as they drove through the familiar streets, past the shops and bars she knew so well that she realised it was true. Here she felt a sense of belonging. London, with all its pomp and grandeur had never felt like home. Here she knew everyone and they knew her. She'd only be staying a short while but it was the perfect place to think about her future.

The car dropped her at the hotel entrance. She stopped to gaze around and breathe in the salty smell of the sea. The familiar sound of the waves filled her ears and a light breeze caressed her face. It was good to be home.

Inside the hotel she made her way upstairs to the family rooms on the top floor.

A flood of warmth enveloped her when her mother greeted her. Pride shone in Violet's eyes as she embraced her. She looks just the same, Rose thought. Unchanged despite the year since I've seen her. It was reassuring. Rose couldn't think why she'd stayed away so long and suddenly wished she hadn't.

"Your room's all ready for you," Violet said. "Welcome home."

Joshua and Florence, home for lunch, greeted her with hugs and questions. "How long are you staying? What's it like in London? Are you a proper nurse now?"

Rose laughed. She'd bought them each a present, a model tank for Joshua and a doll dressed as a nurse for Florence. Joshua thanked her and Florence bounced with delight.

They had lunch together, the children chattering about their school work and Violet telling Rose about the changes to the hotel since she left. Then Violet sent the children back to school.

"I'm afraid I'm going to be busy this afternoon," Violet said. "But I expect you'll want to settle in. I've invited a few people to join us for dinner. I hope that's all right with you. I tend to have a few guests each day. It enlivens the evenings and it's the only chance you get for some convivial conversation."

"I look forward to it," Rose said, guessing they'd be convalescing Officers, probably young and single.

In her room Rose unpacked her bag and changed out of her travelling clothes into something more comfortable. She nodded to a couple of the VADs working there on her way out and passed the time of day. Then she went out for a walk along the front. Dark clouds scudded across the sky, blown on the breeze. An arctic January wind blew in whipping her cheeks to a crimson glow. Flags on the beach fluttered and bent in the breeze. The damp permeated her coat and she was glad of her scarf and boots. She stopped by the railings to gaze out over the water. The pounding of the waves on the rocks filled her ears as she watched the breakers crashing against the shore. She breathed in the fresh, bracing air. She hadn't realised how much she missed it.

She shivered in the cold and walked on into the town where she'd be sheltered from the wind. As she walked past the little shops she paused to look in the windows. Then she called into the bakery and bought a cherry cake. It was Joe's favourite and she planned to call on him guessing that he'd be home by now and could tell her all about his recovery and the stay at the hospital in Kings Lynn. He may even have returned to work at the boatyard.

His mother opened the door and Rose was surprised how worried and shrivelled she looked. She hardly seemed to recognise Rose.

"Good afternoon, Mrs Jennings. It's me, Rose Stone. I've called to see if Joe's home and if he's all right."

Mrs Jennings's face cleared. "Oh it's you, dear. Come in. I'll put kettle on."

Rose went in. "Is Joe home. I expect you're glad of the company," she said.

Mrs Jennings shook her head. "No, love. He's still in hospital. To tell you the truth I'm right worried about 'im."

"Still in hospital? Where? In Kings Lynn? I thought he'd be out by now."

"Aye, me an' all, but they say he's taken a turn for the worse. He's in a place in…" She paused. "Now where was it? Sheldon? Shelby? Somewhere like that. No visitors. I can't even go and see 'im." Tears filled her eyes. She sniffed and turned to the stove. "Poor lad. 'E should be at 'ome. I'd look after 'im."

"Of course you would," Rose said, dismayed at the news that Joe had got worse. "I can't understand it," she said. "He was so well when he left St Thomas'."

"Aye. That's right. I saw 'im in Kings Lynn. He was well on the mend. Then, all of sudden he's took bad and moved to somewhere else. It's fair got me

174

mithered." She took a handkerchief out of her apron pocket and wiped her eyes. "Is there owt you can do for 'im? You being a nurse an' all?"

Rose sighed. She didn't know what to think. Joe Jennings was a strong, strapping lad in good health, except for the wound to his leg. He should be fully recovered and at home by now. "I don't know," she said. "I'll make some enquiries. Where did you say he'd been moved to?"

Mrs Jennings brightened. She waddled into the parlour and pulled open a drawer. "In here somewhere," she said. "Ah. 'ere 'tis." She gave Rose a piece of paper. It read: *Sheldon Auxiliary Hospital* and there was an address.

"Thank you," Rose said. "I'll see what I can find out."

Mrs Jennings served the tea with Rose's cake and they sat in the kitchen to have it, the parlour fire not being lit. "I only lights it when we have company," Mrs Jennings said.

"It's quite all right," Rose reassured her. "I prefer the kitchen anyway, it's cosier."

"You're a good girl," Mrs Jennings said. "Joe always said that."

Rose smiled. Her heart went out to this woman, whose only son had been wounded in the war and now looked as though he may never return to her.

Rose walked back to the hotel deep in thought. She'd never heard of Sheldon Auxiliary Hospital and was confused why Mrs Jennings said he wasn't allowed visitors. Everyone knew that visitors helped keep the patients cheerful and aided their recovery. She could think of no reason why Mrs Jennings wouldn't be allowed to visit her son. Had she got it wrong? She did seem a little confused about the whole thing. It was something Rose vowed to find out.

She still had Joe Jennings on her mind when Major Maitland joined them for dinner. He was the Deputy Director of Medical Services for the area and had an office and two rooms in a suite on the first floor of the hotel. Violet had also invited two convalescing Officers: a young Second-Lieutenant she introduced as Jamie Shaw, a Guards Officer, and a Captain Bryce-Davis, an Infantry man in his forties. A Miss Clara Jones, an administrative VAD, had also been invited to make up the numbers.

"Rose is a nurse," Violet said to the Major as she introduced Rose. "You should have a lot in common."

"Really? Well done. It's good to see our young people being of service," he said.

Rose blushed. "I've just qualified," she said. "I'm sure I have a lot to learn."

The Major nodded. A well-built man in his fifties, he was fit for his age and carried an air of authority with him. He'd seen action in the Boer War, then retired to a country practice, but had re-joined the Medical Corp when war broke out. "Well, please feel free to use my library anytime you wish," he said. "I have a few books and a large collection of medical journals which may be of interest to you."

"Thank you," Rose said. "I may take you up on that." She was just about to ask if he knew anything about Sheldon Auxiliary Hospital when they were interrupted by the arrival from downstairs of the first course. Violet called them all to the table. She sat at the head of the table, with Jamie Shaw and Captain Bryce-Davis either side of her. Major Maitland sat at the other end between Rose and Clara Jones.

Rose chatted to both Jamie Shaw and Major Maitland during the soup. When the main course arrived and Violet was busy bringing it to the table, she took the opportunity to ask Major Maitland if he'd ever heard of Sheldon Auxiliary Hospital.

He frowned. "Sheldon? Hmm. No, doesn't ring a bell. Why?"

Violet put the serving dishes on the table and, there being no one to serve it, they all started handing it round between themselves.

"I have a friend, well an ex-patient, who's been moved there. I just wondered what it was like," Rose said, taking a plate of roast beef from Jamie Shaw.

"Sheldon, Sheldon, let me think." The Major shook his head. "Most of the chaps here come from Norwich or Kings Lynn."

Clara Jones, sitting opposite the Rose said, "Yes, you do know it, Major. It's an old Manor House given over to the Military. A small Auxiliary Hospital. Not many beds. Quite a way out though. A bit rural."

"So it's in our area then?"

"Yes. Definitely one of ours," Clara said, passing the potatoes to Captain Bryce-Davis sitting next to her.

"It's just that his mother's been told that he's not to have visitors. Is that correct? I thought a visit from his mother would cheer him up no end," Rose said, passing the plate of meat to Clara. "It seems a bit strange that's all."

"It does happen sometimes," the Major said, his gaze following the bowl of potatoes around the table. "If the injuries are too horrific they may upset the relatives seeing them. Upsets the patients too." He smiled as Clara put three slices of roast beef on his plate. "And sometimes, when there's little hope of recovery, it's often best."

Rose bridled. "He had a leg amputation. Nothing horrific at all. He was quite well when he left St Thomas'." She spoke more sharply than she intended.

The Major sighed and patted her hand. "He may have picked up an infection," he said. "It's dreadful I know, when it's someone you've nursed back to health, but it happens. Can't be helped, my dear."

Rose wanted to investigate further but the vegetables arrived and everyone was busy passing round the gravy and condiments and Violet steered the conversation to what Rose had been doing in London, so the opportunity passed.

After the meal Major Maitland, Miss Jones, Captain Bryce-Davis and Violet settled down to play bridge. Rose didn't play and neither did Second Lieutenant Jamie Shaw.

"I know it's probably a bit cold, but I would like to take a walk along the front," he said, "and I wondered if you'd care to accompany me. In a nursing capacity of course. I have been told to exercise this leg."

Rose glanced down at his foot and noticed that it was a prosthetic. She hadn't noticed it before. "I'll get my coat," she said. At least she'd done something right, she thought when she saw the smile on her mother's face as they went out.

Chapter Twenty Four

The next morning Rose decided to ask Clara Jones about the Sheldon Hospital as she seemed to know more about it than the Major. She found her in the Major's office. He was out, visiting a hostel for convalescence in nearby Lowestoft.

"I was wondering if you could tell me anything about this Auxiliary Hospital my friend's been moved to," she said. "The Sheldon. I mentioned it last night."

Clara shrugged. "I have heard of it," she said. "We should have a file somewhere." She went to a large filing cabinet and opened it and took out a thin file. She flicked through it. "It doesn't say much here," she said. "Only that it's run by a Medical Officer, Captain Trent. Not many staff. As I said yesterday, it's only a small hospital. The Major would only visit if there was some cause for concern. Sorry I can't be of more help."

"Thank you anyway," Rose said. She had the address. She was determined to go and see Joe, whatever it took. If she couldn't go as a visitor she may be able to get in as a nurse. She'd brought her uniform with her to do some much needed stitching which she hadn't had time to do at Hope's.

Downstairs she checked the route to Sheldon and found she could get a bus from the pier to Norwich and then another bus to the village where the Auxiliary Hospital was based. It would take about two hours, but Rose was prepared for that. She told Violet that she planned a day out visiting a friend in Norwich.

Violet was busy so, thankfully, she didn't question who it might be. Rose changed into her nurse's uniform. With her scarf and coat over the top it would not be visible. She put her nurse's headdress in her bag to put on when she arrived. She pulled on a narrow brimmed woollen hat and set off. A light breeze blew but she felt pleasantly warm as she walked briskly along the front. Pearl grey clouds filled the sky giving off an opalescent light.

She didn't have to wait long for the bus. The journey to Norwich took about half an hour during which she gazed out at bare limbed trees and fields laced with morning frost. In Norwich she picked up a timetable for the local buses. She found one that left in fifteen minutes going to Sheldon village.

During the hour long ride, with the bus stopping every ten minutes or so, she read one of the medical journals she'd picked up in the Major's office. It helped to pass the time.

She'd asked the driver to let her know when she got to Sheldon so she wouldn't miss the stop. When he called her she got off and glanced around. Her first impression of the place was that, in summer, it would be a pretty village and well worth a visit. However, in late January the cold meant the main street was almost empty and people who were out were rushing, heads down against the cold. She walked up the road, looking for somewhere she could find someone to ask the way. A tea room in the middle of the small parade of shops was open, so she went in. Inside a large lady in a white overall greeted her.

"Morning, ducks. What can I get you?"

The journey and the cold had made Rose hungrier than the she realised. She settled for a cup of tea and a cheese sandwich with homemade pickle. Then she asked about the hospital.

"Oh aye. I know it. Military place now. Used to be old man Sheldon lived there. The Manor House. 'E passed on like an' 'is family left for America when war started." She heaved a sigh.

"Is it near here?" Rose asked.

The woman smiled. "Go through the village, about half-a-mile on. Then you'll see a turning off to the right. Half-a-mile or so along there an' you'll see gates." She paused as though having a thought. "Don't see many visitors going there, though. You'd think an 'ospital would have visitors wouldn't you?" She tutted. "Sit down, luv. I'll bring it." She turned to see to making Rose's tea and sandwich.

The cheese and pickle sandwich was good, the bread thick and well buttered. The tea hot and strong. Rose thanked her and went out to find the hospital.

She walked briskly, all the while thinking what she would say when she got there. The roads were lined with trees and a pale sun shone between drifting grey clouds. Butterflies fluttered in her stomach when she saw the wrought iron gates across the driveway. Stopping only to change her hat for her nurse's headdress, she pushed one and it opened. Relieved it wasn't locked she strode on. Trees shaded the long drive then gave way to manicured lawns spread around the building. She felt another flutter of anxiety when she saw the red brick Manor House ahead of her. She could imagine the sort of people who lived there. Then she reminded herself that it was a hospital and she was a nurse. What could be more natural than a nurse coming to a hospital?

Outside the entrance Rose saw a girl standing in a corner out of the wind, having a cigarette. She had a nurse's headdress on and Rose guessed a uniform under her coat. When she saw Rose she took another puff and blew the smoke out. "Hello," she said. She smiled and lifted the hand holding the cigarette. "You won't tell will you? Sister Peters is a right stickler for smoking and it's my first one today."

Rose grinned. "No. I won't tell."

"Thanks," the girl said, stubbing the cigarette out. "I'm Gloria." She frowned. "I haven't seen you around here before. Are you new?"

"Yes," Rose said. "My name's Florrie." It was the first name that came into her head. "First day."

"Best come in then," Gloria said and they went in together. Rose followed Gloria to a cloakroom. Several coats hung on pegs along one wall. Gloria slipped off her coat revealing her uniform, and hung it on a peg. Rose did the same, thankful that she'd be inconspicuous among the other nurses. She took her purse and a small notepad and pencil out of her bag and put them into her pockets. She hung her bag under her coat as she didn't want to draw attention to herself by carrying her bag around the hospital.

"Are you living in?" Gloria asked looking round as though for Rose's luggage.

"No. I've got a room in the village," Rose said, hoping that was allowed.

"Lucky you," Gloria said. "We're all in the stable block across the yard. No heating and not much grub either." She glanced at her reflection in a small mirror on the wall, straightened her hair and rubbed a smudge of lipstick from the corner of her mouth. She sighed as though not quite satisfied, then went out.

Rose followed her into the hall again. "You'd best report to Sister Peters," Gloria said. "Up the stairs, first door on the right. I'm along here." She pointed to a hallway running off the entrance lobby. "The Pharmacy. May see you later."

"Thanks," Rose said.

Left alone Rose took the opportunity to look around. A solid desk stood in the entrance lobby. Papers strewn across the top of it gave the impression that someone should be sitting behind it. The smell of boiled cabbage and overcooked gravy permeated the air. Rose glanced at the watch pinned to her starched white apron. Lunchtime she thought. She hadn't gone any further when a girl in a VAD uniform appeared and took her place behind the desk. She too carried the smell of cabbage and gravy. "Can I help you?" she said.

Rose gave her best smile. "I was looking for Sister Peters," she said. "She's not in her office. I thought she might be down here." She shrugged. "Obviously not." She made her way upstairs. If the Sister's office was up there then so probably were the patients. All she had to do was find Joe Jennings.

She stopped on the landing, relieved that she'd managed to get so far without being challenged or stopped. The first door she passed had '*Sister Peters*' emblazoned on a wooden label on the door. She walked past looking right and left for any sign of a ward full of patients. Several other closed doors led off the corridor before double doors ahead of her prevented her going any further. She guessed they led to the ward where she'd find the patients.

She didn't want to run into Sister Peters, or anyone else for that matter. She looked through the glass porthole in the door. There were eight beds in the room, four down either side, the occupants all lying in bed staring at the ceiling. She pushed the door open. A Nurses' Station by the door stood empty. She glanced around and a nurse came out of a side room. "About time," she said. "I'm starving. No changes to report. See you later." She picked a magazine off the desk and banged her way out of the door leaving Rose alone with the patients. The remains of what appeared to be their lunch sat either on side tables or on trays in front of them. Very few of them had eaten anything.

Rose didn't have long. The relief nurse would be there soon so she went to the first bed. The man lying in it didn't move. She spoke to him. He turned his head, but didn't respond. There was no hint of recognition in his eyes. They continued to stare blankly over her shoulder. She picked up his chart. It wasn't written in any form she recognised. She put it down again. Then she went to the next bed, the same thing happened. She checked all the beds, Joe wasn't among the patients. She was about to leave when the relief nurse appeared.

"Sorry I'm late," she said. "Snagged my stocking. Huge hole. Had to change it. Damn nuisance. Now I'll have to darn it." She glanced at Rose. "Oh hello. Sorry. Are you new? I thought Emmy was on this ward."

"She was. She's gone to lunch now. I'm looking for Joe Jennings. I thought he was on this ward."

The nurse shrugged. "Sorry, I don't know the name. They're all the same to me. Try upstairs. Some of the worst cases are up there. These are the quiet ones."

Rose thanked her and went out. If this hospital was run in the same way as St Thomas' the Sister and the Doctor would go round the wards together either in the morning or the afternoon. If she was quick they could both be at lunch. She made her way up to the next floor. The noise was the first thing she noticed. Someone was shouting and another voice yelling out. It sounded horrendous despite being muffled by the distance.

She walked up to the double doors across the narrow corridor. Peering through the porthole revealed a room set up the same as the one below. She couldn't see the Nurses' Station from outside, so she took a breath and went in. The full blast of the noise filled her ears. She winced. A man at the end howled while another shouted back. Another man was moaning and wailing like a wounded animal. The atmosphere in the ward was one of chaos. She wondered what she'd walked into.

A harassed VAD nurse sat at a desk seemingly oblivious to the noise. When Rose walked in she glanced up from the magazine she was reading.

"Is it always like this?" Rose asked, concerned for the girl's welfare. Supposing the patients became violent?

The girl grimaced. "'As bin since I bin 'ere," she said. "I'm only supposed to 'elp out. I'm not supposed to be here on me own." From her cockney accent Rose guessed her to be from London.

"No. I can see that," Rose said. "Where's the Staff Nurse?"

The girl laughed. "Staff Nurse? You'll be lucky. No proper nurses stay more 'an a day or so in this place. A week at most. Nah. It's VADs keep this place running, though heaven's knows why. These patients should be in a proper facility." She looked suitably cross on their behalf.

"Why? What's wrong with them?" Rose was really worried now. The last time she'd seen Joe he was fine and well on the way to recovery. Something dreadful must have happened for him to end up in a place like this.

"I dunno, but whatever it is they ain't getting any better." She picked up her bag. "Now you're 'ere I can go. I'm due a break. Have fun."

"No. Wait." Sick dread and panic rose up inside Rose. "Please stay. I'm only here to find a man called Joe Jennings. I've been asked by his relatives to look out for him. I thought he might be here."

"Well, lord 'elp 'im if 'e is," the girl said, but she put her bag down. "I s'pose I can stay 'til someone else comes."

"Thanks," Rose said, relief washing over her. She went to the first bed and read the name on the chart. It wasn't Joe, neither was the next one. She found him in the second bed on the other side of the room. He lay mumbling and staring up at the ceiling.

"Joe," she said. "It's me, Rose. Come to see how you are."

A look of sheer terror filled his face, his eyes wide with fear. Then he started shouting and pulled the covers up over his head, ducking under them, calling, "Go away. Go away."

Shocked, Rose could hardly breathe. It wasn't the Joe she remembered. He was clearly on some medication that changed his personality. Cold fury replaced the shock and panic she'd felt earlier. She gritted her teeth and picked up his chart. She didn't recognise any of the prescribed medication so she took out her notebook and wrote them down, copying the words exactly.

Then she checked the charts of the other patients. They were all on the same combination of similar drugs in differing doses. She wrote them all in her notebook.

"Thank you, Nurse," she said to the girl at the desk. "I have all I need."

"Will you send someone up please," the girl said. "I shouldn't be 'ere on me own."

"No. You certainly shouldn't," Rose said, the rage inside her mounting. What on earth sort of place was this? It wasn't like any hospital she'd ever been to.

Chapter Twenty Five

Rose's mind whirled as she left the ward. Outside the doors she heard footsteps coming up the stairs, and voices. She tried the door nearest to her and it opened. She dodged into what turned out to be a storeroom, the walls lined with shelves bearing bed pans and other items. Through a crack in the door she watched two women approach. The older one, well built, her voice heavy with authority, she guessed to be Sister Peters from the scarlet rings on her sleeve. The other, a young girl, her face wearing the expression of a startled rabbit, wore a VAD nurse's uniform. She pulled the door closed as they passed.

Once she was sure they wouldn't see her she slipped out, dashed along the corridor and down the stairs. The last thing she wanted was a conversation with Sister Peters.

As she reached the last flight of stairs a tall man strode into the hall, deep in conversation with a shorter man slightly behind him. Both were in the uniform of The Royal Medical Corps. They stopped by the desk.

"Any messages?" the taller man asked.

"No, Captain Trent," the VAD girl said, almost saluting.

"Good," he said. They resumed their conversation as they came up the stairs, passing Rose without a glance. Her heart pounded, she was surprised they couldn't hear it.

She slipped into the corridor Gloria had disappeared into. As she neared the Pharmacy the door opened and Gloria stepped out to retrieve a trolley standing in the hallway.

"You're too early for the medicine round," she said when she saw Rose. "I've only just got the prescriptions." She pulled the trolley into the Pharmacy. Rose followed her.

Thinking on her feet she said, "I'm not after the medicines for the ward. Emm asked me to get something for her headache. She's not feeling too well."

Gloria sighed. "Emm's always got a headache," she said. "She is a headache. I've told her before I'm not supposed to dispense medicines without a prescription. She should see Sister Peters."

"Sorry. I didn't know."

Gloria smiled. "No. Of course you didn't." She started taking boxes off a shelf over the bench, taking tablets out and putting them into small glass pots arranged on the trolley. Each pot had a different name on it. Each time she put tablets into the pots she ticked off something on the list on the bench.

"What's that?" Rose said, nodding at the box of pills. "I've not come across them before. What are they for?"

Gloria stopped what she was doing and glared at Rose. "What's it to you?" she said. "You shouldn't be in here."

Hot blood crept up Rose's neck to flush her face. "Sorry," she said. "Just asking."

"It's best not to ask too many questions around here," Gloria said. "It'll only get you into trouble." Then she softened. "Look, there are some aspirins in the box on the shelf over the back. In the corner by the window. Tell Emm this is the last time." She finished the box she was holding, ticked off the list and threw the empty box into a waste basket standing on the floor at the end of the bench. She took down another box with the same label.

Rose went to get the aspirins. "I'm not surprised she's got a headache," she said. "The noise in that ward. Is it always like that?"

Gloria shot her a withering glance. Then she shrugged. "Poor chaps. After all they've been through. We try to help them you know, but it's often futile."

"You mean with the drugs?" She was familiar with the use of morphine and codeine in St Thomas' to alleviate pain, but she'd never come across the tablets or the seemingly high doses Gloria was dispensing.

"It's either drugs or electric shock treatment. I know which I'd prefer."

Rose swallowed. This was all wrong. Joe hadn't been suffering from battle trauma when she saw him last. He'd been fit and healthy and on the way to recovery. Whatever they'd done to him had brought on his present condition.

Gloria ticked something off on the paper, reached up and took down a different box from another shelf. "The work Captain Trent is doing here will help hundreds of people in the future," she said in a tone that warned Rose not to ask any more questions.

Rose found the box of aspirins, took two out and put them in a glass pot which she showed to Gloria. "Thanks. I'll tell Emm," she said smiling. Then, making sure Gloria was otherwise engaged and not watching, she bent down as she passed the bin. "Damn," she said. "Snagged my stocking on this bin." She made out she was inspecting the damage to her stocking and picked out the box Gloria had thrown away, slipping it under the bib of her apron.

Gloria only glanced at her for a second. She tutted but carried on putting out the medication.

Rose hurried into the hallway. She wanted to get away from here as fast as she could. She nipped into the cloakroom, put on her coat and picked up her bag. "Just going out for a smoke," she said to the VAD girl at the desk.

Once outside she scurried as quickly as she could without actually breaking into a run. Out through the gates she pulled off her headdress and put on her woollen hat. Then she dashed as fast as her legs would carry her back to the village.

She arrived in the village with time enough to get her breath back and have a cup of tea and an iced bun in the tea rooms before she caught the next bus back to Norwich.

By the time Rose got back to the hotel it was late afternoon. She went up to her room to change. Violet was having tea in the parlour and invited Rose to join her.

"How was your friend?" Violet asked, bringing a cup, saucer and plate in for Rose.

"Err, not too well," Rose said. "I'm quite worried about…her." She took the cup and saucer and poured herself some tea. "I think I'll pop down and have a word with Major Maitland."

Violet smiled. "He's out visiting the hospital in Kings Lynn today, but he's usually back by teatime." She sipped her tea and sat back, looking at Rose. "Have you thought anymore about what you're going to do now you have your Certificate?"

"Not really," Rose said. "Are those Martha's famous fruit scones. I must try one." She took a scone and put it on her plate.

They went on to talk about the hotel and the concert Violet was putting on on Saturday. "You must come," Violet said. Then she went on to tell Rose about William's visit and how he'd entertained the men with Amos.

Rose laughed. "I believe he's really good," she said.

"Yes," Violet said, "I'll give him that, but it's not something to make a living at."

"No. He seems well settled in the Navy," Rose said. "So I don't think you need to worry."

Warmth lit up Violet's face and Rose was glad she'd been able to reassure her about William's future.

After tea Rose went to find Major Maitland. Clara Jones was in her office, next to his. "I'm expecting him back at any time," she said when Rose enquired after him. "Is there anything I can do?"

"I was wondering if I could look at some of his books. He did say."

"Yes. Of course. In here." Clara showed her into the Major's office. A large bookcase took up one wall. "I'll leave you to it," Clara said. "Just yell if you need anything."

Rose studied the books. She searched for something on pharmaceuticals so she could look up the medication Gloria was dishing out. She found several books on the subject, took them down, spread them out on the desk and started reading.

She was so engrossed in studying them that she didn't hear the Major come in.

"Hello," he said, glancing at the books spread out on his desk. "Looking for anything in particular?"

Rose jumped at the sudden interruption. "Sorry," she said, closing the books ready to remove them. "I was looking for some reference to this." She handed him the box she'd picked out of the waste bin at the hospital.

The Major's face creased into a deep frown. "Where on earth did you get this?" he said.

Rose told him the whole story of meeting Joe in St Thomas', visiting his mother and hearing about him being moved to the Sheldon Hospital. "I went to see him," she said. "I got that from the Pharmacy. That's the medication he was being given."

"No," he said. "You must be mistaken."

She showed him her notebook. "I copied the prescriptions from the charts on the beds," she said. "I copied them exactly. I saw a nurse in the Pharmacy making up the doses from prescriptions she'd been given. That's where I got the box."

The Major shook his head, his face filled with concern. "This can't be right. These are hallucinogens and they're being prescribed here with morphine and cocaine. All psychoactive substances. They play havoc with mental ability."

He put his hand to his chin and thought for a few moments, then glanced at the bookcase. "They've been banned for general use since…Let me see." He went to one of the shelves and took down a folder. "Yes. Here we are, Pharmacy Act May 1916. The Army Council issued an order banning any unauthorized sale or supply of psychoactive substances, mostly cocaine, but also methamphetamines, codeine, hemp, heroin, morphine, and opium, to any member of the armed forces, except for medical reasons and only by prescription." He put the folder down and glanced again at the bookcase. "There was a memo from Colonel Wood, Director of Medical Services in this area." He ran his hand along the shelf and called, "Miss Jones."

Clara Jones appeared immediately. "Yes, sir?"

"Memo from Colonel Woods, Director General. Where would that be now?"

Clara went to the bookcase and lifted down another folder. "Here, sir. Filed under Memos from the Director General."

"Ah yes. Quite so," The Major riffled through the papers. "Here we are. Reference to the 1916 Act. Psychoactive substances only to be issued in *extrema fortuna (*extreme circumstances) and when authorised by two doctors." He gazed at Rose. "Are you sure these are being prescribed and in these doses?"

"Yes. I copied the charts exactly and I saw the doses being made up."

He sighed heavily. "Miss Jones, arrange an inspection – no wait – cancel that. Put a call through to Colonel Woods, and see if he's available at 0600 hours tomorrow for an unscheduled inspection at The Sheldon Hospital. You have the address. Oh and bring me the file." He smiled at Rose. "Good chap Oakey Woods. Known him for years," he said.

Miss Jones disappeared and reappeared a minute later with the requested file. The Major sat at his desk and opened the file, the unease on his face deepening as he read it. "Tell me more about what you found when you visited this hospital," he said.

Rose couldn't get the words out quick enough. A great bubble of relief grew inside her. She'd done the right thing bringing it to the Major's attention. Perhaps there was some hope for Joe after all. "Well, the wards were horrible, men lying in bed, mumbling, moaning, some shouting and screaming like wounded animals.

The nurse I spoke to mentioned battle fatigue and trauma, but Joe was fine when I saw him. He wasn't suffering from trauma until he went to that place. She also mentioned electric shock treatment."

His eyes sprang wide. "Did she indeed," he said. He drew a deep breath. "It appears that Captain Trent has overstepped his authority." He closed the file. "Don't worry, my dear. If things are as you say Oakey and I will sort the blighters out and they'll be brought to book."

Miss Jones came in to confirm that the Colonel would be available.

"Good," the Major said, satisfaction clear in his eyes. "Now what did you say your friend's name was?"

"Joe. Joe Jennings. He's in the ward on the second floor."

"Joe Jennings. Did you get that, Miss Jones?"

"Yes, sir."

"Don't worry," he said to Rose. "I'll look into his case personally."

Chapter Twenty Six

That night Rose hardly slept, visions of the day going round and round in her mind. The smell, the pitiable wailing and moaning, the suffering she'd witnessed. Then there was the anxiety. Would the Major and the Director General see what she'd seen on the wards and be moved the way she was moved? Or would the staff close ranks and the atrocities be covered up as so much of what went on in this war was covered up. '*Too much reality for the people at home*', they'd say. '*Undermines the spirit of the nation*', she'd heard given as an excuse for it but surely the families of men at the Front deserved the truth?

She sighed. She trusted the Major and, from the expression on his face when she'd told him what she'd seen at Sheldon, he wasn't a man to be fobbed off. Still, from the brief sighting she'd had of Captain Trent, he wasn't a man to be put off course by a complaint from a chit of girl. Would he persuade the Director General and the Major that he was doing what he could for men who had no other hope than spending the rest of their lives incarcerated for their own good? How much suffering was permissible in the name of research into a hitherto unknown condition brought on by a hitherto unknown type of war?

She'd be depicted as a hysterical young woman too emotionally immature to deal with the rigours of what men went through for their patriotism and too stupid to understand them. It happened all the time, women never being listened to because they were believed to be incapable of rational thought.

Then there was the way she'd uncovered it. She'd gone there on a whim, with no authority. She'd pretended to be one of them, gained confidences she'd never had learned otherwise, but in an underhand way. She should have spoken to the Major first, but then he'd merely have reassured her that '*they know what they are doing*' and say, '*best leave it to the experts,* in his most patronising manner.

She shook her head and told herself to get a grip. The Major wasn't like that. He'd always treated her with respect, if somewhat condescendingly. Then another thought struck her. As well as accusing her of a hysterical reaction to normal medical procedures, Captain Trent could say she had gone there secretly, like a spy, to undermine his work and that her actions were detrimental to the war effort. If they believed him she could even be prosecuted under the Defence of the Realm Act which stated that *'No person shall by word of mouth or in writing, spread reports likely to cause disaffection or alarm among any of His Majesty's forces or among the civilian population'.* Was that what she was doing, causing disaffection and alarm? That would be treated worse than profiteering, possibly even seen as treason.

At best she could lose her job, be stripped of her qualification and barred from the only work she'd ever wanted to do. At worst she could go to prison. A lump of dismay formed in her stomach and rose to her throat. She felt sick.

Fear mounted in her brain and as she dozed off she saw herself being dragged into Court with everyone shouting 'Off with her head,' like the mad Queen in *Alice's Adventures in Wonderland.*

The next morning, long before dawn, she heard car engines running in the road outside. She looked out.

Two cars stood in the road, their engines belching out smoke and vapour into the frosty air. The Major came out of the hotel with several other men in Medical Corps uniforms. They stopped to exchange a few words before getting into the cars and driving off.

She knew Corporal Kerrigan, the Major's driver who was himself a paramedic. If they asked him he'd vouch for her reliability.

She sighed. There was nothing more she could do. She'd started a ball rolling and there was nothing she could do to stop it, even if she wanted to. All she could do now was await the outcome. Her whole body tingled with anticipation. Please God, let them see what I saw and put a stop to it, she thought.

At breakfast Florence and Joshua chatted about the day ahead of them, what they'd do at school and their friends. Rose tried to be encouraging but the nagging worry at the back of her mind prevented her.

Violet noticed. "You look a little tired," she said. "Did you not sleep well?"

Rose took a breath and helped herself to another cup of tea. "No, not very well," she said. "Just a bad dream, that's all."

"The night is full of dark imaginings," Violet said. "Probably the result of spending too much time with the sick and dying. Any plans for today?"

Rose couldn't bear the thought of spending the day in the hotel worrying about the Major and what he would say when he returned. "I think I'll go into town. I need a few things and the fresh air will do me good. Can I get you anything while I'm there?"

"Well, I have ordered some books that need collecting and Joshua's shoes should be ready at the menders. I don't know how he wears them out so quickly."

Probably playing football with the other lads on the way to and from school, Rose thought, but she was happy to be able to add Violet's things to her own shopping.

After breakfast Violet gave her a list. She'd added some ribbons and buttons from the haberdashery she needed too.

Glad to be outside Rose walked along the Promenade, trying to put all thoughts of the Sheldon Hospital and what would be happening there behind her. She tried to focus on the trees that were coming into leaf and the green shoots appearing in the gardens along the front. February meant signs of the spring to come; longer days and cool sunshine, hazel nut catkins and snowdrops alongside the budding hedgerows. Spring meant hope, renewal and better days to come. That's what she was wishing for.

She stopped to watch the hazy sunlight glistening on the water beneath a clear blue sky. The sound of the waves whooshing onto the shore filled the cold crisp air. She took a deep breath, taking it all in.

By the time she reached the shops her face glowed from the cold, but her steps felt lighter and she looked forward to the morning ahead. Her first stop was the haberdashers. She spent a long time choosing ribbons and buttons for Violet and some lace for herself which she could attach to the collar of her favourite blouse. She bought pink wool for Florence, who was knitting a patchwork blanket for her dolls.

In the bookshop she browsed the latest additions to the stock. She found a slim volume of watercolours to send to Peter, simply because she knew he'd appreciate them. She chose the latest Sherlock Holmes mystery for William and picked out a book about ships for Joshua. For herself she decided on *Dear Enemy*, the sequel to the *Daddy-Long-Legs* book she'd read a few years earlier. She thought it might suit her mood.

After the bookshop she wandered along looking in shop windows. She stopped when she came to the photographic studio. She studied the portraits and landscapes on display. She'd read and reread Ferdie's letter many times over and thought perhaps he had a point. Perhaps she could manage something a bit more adventurous if that's what he wanted. Not the underwear, of course, that was going a bit too far, but something a little less formal might be possible. No harm in asking, she thought.

A bell rang as she pushed the door open. Inside the walls held pictures of every size and shape. Pictures of men and women, pictures of families, pictures of groups of people, both women and men, pictures of the pier and the beach and lots of pictures of children and babies. A table in the middle of the room held a selection of albums and photo frames. A shelf near the cash register held camera parts, and various boxes of film.

A woman stepped out from behind a partition. "Good morning, can I help you?" she said. Then she saw Rose. "Oh. Hello, Rose. What can I do for you today?"

Rose smiled. "I was expecting to see Frank," she said. Frank Watson was a photographer and Dora Watson's husband.

"I'm afraid you'll have to put up with me," Dora said. "Frank's gone. He's somewhere on the Western Front with Tommy and Sam." Tommy and Sam were

Dora and Frank's sons. "No idea where, but it doesn't do to dwell does it? What is it you're after?"

Rose blushed.

"Oh I see, a particular photograph for a particular young man I'll warrant," Dora said. "Well, you've come to the right place. What did you have in mind?"

Rose wasn't sure so Dora offered to show her some samples so she could choose a pose for herself. "Whatever you want, my dear," Dora said, handing her a large red album.

Rose sat at the desk poring over the album which contained all sorts of portraits, mostly women. Some head and shoulders, others full length. Some formal, others more casual.

"Is there anything there you fancy?" Dora said after a while. "How about this?" She picked out a photo of a girl in a red satin corset frilled in black lace. Stockings and suspenders covered her shapely legs. "Very popular."

Rose blanched at the thought. "Well…not really me," she said. "Perhaps…how about…something a bit more…erm…classic." She showed Dora a photo of a woman lying on a chaise longue. "How about this?"

Dora grinned. "Good choice," she said. "Come this way."

Rose followed Dora into the studio at the back. Behind the partition she saw the chaise longue on a platform, a rail holding garments against the wall and several boxes overflowing with various props. A pot of tea and a sandwich were set out on a tray on the side. "Sorry I've disturbed your lunch," she said.

"Not at all," Dora said. "I'll get another cup and you can join me. I have some costumes and other props I use." She fussed about getting a chair for Rose and a cup and saucer out of a cupboard over a small sink. "I get them from the theatre. They let me have them after a run's finished. You can look through them and make up your mind what you want."

Rose wasn't at all sure what she wanted or even what was available, so Dora guided her through the possibilities. Everything from Cleopatra to a dancer at the Folies Bergère was available.

"My goodness," Rose said. "Quite a collection."

"Yes. The summer visitors like to dress up a bit in something unusual. A memento to take home, or make into a postcard to send to friends. It's a good part of our trade, or was." She smiled as though lost in memory. "Not now though. With all the men gone I mostly get young ladies like yourself looking for something a bit special for their sweethearts overseas. Quite daring some of them." Her eyebrows shot up and she fanned her face with her hand to show Rose how hot they were. "Now, what's your preference?"

Rose laughed. "I'm not sure I want to be 'quite daring'," she said. In the end, after trying out a few things, she settled for an elegant off-the-shoulder gown in deep crimson. The neckline plunged provocatively and the full length skirt buttoned down the front. She piled her hair on her head with tresses draped over one shoulder. With a little judicious use of paint and powder from Dora's make-up box, Rose hardly recognised herself.

Dora took several pictures of her lying seductively on the chaise longue in different poses, with the skirt left unbuttoned to show a great deal of her long slender legs. If this doesn't get Ferdie's attention I don't know what will, she thought.

It would take a couple of days for the photographs to be developed and printed, so Rose left with a feeling of having done something she wasn't sure about. It was fun and Rose enjoyed doing it, but was it too much? Too tarty? The make-up especially. She didn't want Ferdie to think she was easy. Although, after their last meeting he may already have that idea.

She looked in a few more shops searching for possible gifts to take back for Hope and Cissie. Then she stopped in the tea room for a cup of tea, a toasted teacake and to catch up on the latest town news. The lady owner of the tea room was famous for knowing everyone's business and not averse to passing it on. As it was a quiet afternoon, due to the cold weather, she was happy to sit with Rose and chat for half-an-hour.

Rose called in at the baker's and picked up some fancy cakes for tea before collecting Joshua's shoes from the menders. On the way back to the hotel she ran into Florence and Joshua coming home from school; Florence skipping along as usual and Joshua more serious. He's so like Gabriel, she thought and was glad. It meant he'd grow up a kind, intelligent, sensitive man who'd care for people more vulnerable than himself.

Chapter Twenty Seven

Back at the hotel Rose helped Florence with her knitting while Joshua read his book. While they had their tea she went to see if Major Maitland had returned, anxious to find out what he thought about his visit to the hospital.

"He's not here, I'm afraid," Miss Jones said. "He sent a message to say that he'd be staying with Colonel Woods for a few days."

Rose's heart sank. The anxiety she'd been holding back all day rose up inside her. "Did he say anything about…you know, the hospital?"

Miss Jones shook her head. "Nothing. But then I wouldn't expect him to. It will be highly confidential."

Rose's heart sank further. "Well, if you do hear anything…"

"I promise I'll let you know." Miss Jones smiled.

Rose brooded over dinner until Violet said, "You've hardly eaten anything. Are you quite well?" The look on her face suggested Rose might be suffering from something particular.

She thinks I'm pregnant, Rose thought which made her laugh. "I'm fine," she said. "I just have some letters to write."

"Me too," Violet said. "Perhaps we can sit together after dinner?"

"Yes, lovely," Rose said and went on to tell her all the news and gossip she'd heard in town that morning.

Rose wrote to Peter and sent him the book of watercolours she'd bought. Then she wrote to William sending him his book. As she wrote she thought of each of them and where they'd be now and what they'd be doing. They both seemed so far away.

Then she wrote to Gabriel, a letter to go in with the one Violet was writing, telling him about her day shopping, the fishermen on the beach that morning and the primroses in bud she'd seen on her walk. She didn't mention anything about the photograph she'd had taken, the Major or the hospital. Only good news ever got into letters from home.

As darkness descended and the day ended she said she wanted an early night, so went to bed to read her book.

A couple of days later Rose collected her photographs. Dora Watson had printed out four different poses. Seeing them Rose couldn't believe how alluring she looked. "You've done me proud," she said to Dora.

"I hope your young man approves." Dora grinned.

Rose decided she'd wait until she got back to London before sending a picture to Ferdie. It was bad enough Mrs Watson knowing she had a 'young man overseas'. She'd have to go to the post office to post them and she didn't want to be the talk of the town.

She bought gifts for Hope and Cissie and went to visit Mrs Jennings to see if she'd heard anything about Joe. She hadn't but Rose left Hope's address and asked her to let her know as soon as she heard anything. "Anything at all," she said.

"Do you think he'll be all right?" Mrs Jennings asked, deep worry etched on her face.

Rose didn't know what to say. She hadn't told Mrs Jennings what she'd seen at the hospital, merely that she was looking into it. "He'll be fine," she said as convincingly as she could. "He's a strong lad. He'll pull though." She wished she could be sure of that.

All too soon Rose's leave came to an end. She had to return to her job at the hospital. She'd enjoyed spending time with the family, the change of scene and the chance to relax, but now she was getting restless and anxious to get back to work.

Violet helped her pack and gave her some soap, toiletries and stockings she thought might come in useful. She also made sure she had something to eat on the train.

"The children will miss you too," she said when the time came to say goodbye.

Rose kissed her mother. "I'll write," she said. She waved as she walked away to go to the station. Why did partings always have to be so sad, she thought.

When she arrived in London, among the pile of letters Hope had put aside for her she saw a hand delivered note. She recognised the handwriting as Ferdie's. She ripped the envelope open. Ferdie had written that he'd been in London on leave and was sorry to have missed her. He enclosed a photograph of himself in uniform, signed '*With love, Ferdie, XXX*'.

Her heart plunged at the thought of him being here and her missing him. If only she'd been home, she thought, but the fact that he'd called anyway cheered her. He'd made the effort to see her. That must mean something. She smiled, kissed the photo and ran upstairs to her room to write to him. She had a surprise for him. In her letter she wrote that she was devastated to have missed him and hoped he'd be back in London before too long. Then she went through the photos Dora had taken, picked out the most glamorous, signed it with love and kisses and put it in the envelope. She sighed as she posted it.

The February weather was dull, misty and often wet. Most days she found her shoes and coat were soaked by the time she arrived at work. She soon fell back into the routine of the hospital. It was good to see Cissie again and catch up with all her news. The days passed quickly with Rose working long hours and the seemingly endless stream of casualties arriving from Clearing Stations on the Continent.

A month went by before she heard from Major Maitland. The official looking letter bore a Great Yarmouth postmark and her hands trembled as she opened it. Her heart lifted when she read that Sheldon Hospital had been closed and the patients transferred to other hospitals in the area. The Major thanked her for having the courage to bring the situation at the Auxiliary Hospital to his attention and assured her that a full investigation had been carried out. Due to the unconventional (for this she read devious, underhand and bordering on criminal) manner of her discovery he thought it best to keep any mention of her part in it out of any reports. It would be logged as a routine inspection that had uncovered practices that fell below the standard expected of an Auxiliary Hospital serving the Military.

His letter said he had looked personally into the case of Joseph Jennings and was pleased to report that he had been moved to Kings Lynn Hospital where he was expected to make as full a recovery as his disability would allow.

He wished her well in her nursing career and hoped to see her again should she return to Norfolk.

Miss Jones's letter, which arrived the next day, told her (in the strictest confidence) that Captain Trent had been charged with Conduct Likely to Endanger

Life in that he carried out unauthorised research, the methods of which were prohibited. He'd been found guilty, demoted and sent to a base hospital at the Front where his expertise would be most useful. Thank goodness, Rose whispered when she read it. Perhaps if he sees the trauma the soldiers go through first hand he'll be a bit more sympathetic. She thought of the nurses who would be relieved to be moved to a proper hospital too. Overall she was pleased with what she'd done. She'd made a difference. That's what she'd always wanted.

April brought good news in the form of a letter from Alfie announcing the birth of his and Jenny's first child. '*We're naming her after the dearest people in both our lives*' Alfie wrote. Hope beamed with delight when she read that they were naming her Eva Hope Daniels, Eva being Jenny's mother's name.

Alfie said he hoped that Hope and Silas would stand as Godparents for the child. Hope wrote back saying it would be an honour and a privilege. They'd look forward to the Christening as soon as it could be arranged.

"Another niece," Hope said to Rose. "I'm so happy for them."

Rose too congratulated them and sent a pair of knitted bootees for the baby.

Spring turned to summer, the days became warmer and the evenings lightened. Rose and Cissie went dancing and to the cinema. Their second summer in the city was more satisfying than the first now that they were qualified and could undertake more rigorous work on the wards, often unsupervised.

Rose wrote to William and he wrote back telling her how well he was doing, and sending love from Amos. He also mentioned Glyn saying he looked forward to seeing her and Cissie again. Gabriel and Violet wrote regularly. Violet's letters always enclosed carefully written notes from Joshua and Florence. Rose could see Ma standing over their shoulders while they wrote them.

She wrote to Ferdie sending him biscuits and a silk scarf she'd found in a sale. She hoped he'd wear it and he'd think of her. Hope shared news from Silas about time he'd spent in Paris with his sister, and the war went on.

During long summer days and warm summer nights, trees broke into leaf, flowers blossomed and, despite the shortages and difficulties, Rose thought everyone smiled a bit more in the sunshine.

Peter came home for a few days leave in June. He escorted Rose and Cissie to dances and nightclubs. He cut quite a dash on the dance floor and was popular with all the young ladies.

"He's bit of all right," Cissie said when she met him. "Where have you been hiding him?" Rose laughed but warmth and pride flowed through her.

On their afternoon off he treated them to ice creams and took them both rowing on the Serpentine in Hyde Park. He made them laugh and Rose couldn't remember when she'd had such a good time. His leave was all too short and Rose felt a thud in her heart when they said goodbye.

Chapter Twenty Eight

When Peter rejoined his unit he found they'd merged with several other units who'd been similarly decimated. Men he'd come to know, men he'd trained with, worked with and shared experiences with, men he'd lived with in filthy, stench filled dug-outs crammed with blood, dirt, lice, disease and death, men he'd talked with and laughed with, men whose names he knew and would never forget, had disappeared to be replaced by spotty, half-trained eighteen-year-old conscripts who had no idea why they suddenly found themselves there.

It was his job to inspire them to do what was expected of them and what they'd come to expect of themselves and each other. To be the best version of themselves they could be.

They were moving up the line again. Word in the camp was that something big was coming. The roads were full of men marching, trucks carrying troops, large gun emplacements being moved. Vast numbers of conscripts were being shipped in and streams of experienced men were amassing in greater numbers than he'd ever seen before. They lay in the sun, smoking, talking and waiting, preparing for the Big Push that was bound to come. God knows how the word spread, he thought, but it did.

Even he, who prided himself on remaining calm in the most difficult circumstances, felt a prickle of anticipation, wary of what lay ahead.

This had been his life for almost three years now, fighting this war, often over the same piece of muddy, tortured, barbed-wire infested ground littered with shell holes and craters. He had great admiration for the infantry brigades on the front line, living in trenches, their risks the highest, their losses by far the greatest and yet they retained their sense of humour, their innate resilience, stubborn pride and confidence in their own abilities to weather the storm and survive it. He'd sat with them in the dug-outs playing cards, talking, laughing and singing, *we're here because we're here, because we're here...*all resigned to certain death.

Their courage and fortitude overawed him as he watched from his position on the hills and ridges above the battlefield. He saw them climb out and move forward over churned up, bomb-cratered ground facing shelling, barbed-wire and rifle fire at Passchendaele. He shouted encouragement to his men as they loaded, fired and re-loaded guns that provided the barrages ahead of the push from the trenches into the German lines.

July brought weeks of incessant rain and the heaviest and most accurate German barrages he'd seen so far. They lost men and batteries. Brimming craters pock-marked the desolate landscape. Water-logged shell-holes filled with the dead and dying. The roads became impenetrable; the heavy artillery bogged down and had to be hauled out by horses over terrain unfit for motor vehicles. He worked tirelessly going from emplacement to emplacement, digging out casualties and having them transported to clearing stations. He searched for safer placements, moving when required through impassable roads. After a month of non-stop barrages of shelling and bombing he was bloodied, muddied, frustrated, bone-weary with exhaustion and amazed by the pounding men could take without breaking.

At the end of the month his unit were sent to the Reserve. A chance for respite. He was allowed a three-day pass. The first two days day he bathed, slept and ate a half-decent meals in the Officers' Mess. The third day he packed his sketch pad and a supply of pencils into his pack and caught a ride out of the camp into the nearest town. He liked to sketch the places he visited, peaceful places which, in normal times would be picturesque and which still held a little of their peacetime appeal. In a small village west of Ypres he ran into a man he'd trained with. Buffy Parsons had been wounded, marked unfit for front line duty and moved to a Transport Station. They greeted each other warmly.

"It's amazing who you run into out here," Buffy said. "Small world."

Buffy was billeted nearby and knew the best place to go for a drink. He took Peter to a bar next to the local brothel, both frequented by soldiers from the camp. A queue of men formed outside the brothel. Buffy noticed Peter's raised eyebrows.

"Who can blame them?" he said. "Looking for a little pleasure? I see them all, you know. They all pass through here on their way to the next place."

Inside the bar a rowdy group of soldiers sat at a table, drinking, making jokes and laughing. Another soldier sat at the bar. Every now and then one of the men from the table would go up to him, they'd talk for a while then they'd go back to the table, a satisfied grin on their face.

Buffy got the first drink. "7th Irish," he said, nodding at the group at the table. Infantry. Chap at the bar's their Corporal. They'll buy him drinks all night in the hope he won't report them for their misdeeds. He probably will."

"You know him then?"

"Know of him. Not the same thing. They'll have been in the brothel, or waiting their turn."

Peter glanced over at them. Who was he to begrudge them a bit of pleasure? "You don't…?" he nodded towards the brothel.

"Me? No. Might come out with more than I went in with," Buffy said. "But if you want to…"

Peter chuckled. "No." They drank and talked about the people they knew and what had happened to them, but not in a sad way, just remembering the best of them, their antics, their humour, their kindness and their unfailing optimism.

"Another?" Peter said.

Buffy handed him his empty glass. Peter went up to the bar. He stood next to the man sitting there and noticed he had a pile of photographs on the bar in front of him. Peter smiled at him, after all they were fighting the same war.

The man nodded back. "Afternoon," he said in a thick Irish accent. "Sir," he added seeing the insignia on Peter's shoulder.

Peter ordered the drinks for himself and Buffy. "Can I get you another," he said, being friendly.

"Thank you kindly." The man pushed his glass forward. "Sir," he said. "A beer, thanks." He spread the photographs in front of him across the bar. "Can I interest you in a photo for your billet, sir? Take a girl home with you tonight? Very reasonable price."

Peter shook his head. "No thanks," he said as he watched the girl behind the bar pouring their drinks.

"Are you sure now, they're very popular, very clean girls, young and pretty."

Peter glanced at the photographs spread out on the bar. They were all young girls wearing very little, their bodies clearly visible through the lace of their underwear. His eyebrows rose.

"No. Really," he said.

"Shame," the man said. "A lot of young men like yourself enjoy having something to look at in their billets."

Peter smiled. He could see why young lads away from home for the first time might be attracted to pictures of nubile young girls to feed their fantasies, or even to help them feel as though they 'fitted in' with men who'd been there longer and were more experienced. "No," he said. The barmaid placed their drinks on the bar. Peter paid for them.

As the man gathered up the photos Peter caught sight of a picture of a girl in a white blouse, her chestnut hair swept up and pearls in her ears. Shock struck him like a punch to the stomach knocking the breath out of him. He picked the picture up and stared at it unable to believe his eyes. Thoughts buzzed through his head like angry bees. How had this vile creature, the most squalid of squaddies, got hold of a picture of Rose?

"Ah!" Ferdie said. "I see that one's caught your eye. A good choice for a gentleman like yourself. Sir. An innocent beauty and only five shillings."

"Five shillings!"

"Erm." Ferdie swallowed. "Half-a-crown to you, sir."

Peter's first instinct was to punch him in the face, but he clenched his fists and managed to control himself. It wouldn't do any good and six of his mates were sat at a nearby table. He took a breath. "Do you…do you have any more pictures of this young lady?" he asked as lightly as he could.

Ferdie grinned. "A bit more – risqué – shall we say? Is that what you're looking for?"

"I asked if you have any more," Peter said trying and failing to keep the anger out of his voice.

Ferdie shrugged, quietened by Peter's tone. He glanced around as though making sure they weren't being overheard. "I'm working on it," he said.

"If you do get any more of this particular girl – only this one mind – will you let me know?"

Ferdie grinned. "My pleasure, sir."

Peter gave him his card and slammed five shillings on the bar. "Let me know," he said. "And only me. Got it?"

"Got it. Sir," Ferdie said.

Peter paid for the drinks and took his and Buffy's back to their table, his heart pounding, his head buzzing with of thoughts of Rose.

Chapter Twenty Nine

Rose made her way to work along streets humid with August heat. Even walking by the river felt airless. No breeze ruffled the trees but she shivered as a sudden chill engulfed her. She tried to shrug it off. Someone's walked over my grave, she thought as she shivered again.

The feeling dogged her all morning. Even in the ward when Cissie complained of the airless heat, Rose shivered with cold.

"You're unwell," Cissie said, seeing Rose's face as pale as parchment.

"It's just a summer chill," Rose said. "I'll be fine," but the feeling persisted along with the notion that something wasn't right. She had no idea what it could be. Again she shrugged it off, until the Sister sent her home.

"Hot milk and honey," she said. "And go to bed. A good night's sleep and you'll be better in the morning."

The next day she felt a little better but the feeling of something being wrong still troubled her. Try as she might she couldn't shake it. All day long she was besieged by sudden chills and knees like jelly so she had to sit down. Anxiety churned inside her but she couldn't think why. Something was wrong, terribly wrong, but she didn't know what.

Gabriel, at the docks in Boulogne to pick up a shipment of corrugated iron to be transported to the troops at the Front, stopped what he was doing when he received an urgent message, wired from London to Transport Headquarters and brought to him by a motorcycle courier. His hand shook as he opened it.

When he read it a chill rang through to his bones. His heart stuttered. His first thoughts were of Violet and home and how he could get there as soon as possible. After passing orders to his next in command he managed to book passage on the next ship out.

Five hours later he was in Dover. He made some phone calls, then got the train to London, arriving just as Rose came home from the hospital.

"Pa," she said, running towards him. "You're home. I didn't expect…" her voice faded when she saw his face, twisted in pain.

"What is it? What's the matter?" Her heart hammered.

"You'd best come inside," he said, putting his arm around her to usher her up the path to where Hope stood by the open door.

Inside he showed them the message he'd received from his friend at the Admiralty.

'Ships Sea Hawk and Albion sunk in the Med. No details yet. Thought you should know. Eyes Only. TF'

"But that's William's ship," Rose said. She gasped, her hands flew to her mouth and she dropped onto a chair as the news sunk in. "No," she said. "It can't be right. Not William." Tears pricked her eyes. It isn't true, she thought. It can't be true.

"He only says the ships were lost," Gabriel said, hope lighting his face. "I spoke to Toby at the Admiralty when I landed in Dover. He said some crew members were picked up but they don't have a list as yet."

"So there's a chance…" Hope said.

"Yes. Let's hope it's a good chance," Gabriel said. "William's the most resourceful lad I know, and the best swimmer. We can only pray…"

Rose shook her head. "Not William. It can't be William. He's alive. I know it. I'd know if he wasn't. I'd feel it. In here." She beat her chest. "I'd know if anything…" A dark wave of despair engulfed her. "It can't be true. It just can't," she said and threw herself, sobbing, into Gabriel's arms. "I won't believe it, I won't believe it," she kept repeating, her fists hammering his chest.

Gabriel held her until her tears subsided. "I pray that you're right," he said.

"Ma!" Rose gasped, her eyes wide. "She'll be…does she know? Will they have told her?"

"Toby said they'd be releasing it to the press tomorrow for the evening papers. He'll let me know when he gets the list of crew picked up. If he's not on it he'll be posted Missing. Then the telegram would be sent to your mother, his next of kin."

"Here, I think we all need this," Hope said, handing them each a glass of brandy.

Gabriel gave a wan smile. "Thanks. If worst comes to worst I want to be there," he said determination in his voice. "I'll get the train tonight. Do you want to come with me, Rose?"

Rose took a swig of brandy and shook her head. She didn't think she could face seeing her mother when she got the news. "I think me being there would make it worse," she said. "William always was her favourite."

"That's not true," Hope said. "She loves you both."

Rose shrugged.

Gabriel took her hand. "I think we should all be together as a family," he said, gently. "She'd want that."

Rose gazed at him with tear-filled eyes. She nodded. "Of course," she said. "You're right. I'll get my things."

The journey north was the most dismal Rose had ever undertaken. A great stone of dread sat in her stomach, although part of her still didn't believe it. Surely she'd know if ...they were so close. There was an invisible tie that bound them, a tie formed before they were born. She knew his thoughts, his feelings, she hurt when he hurt, she cried when he was sad... surely that counted for something?

Then she remembered how she'd known there was something wrong... something...but not William's...she couldn't even think the word. In her head she had visions of him, thrown into a swirling sea, trying to swim against surging banks of water as high as the sky, struggling to breathe, the waves overtaking him. No, it wasn't right. She'd never believe it, never.

They arrived at the hotel later that evening. Violet's dinner guests were just departing. Her face lit up with surprise when she saw them, then, when she saw their faces, the smile dropped from her lips. Fear filled her eyes. Her hands flew to her mouth. "No," she said. "No, not William." She stood frozen to the spot.

Gabriel stepped forward to embrace her. She pushed him away. "I knew it," she said. "I knew it as soon as he joined up. I knew." Despite the words disbelief shone in her eyes.

"It's not certain," Gabriel said, hanging on to a wisp of hope. He handed her the message he'd received. She sank down onto a chair and stared at it. "No," she said. "Not William's ship."

"I rang Toby from Dover," Gabriel said. "He said there were survivors."

"William?" Her face lit up with expectation.

"We don't know," he said.

Violet's fear turned to anger that twisted her face. "What do you mean you don't know? Is my son alive or dead?" She stared accusingly at Gabriel.

"He's alive," Rose said. "He must be. I can feel it, here." She touched her chest. "I'd know. I'm sure I'd know." A surging wave of deep emotion threatened to overwhelm her.

Violet stood up and hugged her. "Of course you would," she said. "You two were always close." She took a deep breath and stroked Rose's hair.

She glanced at Gabriel. "I'm his mother," she said. "Surely I'd feel it too? I'd know if something so terrible had happened, just as Rose would." She managed a brief smile and Rose watched her blink away the tears brimming her eyes.

"We'll know for sure in the morning," Gabriel said. "They'll have the list then."

Violet led Rose to the settee where they both sat. She produced a handkerchief and handed it to Rose. A chaos of conflicting emotions battled across her face. "This will be hardest on you," she said.

Rose sniffed, fighting back the tears. "And you, and Joshua and Florence," she said. "Until they confirm he's safe it'll be hard on everyone."

"Of course," Violet said. "There's nothing more we can do tonight then, other than pray." She took a deep breath. "I'll make some tea and you'll both have some supper before bed. It's going to be a long night."

By midnight Rose was so tired Violet insisted she go to bed. "Try to sleep," she said. She hugged Rose again, but there were no words she could say to make anything any better.

Rose didn't go immediately to her room after saying goodnight. She went instead into William's room, closing the door behind her.

Everything looked exactly as he'd left it. The model boats lined up on the windowsill, the brushes on the dressing table, his shoes by the bed, a jacket thrown carelessly over a chair. She picked the jacket up, hugging it to her face, breathing in the lingering smell of him and her heart turned over.

She sat on his bed trying to make sense of it. In her mind she saw the beguiling smile on his face when he got the news that he'd been accepted for Naval Training, saw him walk away to the station, eager for adventure, saw him again in London, laughing and teasing her over that damned letter from Ferdie, saw him, dashing in his uniform, dancing with Cissie.

Cissie?

Hope was sending a message to the hospital so Rose could take compassionate leave. Would Cissie realise why? What would she think? How would she feel? Then there was Glyn. He'd have been on the ship with William. Was he safe? Thoughts ran through her head like wild hares across a field, going hither and thither. Tears rolled down her cheeks. How could something like this happen? How could something so full of life and joy be snuffed out like a candle flame and her not feel it inside?

"I won't give up hope," she said aloud to the empty room. "I won't believe it until I see it with my own eyes."

She hardly slept that night, but when she did she dreamt of William, the happy cheeky inquisitive boy she'd loved from birth, then saw him lost in a raging ocean surrounded by bombs and debris, swimming towards a distant shore that kept moving further and further away.

When the telegram did arrive Violet was so shaken at the finality of it she couldn't open it. She handed it to Gabriel. "I can't," she said. "You do it."

Rose stood holding her hand while he opened it.

He read aloud, *'We regret to inform you that Leading Hand W. Addison Stone was lost at sea on 25th August 1917 and has been listed as Missing'."*

Violet gasped. Rose shook her head and took the telegram from him as though she didn't believe what he'd read. Her heart faltered and fell into her stomach. "Missing," she said. "That means still alive. No body. He hasn't drowned. They'd know if he'd drowned wouldn't they? He's alive I know it."

Gabriel hugged them both. "Yes. We have to keep believing that he's alive somewhere. He'll come back to us. I know it too."

"What'll we tell Joshua and Florence?" Rose asked. "Do they have to know?"

Gabriel sighed. "I'm afraid they do. The whole town will know. Word always gets around, God knows how, but it does. We have to prepare them."

Joshua and Florence were kept home from school for a few days until the news sunk in and the town gossip faded. He'd be remembered as one more of the town's young men lost to the war. The next few days were the hardest in Rose's memory. She felt she had to carry on as best she could for William's sake. "He wouldn't want us to be sad," Violet said. "He was doing what he wanted and enjoying his life, we have to cling on to that."

"You talk as though he's already gone," Rose said in a rare outburst of rage at her mother. "He isn't. I know it. He'll be back."

Everyone in the town knew and liked William. He'd grown up there and was popular. Several visitors came to pay their respects. Rose always thanked them but told them he was 'Listed Missing' and was sure to be found alive eventually. Nesta called to sit with Violet who put on a brave face.

"There's no need," she said. "I'm fine. We all believe he'll come through this and we'll see him again. You know William, always getting into scrapes but managing to survive them. Now, let's have some tea and refuse to worry about it."

Gabriel accepted that Rose, being William's twin, would have feelings about him that no one else could comprehend. They'd always had a closer connection and understanding than most brothers and sisters. Rose was the level-headed one, a perfect foil to his impatience and impulsiveness. But he worried about Violet's refusal to accept that anything could have happened to William. He realised that, if she acknowledged it, her sorrow would be so deep she'd fall apart and she couldn't afford to do that. Not with Rose, Joshua and Florence to think about. He admired her for that. This was the Violet he'd fallen in love with. The woman who wouldn't let anything defeat her. Only himself and Rose would know how deeply she felt the loss. How the thing she loved most in the world had been snatched from her. How her life would never be the same again and how she, like Rose, would never give up hope.

Chapter Thirty

The next few days merged into a blur for Rose. She felt lost, not knowing what to do for the best. Every day she walked along the seafront, staring out at the vast expanse of water. "Where are you, William?" she whispered into the wind. "I wish you'd come home." If he was out there she felt sure he'd hear her, or at least know she was thinking of him. That's how it was with them, they knew each other's thoughts and wishes.

In the evenings she went out and gazed at the moon and stars thrown across the sky like jewels scattered by a fleeing thief. Knowing he was under the same moon and stars gave her some comfort. Was he gazing at the sky and thinking of her?

She walked into town on errands for Violet, seeing familiar faces, but it felt very different. People stopped to say how sorry they were to hear…or sometimes they wouldn't say anything, just smile with sadness in their eyes. She could see them thinking, 'another one to add to the list of men who'd gone to war and never come back'. But William was different, he was missing. He would be coming back. He had to come back. Life would be unbearable if he didn't.

Violet busied herself with duties in the hotel, but Rose knew William was never far from her mind. Gabriel telephoned the Admiralty every day, but there was no news.

After a week of sitting around, helping Violet in the hotel and wandering through the streets, Rose became restless. She needed to keep busy and she wanted to get back to work, where at least she'd feel useful.

"It was good to have you here," Violet said when she told her. "I'm sure we'll get some good news soon. I'll telephone as soon as I hear."

"I'll come back at Christmas if I can," Rose said. "Perhaps we'll all be together then."

Gabriel had to return to duty too, so, after saying goodbye to Violet and the children, they travelled back to London together.

Being back at Hope's the news about William seemed to belong to a different world. Rose threw herself into her work taking comfort in its routine, familiarity and unchanging certainty.

Seeing Cissie for the first time was difficult, but Rose told her, "He'll have been picked up by another boat, one that hasn't reported it. We just have to wait until they do."

"I'm sure you're right," Cissie said, although Rose heard the doubt in her voice.

"I'd know if…if anything really bad had happened to him," Rose said, still not able to face the possibility or the words that burned her tongue. "Ma agrees with me. She'd feel it too. She's his mother, she'd know."

"I hope you're right," Cissie said. "Look, we both need cheering up, and going dancing's not the same without you, so, why don't we hit the town tonight and drown our sorrows?"

At first Rose thought that a little insensitive, but then she saw Cissie's robustness and practicality in a different light, recalling that Cissie had lost a brother at Ypres and had two others still overseas. She smiled. Perhaps it was just what she needed. "You're on," she said.

That night they went dancing and the trips to the cinema and dances soon became something Rose

225

looked forward to again, away from the clamour, tension and heart-rending sights of battle-scarred men in the wards.

As she fell back into the rhythm and routine of the hospital worries about William faded. When she thought of him now it was on the ship, sailing around the world, something he'd always longed to do.

In September, the days became shorter, trees put on their magnificent autumn tapestry and dusk turned hot summer evenings into warm twilights. Rose enjoyed the walk to work and back watching the boats on the river making their way to the docks. She often stopped on the bridge to watch the sun set, painting the sky with glorious golden rays spread over the city. On nights like those the war felt a long, long way away.

One night Rose and Cissie went to a hotel in the Strand, dancing. Halfway through the evening Rose went to visit the powder room. On her way back to the dance hall a man stepped out in front of her.

"Good evening, Rose," he said. His thick Irish accent sounded familiar. "Remember me?"

Rose gasped. Her heart leapt. "Ferdie," she exclaimed her lips spreading into a smile.

"Give us a hug," he said, moving towards her and taking her in his arms. His lips brushed her neck. Her pulse raced. He glanced around. "Can we go somewhere? Just the two of us?"

"Erm," Rose was conscious that Cissie would be waiting for her.

"Come with me, Rose. Let's have a drink. Somewhere we can talk."

"Talk? Where?"

"I have a room. It's not far."

"A room?" Her voice rose at the thought.

"I just want to get to know you better." He touched her cheek and his eyes held the promise of pleasures to come.

Rose wanted to get to know him better too, but going back to his room, especially after what Cissie had said about him? She wasn't sure.

"Don't you trust me, Rose?" he said. "We'll just have a drink. I won't do anything you don't want me to. Cross my heart." He crossed his heart. His summer blue eyes twinkled and Rose felt foolish for refusing. Am I being prudish, she thought. It's just a drink.

"Last chance," he said. "I go back overseas tomorrow."

His confident smile and handsome face won her over. He was fighting for his country and could even be killed. How could she deny him a little pleasure? "I'm with Cissie," she said.

He leaned forward and kissed her neck sending a thrill like an electric current thought her body. "Tell her you don't feel well and want to go home."

The touch of his lips sent all rational thought flying from her head. "I'll get my coat," she said.

As she left Ferdie took out a cigarette and lit it, drawing the smoke deep into his lungs with a satisfied grin on his face. A man, who'd been standing in the shadows by the bar door and had overheard every word of the conversation, stepped forward and grabbed his shoulder, swinging him around.

Startled, Ferdie was about to protest when a spark of recognition reached his eyes. "Lieutenant," he said. "After some more photographs. You're in luck. Tonight I'm hoping to get some really juicy ones."

The punch came out of nowhere connected with Ferdie's jaw and sent him sprawling on the floor.

Peter, fists still clenched, a cauldron of rage bubbling inside him, stepped next to him, bent over, grabbed the lapels of his coat, lifted him off the floor and dragged him out of the door.

Outside the hotel, fierce fury burned inside him. The survival instinct of the street-boy he used to be rose up, giving him strength and purpose. His coal black eyes sparked fire. He leaned close to Ferdie's ear. "Rose is family," he whispered through gritted teeth. "Come near her again and I'll have your balls in a bag. Understand?" He jerked Ferdie's coat up so it nearly choked him. "Touch her again and you'll wish the Hun had killed you." He pushed him against the wall, his arm across his throat, holding him there, putting all his weight behind it. "I've met your type before," he said. "I know all about the pictures you sell to lads too young to figure out how you come by them. Keep away from here." He punched Ferdie again, under his ribs, making him gasp for breath. "If I find you've been preying on young girls again I'll track you down and see to it that you spend the rest of your life being wheeled around. Got it? Just so you don't forget." He raised his knee sharply into Ferdie's groin.

Ferdie doubled over in pain and fell to the ground. "Don't let me see you round here again," Peter said.

Ferdie stared up at Peter, deep hatred in his eyes. "Bastard," he yelled. "I'll get you."

Peter shrugged and walked back into the hotel.

"Everything all right, sir?" the doorman, who must have seen everything, said.

Peter rubbed his knuckles, still sore from the punch. He straightened his uniform. "Perfectly fine," he said as the anger ebbed out of him.

Rose came out of the dance hall, carrying her coat. "Peter," she said, glancing over his shoulder as though looking for someone. "What are you doing here?"

"Just got home on leave," he said. "Ma said you'd gone dancing. I thought I'd come and find you. Shall we?" He offered his arm.

Rose hesitated and glanced around again. Anxiety twisted inside her. Where was Ferdie? Where had he gone?

"Expecting someone?"

"No. No of course not," she said. "Just surprised to see you."

"And delighted, I hope."

She smiled hesitatingly, still glancing around. There was nothing for it so she allowed him to lead her back into the dance hall to the table where Cissie sat.

"Feeling better?" Cissie asked, eyeing Peter up. "I suppose the chance of dancing with this handsome devil would make anyone feel better." She laughed.

Peter took Rose's coat and placed it on a chair. "She's quite recovered," he said. He guided Rose onto the dance floor. The band played a slow waltz and he pulled her close, their bodies moving together to the music.

Rose breathed in the clean, fresh smell of him. In his arms she felt safe, protected and cherished. She sensed the warmth and closeness of him as they danced and her worries about what had happened to Ferdie melted away.

After the dance Peter walked her home. The heat of the day lingered as they strolled by the river. Moonlight shimmered on the water beneath a canopy of stars. The sound of waves lapping against the hulls of boats moored by the bank filled the still night air.

Rose wondered what had happened to Ferdie. He'd seemed so keen to be with her. Was Cissie right? Was he playing fast and loose with her? He wasn't short of admirers, she knew that. Had a more attractive opportunity presented itself? Had he gone off with someone else? No, she wouldn't believe that. He must have been called away.

"I was sorry to hear about William," Peter said, bringing her out of her reverie. "It must be especially hard on you, you being so close."

Rose shrugged. "No harder than on other families who've lost loved ones. At least there's a chance William will be coming home. We have to believe that."

"Of course."

"So, how long are you home for this time?" she asked, changing from a subject she didn't want to talk about.

"A flying visit, I'm afraid," he said. "I've had another promotion. First Lieutenant, and I've transferred to the Tank Corps. Tomorrow I'm off to train on tanks."

"Tanks?

"Yes." Enthusiasm lit his raven dark eyes. "Tanks are going to win this war for us," he said. "Or at least shorten it."

"Do you think so?" she said, picking up his enthusiasm.

"Oh yes. I saw Pa when I was in France. He agrees with me. Tanks can overrun the German lines with little loss of life and…" He stopped. "Sorry. Probably not an appropriate conversation to have with a beautiful girl on a moonlit night under the stars."

Rose laughed but warmth flowed through her at the words 'beautiful girl'. "So, what would be appropriate?" she said.

Peter pondered. "Well, we could talk about you and what you and Cissie get up to while us men are away."

Rose giggled. "Oh no. Far too racy for the delicate ears of a newly promoted First Lieutenant in the Tank Corps," she said. "Tell me about seeing Uncle Silas in France. How is he?"

"He's well, under the circumstances. Working too hard of course, but you know Pa." He then went on to tell her about the meal they had together in a restaurant in a small village near Arras, the people he met, and the extraordinary beauty of the countryside. He even told her, as they gazed up at the night sky, that Ox had described the September moon as the 'Harvest Moon' because that's when the crops were ripe for gathering. He didn't tell her about the death and destruction he'd seen, the noisy chaos and fearful ferocity of battle or the filthy, degrading living conditions they had to endure. Those things he kept to himself.

Lying in bed that night Peter replayed the events of the evening over in his mind. He'd seen Ferdie Giggs going into the hotel and recognised him immediately. The memory of the scantily dressed girls in the photographs he was selling to the new conscripts filled his mind. Intrigued, he'd followed him into the bar and watched him choose a table by the door where he could watch the comings and goings in the lobby. When, after an hour he got up to speak to Rose, Peter's blood began to boil. He listened to the conversation and realised he intended to lure Rose to his room where, no doubt, he had a camera set up. His promise of 'juicy photographs' rang in Peter's ears and the ferocious fury he'd felt rose up inside him again. Ferdie Giggs wasn't the only man in the trenches making money out of naive young conscripts desperately trying to be whatever was expected of them, not by any means, but exploiting young girls to do it – Peter couldn't countenance that.

When he saw Giggs with Rose his hands had curled into fists. All the hurt and pain of his early years on the street came back, bubbling up inside him. He was a fighter, he'd always been a fighter, his earliest memories were of the struggle to survive. He may have been a bit of a scrapper when he was young, but the army had honed his reflexes and trained him well. He could easily have killed him.

Then he thought of Rose and the feelings she evoked in him. The thought of that man's hands touching her sickened him. All he wanted to do was protect her. Or was it? Was it that he wanted her for himself?

Chapter Thirty One

The next morning Rose rushed to get the post when it arrived. She expected a note from Ferdie explaining why he'd had to leave in such a hurry. He'd seemed so keen, then he'd let her down. She couldn't go back into the dance after lying to Cissie, she'd look like a fool. She'd felt humiliated. How could he walk away and leave her stranded? If it hadn't been for Peter being there to rescue her she'd have had to leave early and walk home alone. As it was Peter had saved the evening and, in the end, she really enjoyed it.

She didn't know whether to write to Ferdie and ask him. He owed her an explanation after all, but she didn't want it to appear as though she was chasing him. She had too much pride for that. Anyway, it wasn't the girl's place to chase the men they were attracted to. Their role was to wait until asked. The gentlemen had to approach them, that was how it was done. Did that apply in this case? She knew better than to ask Cissie's advice, or even Hope's. Part of her longed to see him again. He'd aroused feelings in her she'd never experienced before. She recalled the storm that raged inside her when his lips touched her skin and the way her heart leapt when she saw him. Was she in love with him and, more importantly, did he feel the same way about her?

She shuffled through the letters. There was nothing in Ferdie's handwriting but there was a letter addressed to her with a Naval Post Office postmark. Her hands trembled as she ripped it open. She felt a thud in her heart when she saw it was from Glyn. She'd been so sure it would be from William, then she remembered he wasn't a keen letter writer. Much more likely to send a telegram or even telephone.

She read the letter with a heavy heart, glad that Glyn was safe, but still fearful for William. Glyn said he'd heard William was missing. He was sorry he had no news of him. He'd been injured in the blast that sunk the ship and another vessel had picked him up. They had taken him to the Naval Hospital in Gibraltar. He hoped to be able to call on her as soon as he returned to England. Meanwhile he was thinking of her and sent his best wishes to her and her family.

Rose sighed. She wasn't sure whether hearing that Glyn was safe made her feel better or worse. Why wasn't it William?

When Glyn arrived at the hospital the week before Christmas, a light drift of snow covered the landscape, frosting the trees and muffling the rattle of traffic. As dusk fell the late afternoon sunshine dropped softly over the buildings embracing them in its golden glow. A sharp breeze from the river chilled the air.

Rose was called down to the reception to greet him. He looked a lot thinner than she remembered, haggard even and at least ten years older. The spark had gone from his soft brown eyes, shadowed by dark hollows and a livid scar ran from the middle of his forehead to above his left ear. His face bore the look of a man who'd suffered and seen too much, which he probably had. He had a kit bag with him.

"I finish at six," Rose told him.

"I'll wait," he said.

"There's a canteen. Go and have some tea. We'll meet you there."

He nodded.

Later, Rose and Cissie joined him in the canteen. He told them as much as he remembered about the ship going down.

"I'm lucky to be alive," he said. "All I remember is an ear splitting explosion, then total darkness and cold, excruciating, debilitating, cold. I didn't see William. Everything happened so quickly, although it plays in slow motion in my mind. I keep seeing it, the flashes of light, then the dark. There are bits so foggy they're just out of reach and I can't get to them. I'm sorry I can't tell you more."

"It was good of you to come to see us at all," Rose said.

He took her hand. "Don't give up. I was picked up. There's a chance William was too. There were ships all around. Not only British Naval ships. He could be anywhere."

"That's what I think," Rose said.

"So, what are you going to do now?" Cissie asked.

"I'm going home." He touched his head. "I get headaches, memory loss, lose concentration. Sometimes my co-ordination goes haywire. It's a long road to recovery they tell me."

"Is there anything we can do?" Cissie asked, touching his hand. Rose saw Cissie's softer side as she spoke to him, the side she showed when dealing with the sick or injured, the caring side of her nature which she mostly kept hidden. Perhaps it's because they're both from Wales, she thought. They'd share a similar upbringing and sense of loyalty.

His lips struggled into a smile. "You could write," he said.

Cissie wrote down his home address. "I'll do better than that," she said. "I'm going home for Christmas. It's not far from you. I'll visit."

Light warmed his gentle brown eyes. "I'll look forward to that," he said.

They walked with him to the station to get his train home and Rose wondered what sort of future lay ahead of him.

Rose too went home for Christmas, just as she'd promised. It felt especially poignant as it would be her and William's eighteenth birthday and he wouldn't be there to celebrate it with her. She felt as though part of her had been wrenched away and she wasn't sure how she'd manage without it.

Gabriel being home on leave helped. She'd always got on better with him than with her mother but it was only now she came to appreciate his steadfast presence and understanding. She realised how much Ma depended on it too.

Spending time with Joshua and Florence softened the swirling sadness that invaded her at odd intervals, when she saw something William would enjoy, or they had a meal that had been his favourite. She got caught up in their resilient optimism and animated chatter. They worried about what they'd get for Christmas, who would come, how their friends were and a thousand other things that, although trivial, saved her from sinking into other deep obsessive thoughts. Their lives were moving on so quickly. Why couldn't hers?

Christmas Eve she had some last minute shopping to do so went into town. Seeing Lenny's dolls in the shop window jarred her heart as memories of Amos sprang to mind. He'd be lost too, she thought.

After shopping she went to visit Mrs Jennings.

"Come in, me dear," the old lady said. "Joe's not here. He's at work in the boatyard, but you're welcome to stay for tea."

In the cosy front room she noticed Joe's medals in a case over the mantle-shelf with his picture. "You must be proud of him," she said.

"Oh Aye. And it's thanks to you that 'e's here to tell the tale," she said. "If you hadn't got 'im transferred from that 'ospital, well, I'd 'ave gone out of me mind I would."

Rose wasn't sure she deserved the thanks.

"Your ma's invited me for tea and a concert at the hotel this evening," Mrs Jennings said. "Good of her ain't it?"

Rose smiled. "She's invited a few of the women in town with husbands and sons away fighting overseas. She wanted to do something special for them."

"Well, she'd know what it's like, wouldn't she? The worry and that, what with Mr Stone and your William going. Eh. I was sorry to hear about young William. He was a good lad. Everyone says so."

Rose sighed. "We still hope he'll be home," she said, aware that a lot of the women in town didn't even have that uncertainty to cling to. Their men were gone forever.

"Oh aye. Listed Missing weren't 'e? Well, there's 'ope then." She didn't sound convinced.

They sat and chatted for a while until Rose said she'd go and see Joe at the boatyard.

"Aye. 'E'll be glad to see you an' all," Mrs Jennings said. "Never stops talking about you and saying as how you visited him. 'E appreciated that."

Walking to the boatyard brought another deluge of memories of William and the time he spent there. She told herself they were happy memories and that's what she should cling on to.

Joe and Lenny were welcoming. "Come in, lass an' have a cup of tea," Lenny said. "Not every day we get a visit from an angel of mercy who, Joe's ma tells me, saved this 'un here."

"I'm not sure I can take all the credit for that," she said. She didn't want to go too far into her part in having the hospital closed down. "How much do you remember, Joe?"

"Me? I don't remember nowt. It's all a blur from when I left London 'ospital to waking up in Kings Lynn. Ma told me I was in another 'ospital in Sheldon, but I don't remember that."

That's probably just as well, Rose thought but said, "Well, I'm glad you're better now."

"Yeah. I'm good as new," Joe said, slapping his false leg. "An' they was right about the bunions an' all."

The afternoon of the party Rose helped Violet set up the tables and decorate the room.

Martha made sandwiches, scones and cake. The tea would be served first. Joshua and Florence would help serve, then the concert would begin.

Violet had arranged for various acts to perform, including a comedian, a juggler and a man with a performing dog.

Rose worried when she saw the townswomen filing in, but she needn't have done. The evening was a great success. Seeing the women able to forget their worries, relax and enjoy themselves brought an avalanche of admiration for her mother, who'd arranged it.

She even persuaded Nesta to sing an old Music Hall favourite which had all the ladies in the audience joining in and laughing. At the end of the evening, after the professional performances, the ladies themselves were invited up onto the stage to 'do a turn' which resulted in surprisingly bawdy songs and much hilarity.

Dora Watson, from the photographic shop, sung a particularly saucy ditty that brought a blush to the younger ladies' faces.

Violet went from table to table, chatting, sharing their joys and sadness. Rose watched her lift their spirits with a few well chosen words.

"She's got a talent for making people feel better," Gabriel said to Rose as they stood by the bar.

"I think she feels she's doing her bit," Rose said. "Doing what she's good at to raise people's morale."

"Yes," Gabriel said. "We should never underestimate the importance of that and the difference it makes to people's lives."

Seeing the smiles of the ladies as they left, all congratulating Violet on a wonderful evening, Rose knew Gabriel was right. Violet was making a difference to people's lives.

Violet insisted that Christmas Day should be for the family. "After all," she said, "we've spent so much time apart."

They attended the Christmas Day service at the church together, then after dinner they exchanged gifts. Violet and Gabriel gave Rose a silver fob watch for her birthday. One she could pin onto her nurse's uniform. Rose was touched when she read the card, '*To our beautiful daughter, Nurse Addison Stone, on her Eighteenth Birthday, Love Ma and Pa.'*

They'd bought William a pocket watch which they said they'd keep for him until he came home. William's absence tinged the day with sadness, but Rose was convinced she'd know if he wasn't coming back. She'd feel it in her heart and her heart told her there was still hope.

She sat on the floor with Florence helping her set out a tea party for her dolls, while Violet, Gabriel and Joshua played board games. After tea, when Joshua and Florence had gone to bed, they had a sing-song around the piano.

Before Rose went to bed that night she wrote a note to Ferdie. Nothing dramatic, just wondering what had happened to him and hoping he was all right. She'd post it when she got back to London.

Chapter Thirty Two

Peter also managed to get home for Christmas, despite having been injured in Cambria in November.

He'd been in one of the tanks in the initial assault, advancing under heavy artillery fire when his tank was hit. Having flattened the German wire they came under sustained shelling. He couldn't remember much about the attack, it was all a blur. All he recalled was an almighty bang, flashes of light, the rush of wind like a flight of wild geese, the smell of cordite, pain and incredible heat engulfing him. He didn't even know who pulled him out, or how he got to the nearby field hospital but, as he lay in bed he pledged to find out and thank them.

His legs burned, swollen and blistering. It made it difficult to walk. His ankle throbbed with pitiless, pounding pain. "You're lucky," the doctor said. "Second degree burns. They'll heal in time. The pulled ligaments in the ankle too will recover. It's not a Blighty wound." A Blighty wound meant a passage home and a Medical Discharge. "They'll assess you when your ankle heals, but I've no doubt you'll be back in your tank in a month or two."

Peter thanked him. He didn't know whether to be sad or happy about his future prospects.

He lay back and thanked his lucky stars. His ma and pa were still looking after him, he thought. Half his uniform had been burned away and bandages replaced his trousers. He could bear the pain. It meant he could feel something, therefore he must still be alive.

"You'll be here for a few days," the doctor said. "Best get used to it."

He was allowed out of bed on the third day and given crutches until his swollen ankle went down. He'd be moved to a recovery station for assessment as soon as they could find transport.

The sight and smell of the hospital sickened him. He wanted to get out.

In the receiving station the air was diamond hard with cold, but fresher. He preferred it to the stench that permeated the tented ward. He watched the casualties being brought in and others being shipped out. He could share a smoke with some of the other men waiting for transportation.

One day he was standing there when a stretcher bearer almost slipped on a patch of ice by the door. Peter stepped forward to catch the stretcher before he went down.

"Thanks, mate," the bearer said. He nodded to the casualty. "Poor devil. Saved two of his mates then caught it." He shook his head. "Damned unlucky."

Peter looked at the casualty and felt a punch like a fist to his stomach that took his breath away. Under the dirt, blood and grime he recognised the face of Ferdie Giggs.

The receiving doctor must have seen him stare.

"Know him do you, Lieutenant?"

Peter continued to stare. Rational thought flew out of his head like swarming bees. "Sort of," he said. "What are his chances?"

The doctor sighed and shook his head. He nodded to the stretcher bearers who carried Giggs away.

Nausea churned in Peter's stomach. Sickness rose up towards his throat. He swallowed it back. The doctor watched him.

The next morning Peter heard Giggs had died. The doctor approached him. "Sorry if he was a friend," he said, handing Peter a canvas bag. "His possessions. His CO and half his platoon have been wiped out. Can you write to his family? It's always better coming from someone who knew him. More personal. Thanks."

Peter stood stunned. Thoughts whirred through his brain. Memories of the fight, of seeing Giggs with Rose, all mixed up with the sight of his bloodied face as they carried him away.

He went back to his bed in the ward and sat with his head in his hands, not knowing what to think. He'd seen death before, many times, comrades-in-arms, men he'd lived with, sat in batteries with, even men he'd been beside when shrapnel shattered them, but the thought of Ferdie Giggs's…

He recalled the first time he'd seen him standing there, photographs spread out on the bar in front of him. How he'd felt seeing Rose's picture among them. He'd felt betrayed. He remembered Giggs in London, trying to lure her to his room where he would have taken her innocence for his sordid trade. Clearly that was his plan. A frenzy of fury rose up inside him, clenching his fists again at the memory. Still he couldn't find it in his heart to hate a man who had died fighting for his country. Wasn't that what they were all there for?

Ferdie Giggs was a man who did bad things. He was also a man who'd lost his life saving his comrades. Was he a bad man, when he did good things too?

There were men in the trenches doing far worse than Giggs, whose enterprise would be seen by many as a bit of fun and a badly needed morale boost for fighting men away from home. Peter had only been disgusted by it because of Rose. He wouldn't have thought twice about it if he hadn't seen her picture. Did that make him any better than any of the other men buying the photos or even Giggs, selling them? Peter's reflection of himself, who he thought he was, began to dim. Who was he to judge others?

He sighed, and, with a heavy heart, opened the bag. Inside he found Giggs's notebook and official documents. A letter marked *'To be sent in case of Death'* and his collection of photographs. Peter shuffled through them. The girls were all smiling. They looked happy to be posing. That puzzled him. Had he got Giggs wrong? Then he saw Rose, posing seductively on a chaise longue in a low-cut dress, buttoned down the front with the bottom buttons left open to reveal surprisingly long legs. The photo was signed *'With Love, Rose'* and there were three kisses.

Shock, like the kick from a wild horse, knocked the breath out of him. She looked so beautiful, so calm and serene, a world away from the dirt and muck surrounding him. Tears rose unbidden to his eyes and rolled down his face in an unstoppable torrent. All the pent up emotion of the last years gathered inside him like a summer storm. He put his head in his hands and wept for all the lives they had lost.

Later that day he was transferred to an Officer's Recovery Centre in a country house several miles behind the lines. The walls were solid and thick, the rooms clean and comfortable, despite being overcrowded with beds haphazardly push into rooms once spacious and ornately beautiful. The ward he was in was on the ground floor with long windows overlooking the garden. Bare branched trees, silvered with ice, surrounded a lawn where chickens pecked at the frost-hardened ground. It was the complete opposite of the noise and confusion of the battle still raging a few miles away.

After settling in he began to heal and to feel human again. He found out as much as he could about the 7th Irish's skirmishes along the Front before he sat down to write to Giggs's family. He went through his possessions again.

In his wallet he found a picture of a couple that could only be his parents. His mother was noted on his record as next of kin.

He shuffled through the other photographs, slipped the photograph of Rose into his pocket and burned the rest. He flicked through the notebook and debated whether to send it. There were names and addresses and, to his surprise, several short, romantic poems. Nothing that would threaten security if published. He put it into an envelope with the 'In Case of Death' letter. He'd written letters before to bereaved families, it was part of his job as an Officer in charge of men, but none disturbed him as much as this one.

In the end he wrote of Giggs's courage in battle, his unselfishness, his popularity with his comrades. He told them two lives had been saved due to his actions and their son had died as he lived, bravely and with honour, thinking of others. They should be proud of him.

It was only much later that he learned that Cpl F Giggs of the 7th Irish Fusiliers had been posthumously awarded the Military Cross.

Chapter Thirty Three

Hope noticed the change in Peter when he arrived home for Christmas with a second wound stripe on his sleeve. He looked thinner, paler, a shadow of his former self. His eyes were hollowed with pain and exhaustion. Her heart went out to him.

His burns still needed medical attention so she called Doctor Matthews, but it was clear to Hope that more than his wounds troubled Peter.

"The spirit has gone out of him," she said to Silas, home on a forty-eight-hour pass while his division waited for supplies. "He has the weight of the world on shoulders too young to bear it. I hate to see him suffer."

Silas nodded. "He's seen too much for too long," he said. "Endured hardships that would break older, more experienced men. Three years at the Front. It's bound to take its toll."

"I think there's more to it than that," Hope said. "A deep melancholy, so unlike his nature. He was always a serious boy but he had a light inside him, a spark of impudent humour and intelligence."

"Yes," Silas said, smiling broadly. "I remember. He was a cheeky young street urchin brimming with bravado and pride who defied all attempts to mould him."

Hope laughed. "But we tried and I think we succeeded," she said. "He grew into a fine young man we can be proud of. Can you speak to him? He listens to you."

"I'm not sure that's true," Silas said, "but I will have a word if it pleases you."

Hope kissed him and thought again how lucky she was to have married him.

After examining Peter, Doctor Matthews spoke to Hope. "His burns are healing well, but it takes longer for what's inside to heal. At least he's still young with his whole life ahead of him. He needs rest, time and something to remind him that life's still worth living. The good times will come again."

"Thank you, Doctor Matthews," Hope said. "That's just as I thought."

When the doctor had gone Silas took Peter to The Grenadier, his gentlemen's club, now used by Officers. Peter recalled the last time he'd visited. How different he'd felt that afternoon sitting with Major Fortescue. The war had felt like an adventure that was sure to end in victory. It didn't feel that way now.

Silas bought them each a beer and found a table where they could talk. "So, what's on your mind, son?" he said.

Peter sipped his beer. How could he tell this man, the man who'd taken him off the street, who'd provided for him and loved him, who he loved and respected in return, a man whose strength, steadfastness and compassion had been the constant, steadying backdrop to his growing up, how could he explain something he didn't understand himself?

"You know we've always been proud of you," Silas said. "Proud of the man you've become. There's nothing you could do or say that could change that."

"I know," Peter said. "And I'm grateful."

"The gratitude is ours," Silas said. "Gratitude for the joy you've given us over the years. Ma loves you beyond measure, son. As do I."

Peter sighed. "How did you know you were in love with Ma before you married her?" he asked.

The anxiety that had clouded Silas's face cleared. He smiled. "Ah. So, it's a girl?" he said. "Well, I'm not sure I'm the best person to advise you. The ways of women are a mystery to me, but if it helps…"

He took a deep breath, a swallow of beer and leaned back in his chair. "I fell in love with Hope the first time I saw her. She was working in her father's pub, clearing glasses, sweeping, cleaning the bar. She was holding a broom and wearing an old, blue dress so worn you could see the threads in places. Tresses of golden blonde hair had escaped from an untidy knot on her head to frame her face and curl on the nape of her neck. She had amazing sapphire blue eyes that glinted like a faceted gem." His voice softened with deep admiration as he spoke. "I was a successful businessman. I had wealth, power and influence and she treated me with such disdain." He chuckled at the memory. "Not only was she beautiful, she had intelligence, wit and a capacity for kindness that took my breath away. Still has. You've probably noticed."

Peter nodded. "I have," he said.

Silas became serious. "She's something special. I was lucky to find her. She had an indefinable quality I couldn't quite put my finger on. I couldn't get her out of my head, knew I'd do anything for her, just to spend time with her. I couldn't imagine a life without her in it." He paused and sipped his beer. "I was used to getting everything I wanted in those days, and I wanted her, but she didn't want me. Not then. That came gradually over time, I think. She must have come to appreciate my sparkling personality." He laughed and his striking blue eyes twinkled with warmth.

"Although, she'll tell you I pursued her relentlessly until she gave in." He drained his glass and held it up. "Another?"

Peter nodded, finished his drink and handed Silas the empty glass. Silas got them another beer each.

"Now, do you want to tell me about this girl?"

Peter shook his head. "Not yet. I've something to sort out first." Rose's photo burned in his pocket. He still had to see her and tell her about Ferdie Giggs's death. It wasn't something he looked forward to.

They walked back to the house together. Silas went in but Peter wanted to walk on further. Walking by the river was a good place to think and he needed to think. His feet took him along to the stretch of river where he could see the hospital where Rose worked. He found a bench and sat looking across the water. He imagined her there, in the ward, ministering to the sick and wounded. She was something special. He knew that. He thought back over the years growing up, holidays with Rose and William, always full of laughter and happiness. He'd felt like part of the family. The difference between them had never bothered him then. It was the encounter with Ferdie Giggs that brought it back into focus.

Giggs brought out the worst in him. The fight was out of character. He'd reverted to the law of the street and he didn't like it. Would he have acted the same way if it had been a girl other than Rose? Would he have merely seen a soldier, asking a girl out for a drink and thought nothing of it? Probably. Then he recalled Rose's face when she saw him waiting for her instead of Giggs. The smile had fallen from her lips, the joy and expectation in her eyes had dissolved like sugar in hot tea. His heart lurched at the memory.

Ferdie Giggs's death disturbed him more than any other. He took out Rose's photograph. She looked happy and relaxed. It was signed *'With Love'*.

He knew Rose rushed to get the post each morning. Was she waiting for a letter from him? She wouldn't know of his death. If he didn't tell her no one else would. How long would she wait, hoping to hear from him, wondering why he hadn't written? Would her concern for him blot out all thought of anything else, any other chance of happiness? He'd heard of women who spent their whole lives waiting for men who left and never returned. Would Rose become one of them?

He sighed. She was away, visiting her family for Christmas, but when she returned he'd have to tell her. It was the least he could do.

Rose returned after New Year. She kissed Peter on both cheeks and told him how pleased she was to see him. She asked about his wounds and offered to get him anything he needed.

"I'm fine," he said. "Swinging the lead really." It wasn't true, he wasn't fine, far from it but he couldn't tell her that. Not yet.

He waited until after dinner, when Rose had told them all about her visit, how the family were and shown them the gifts she received both for Christmas and her birthday. Peter gave her a rose coloured silk scarf he'd bought in France.

"It's beautiful," she said. "You're so clever, Peter," and she kissed him again. His heart crunched.

Olivia and Sean went to bed, Hope and Silas retired to his office to go through some paperwork that had piled up in his absence before he left to return to duty the next morning. Peter was left with Rose to have coffee in the drawing room. Rose poured the coffee.

"We have to talk," he said.

"That sounds ominous. Nothing bad I hope," she said.

He hadn't counted on her buoyant optimism.

"I'm sorry," he said.

"Sorry?"

This was more difficult than he'd ever imagined. "I came across a chap in the hospital. He had this." He showed her the photograph.

Rose took it. Blood drained from her face and she sank into a chair. "Where…"

"His name was Ferdie Giggs. He died. I found it among his possessions."

Rose stared at him, her eyes wide but blank of emotion. "I don't understand," she stammered.

Peter moved beside her. "I think you knew him. You've been seeing him."

"Knew him? Ferdie? You mean – he's dead?"

"Yes. I said. He died in the hospital. They gave me his possessions. I found your photograph…"

Rose stared at him, then the photo. Her eyes bright with confusion as the news sunk in. "He's dead?" she whispered.

Peter nodded and put his arm around her. "I'm sorry, Rose." He touched the photograph in her hand. "You signed this photograph '*With Love*'. How long had you known him?"

Rose stared at him, the confusion on her face turning to mounting anger. "I loved him," she said, and Peter's heart broke.

Chapter Thirty Four

Upstairs in her room Rose struggled with her conscience. Memories of Ferdie ran through her mind. She rummaged through his letters, took out his photograph and propped it against an empty vase on top of the chest of drawers.

She sat looking at it for a while. He was gone. That was hard to believe when he'd been so full of life. She felt as though a light had gone out, someone switched it off. She saw his smile, heard his seductively persuasive voice, soft, insistent, caressing, remembered the thrill of his touch.

Peter showing her that photograph shocked and surprised her. Scorching shame flushed her cheeks. She remembered Dora Watson taking it when she was in Great Yarmouth. It had felt brave and daring. Now, looking at it she wasn't so sure. It wasn't like her. The dress was cut too low, just the right side of decent and the legs – well. The look on her face, which at the time she'd though alluring, in the picture just looked sleazy. The thought that this was how Peter had seen her in a picture taken from another soldier's possessions made her shudder. Why had she had it taken? Because Ferdie asked her to. She'd signed it *'With Love'* and added the kisses because he had.

She sat on the bed and reread the letters. Every one asked for a photograph *'to keep by me to remember the delight that awaits my return'*, or *'just for me, something special'*. Then there was the underwear he'd sent *'looking forward to seeing you in it'*.

There was nothing else. No great protestations of love or promises of a future together. He said he looked forward to seeing her again, but that was all.

Merely everyday chit-chat from a bored soldier with time on his hands.

Oh he was exciting. She thought back to when she first met him. She'd felt so proud being picked out to dance with him, the handsomest man in the room. Then Cissie's warning had added to his appeal. That evening in the alley she'd drunk too much and got carried away. His ardour had taken her by surprise and she'd let him go further than she should, so she'd dressed it up as something it wasn't. That way she could live with it.

There'd never been anything more than a quick fumble between them, two brief encounters, a few letters written in the tedious hours waiting for action in the trenches and the exchange of a couple of photographs to give pleasure to a man away from home. It was easier to call it love than admit the truth, even to herself. She now realised how tawdry that was.

Then she remembered how he'd stood her up after asking her to leave the dance. He hadn't written or given any excuse and she'd hardened her heart against him putting him out of her mind.

She took down his photograph, tears stung her eyes. "I'm sorry, Ferdie, so very sorry," she said. "The world will be a sadder, duller place without you." She sniffed to hold back the tears and ran her finger over his cheek. "I'll never forget you," she whispered.

A flush of anger mixed with deep grief ran through her. Damn this war, she thought. It's taken the brightest and the best. Will it never end?

She put the photograph back on the chest of drawers and sat for a while, head in her hands, sorting out her thoughts and feelings. She was deeply sorry, of course, but she felt no greater sense of sorrow than she did when they lost a patient. She'd expected to feel more devastated than she did. One more brave soldier's life given away so cheaply. Every man lost was a tragedy, but she didn't feel the shattering sense of loss she'd felt when she heard William was missing, or the overwhelming grief she'd have felt if it had been Gabriel or even Peter. That would have overshadowed everything.

She'd treasure the memories of the moments they'd shared, but she didn't love him. She knew that now. She didn't know him well enough for that. A crush perhaps, nothing more.

So why had she said that to Peter? It had just come out. She glanced at the picture of herself draped over the chaise longue. It was justification. Her defence for the shame she felt at posing like some brazen tart and him seeing it. His kindness had only made it worse. When he asked how long she'd known him he'd drawn his brows together the way she remembered he used to do as a child when she or William said something that puzzled him. The memory felt like a knife in her heart.

She'd hurt him. She saw that in his face and she regretted it. She felt bad. He'd shown her nothing but kindness all her life.

She hardly slept that night. Peter filled her dreams. Peter, the shabby, undernourished ragamuffin with defiance shining in his eyes. Peter, the holiday companion, daring and funny, his face lit up with a hard won smile. Peter, whose opinion she valued above all else. Peter, the soldier with a scar on his cheek and wound stripes on his sleeve and Peter, the caring friend who'd struggled to tell her the man he thought she loved was dead.

Her heart swelled with love and sorrow. She'd hurt him and she'd never wanted to do that. She recalled the lurch in her heart when she saw him standing by the cab when he arrived home on leave. The way her heart lifted in his presence, the way the world seemed a better place when she was with him. The way his face appeared unbidden into her thoughts, how every judgement she made was measured against his opinion.

She'd been naive and stupid to believe there could ever be anything between her and Ferdie Giggs, other than his lust. She'd been sixteen and unaware of the ways of men, and first love is often fleeting and ill advised. Now she was older she could see her infatuation with Ferdie for what it was. A young girl's foolish dream.

She knew she had to apologise to Peter. Tell him the truth. She was ashamed of the photograph, it was a mistake. She hadn't meant what she said. It was the shock of him having the picture. She hadn't been prepared for that and she was sorry. First thing in the morning she'd apologise, tell him the truth and put the record straight about Ferdie Giggs.

"Is Peter up yet?" she asked Hope at breakfast next morning. "I wanted a word with him."

"Well, you're out of luck," Hope said. "He was up hours ago. He's gone to see Doctor Matthews."

"Oh. I'm sorry. I'd forgotten how badly he was hurt."

"Yes. Lucky to be alive," Hope said. "I'm glad he's out of it for now at least. I wish he'd never go back."

Rose thought about William and understood that very well. The fear of loss was ever present.

"Doctor Matthews won't sign him off until he's fully fit," Silas said. "So there's no need to worry about that in the near future. But I have to be on my way."

"I wish you didn't have to go either," Hope said.

"I know," Silas said. There was a depth of understanding in his eyes, the affection between them was clear. "I'll write as soon as I get there and don't worry. It'll take more than a few Germans to kill me off."

"Take care, Uncle," Rose said kissing his cheek.

Hope went to see him off.

"It's my afternoon off. I'll see Peter then," Rose said when Hope returned.

When she got to work the matter of the photograph still played on her mind. The morning dragged, only brightening when she saw Cissie who looked fresh as a newly opened bud.

"You look blooming. Did you have a good holiday?" Rose asked.

"The best," Cissie said. "I saw Glyn. Spent a lot of time with him actually." A blush coloured her cheeks. "And I've got some news."

"News? Do tell. I could do with cheering up."

Cissie took a breath. "I've told Glyn that I'm going to give my notice in here and move home to Wales."

Rose's heart sank at the thought of losing her friend. She gasped. "Wales, but I thought…"

"That I preferred London? Yes I did but me and Glyn, well, you know." Her eyes shone with happiness. "I'm going to take a midwifery course so I can carry on working when we're married."

"Married?" Rose's jaw dropped. Delight bubbled inside her. How could she be anything but glad for her friend? "That's wonderful. I'm so happy for you," she said, hugging her. "I'll miss you but…Oh it's so exciting… He's lovely and I know you'll both be very happy. You must tell me all about it."

Cissie told her about seeing him over Christmas and finding they had a lot in common. "Mam and Da thought we were rushing things, what with the war and everything – but I've never been more sure of anything in my life and we could all be dead tomorrow."

Rose felt a thud in her heart thinking of Peter.

"He's a good man, Cissie," she said, kissing her cheek. "You'll do very well together."

"I enjoy his company, he makes me laugh. It was like I'd found a part of me that had been missing for a long time. I fell in love, Rose. You should try it."

Rose sighed. "No chance," she said. A lump of misery formed in her stomach. "I've done something stupid and I feel bad about it."

A look of concern crossed Cissie's face. "Something stupid? What?"

Rose's stomach churned but telling Cissie about it would be a load of her chest. "I sent some photographs to a soldier," she didn't say it was Ferdie, "and Peter somehow got hold of them."

"Peter? Your dashing cousin?"

"Step cousin. Well, adopted cousin. Yes."

"And the problem with that is?"

"They were a bit…you know…sleazy, so I felt bad about him seeing them. The only excuse I could come up with was to tell him I loved him – the soldier." As she said it the hurt in Peter's eyes came back to her.

257

"But it wasn't true. I don't know why I said it. I've hurt Peter and I didn't mean to."

"Hmm." Cissie stared at her. "So you told cousin Peter, who is in love with you, that you loved someone else but you don't. Is that it?"

"Peter isn't in love with me," Rose said.

"Of course he is, cariad," Cissie said. "You can see it in his eyes when he looks at you. The last time I saw him with you at that dance, he never took his eyes off you all evening. I've never seen a man so smitten."

A maelstrom of emotions swept over Rose. Her heart faltered. Peter in love with her? Was he? That would make what she did worse, far worse. She had to know for sure. She undid her apron. "Tell Sister I'm sick and I've gone home," she said. "I'll see you tomorrow. I have to see him. Put things right between us."

Hurrying home she thought about all the times they'd been together, how she felt in his company, how her heart lifted when she saw him. How life always felt more worthwhile when he was around. Next to William he was the person she cared most about. She remembered how his eyes sparkled like fireworks in the night sky when he saw her, the magic of his swift smile that made her feel as though the sun had come out, the ripple of his laughter. He was kind, reliable, funny, clever too but never arrogant about it. He was the person whose opinion mattered most to her. No one made her heart beat faster the way he did and she'd hurt him with three careless words that weren't even true – that was unforgiveable.

When she got home she called his name, but there was no reply. She found Hope in the kitchen, making bread.

258

"Is Peter back? I need to speak to him."

"No," she said, her voice choked with emotion. "He's gone back to the war. I tried to stop him, as did Doctor Matthews, but he insisted." She banged the dough she was kneading hard on the table, sending a flurry of flour up into the air. "Sometimes he's so mule-headed and stubborn. If he gets an idea in his head it would take a mountain of dynamite to shift it." She glanced at Rose. "He hasn't been the same since he came back this time. There's something got inside him and I'm damned if I know how to fix it." Tears shone in her eyes as she pounded the dough with her fists. "As if he hasn't been through enough."

Rose swallowed. "When did he go?"

"About an hour, maybe two."

Rose's heart turned over. Peter was gone and it was all her fault. She forced a smile to her lips. "Thanks," she said.

An hour, maybe two, if she hurried …

Chapter Thirty Five

Peter gazed out of the window of the train as it sped through the countryside towards Dover. His heart had shattered when Rose said she loved a man he had so little regard for. He could have born it if he'd been a decent man, a man who'd love and care for her, cherish and protect her the way he would have done. A man she could turn to for reassurance when things went wrong. Then he would have sympathised and mourned with her, but Ferdie Giggs didn't strike him as a man able to do that. The memory of the girls in the photographs haunted him.

He wasn't sure he could stay in the house, seeing her every morning, living with her grief. So, he'd got up early, packed his things and gone to the doctor to get signed off. Then he could go back where he belonged.

Doctor Matthews had been surprised to see him so early. "You're not fit. I'll sign you off for another month," he said, but Peter insisted.

Then he'd gone to the churchyard to his parents' grave to say goodbye. He left lilies and stood there a long time, thinking. The sky lightened, opalescent clouds drifted like stately ships crossing a calm grey ocean. A sharp breeze scattered fallen leaves in patterns of red, gold and brown around him, lifting them to swirl in the air before falling back to earth. The desolate churchyard dripped with morning dew.

He shivered. The air was cold, but not as cold as his heart. "I'm off again, Ma, Pa," he said. Resolve grew up inside him as he spoke. He thought of his parents who'd lain here most of his life. It was as though they were talking to him. He was young. He had his whole life ahead of him. One setback shouldn't stop him making something of himself. That's what they would have said. A feeling of deep peace settled over him like a cloak. "I'll be back," he said. "I'm definitely coming back."

That decided he made it to the train in a better mood. He was going back to where he could be of some use to work with men he admired and camaraderie he enjoyed.

On the train he tried to put thoughts of Rose out of his mind but he couldn't. He kept seeing her face when she'd said she loved Giggs. He thought about it rationally as he always thought about things. He could see Ferdie would have been handsome and full of Irish magnetism, enough to charm a young innocent like Rose. He wouldn't have been steadfast though, he lacked commitment and he'd have let her down eventually. She'd have found out what he was really like. The thought comforted him. At least she'd been spared the pain of that, which could have been greater than the current loss. She could still see the good in him, what there was of it, and keep her illusions, her memories unsullied.

He loved Rose, he realised he'd always loved her, since the first time he saw her, but what did he have to offer? A broken, scarred body and an uncertain future. He wasn't the man he was before the war, he knew that. He'd changed, become tougher, more resolute and determined, but also damaged, as they were all damaged by what they'd been through. Still, he retained the unswerving devotion he'd always felt for her. Giggs was dead. How could he compete with a dead hero?

Silas's words about relentlessly pursuing Hope until she gave in came to mind. He smiled. He admired Silas; would do anything for him. Perhaps there was a chance, if he came through this war. Even as a five-year-old Rose had had a practical streak. Surely she'd realise that a live hero is better than a dead one.

Rose caught a cab to the station, then the train to Dover. That's where he'd embark. He'd have to wait for the boat. There was time.

She gazed out of the window as the countryside sped past. Cissie's words 'we could all be dead tomorrow', never felt more true. Peter was going back to face death and it was all her fault.

Her mind filled with memories of Peter when they were growing up. William worshiped him. A couple of years older, Peter had shrewd resourcefulness and an instinct for survival. She hoped that was still the case. Clever and daring, nothing fazed him. She recalled his kindness, his confidence and his steadfast personality. Memories of magical summer days filled her mind. She felt closer to Peter than she did to anyone, except perhaps William.

She sighed. They were both grown up now. She should have known better.

The train pulled into the station in Dover with a hiss of steam, a screech of brakes and clouds of smoke. The station platform hummed with soldiers and women come to see them off moving slowly out of the station. She followed the crowd to find the way to the quay where troops would board ferries for France. At the docks she looked from side to side, pushing her way through crowds of embracing couples saying goodbye. A troop ship stood in the dock ready to depart.

As she neared she saw a queue of uniformed men, heads down moving towards the gangplanks. Her heart pounded. Was he still here? Had she missed him? Her gaze frantically searched the faces of the men ready to leave. Then she saw him, in the line.

"Peter, Peter," she called. He turned. The surprise on his face turned to a glow of pure pleasure.

"Rose? What on earth…What are you doing here?"

"I came to apologise." Her breath came in quick gasps. She couldn't get the words out quick enough. "What I said about Ferdie Giggs. It wasn't true. I don't love him."

He drew his brows together in that quizzical look she remembered from childhood. She threw herself into his arms and kissed him. Relief and joy flowed through her when she felt his arms tighten around her and his lips respond to hers. In his embrace all her worries and fears floated away.

A man in uniform, who'd been standing by the gangplank seeing the soldiers onto the boat, tapped Peter on the shoulder. "Come along, sir," he said. "You're holding up the war effort."

Peter let her go, "I have to…" He kissed her quickly again and turned to go.

"I love you," she called as he moved off. When she saw him on the gangplank she waved and shouted again, "I love you." The words caught on the wind and drifted away, but not so far that Peter didn't hear them.

On the ferry, during a turbulent crossing, Peter wrote to Rose:

My darling Rose, Seeing you there on the quay was a wonderful surprise. Did you mean what you said? Holding you in my arms, kissing you, was one of the best moments of my life and I'll never forget it. I'll carry the memory of it with me to sustain me through what lies ahead. I've loved you forever but only realised how deeply when I came home and saw what a beautiful, kind, compassionate person you've become. I've thought of no one else since that moment and hoped that, in time, you might come to feel the same. Hearing you say you love me was more than I could ever have wished for. Nothing in the world could have made me happier. You are so special and I can assure you I'll strive every day to be worthy of that love. I'll be counting the days until I can return to be with you. I hope you feel the same. All my love, always, Peter.

He posted the letter as soon as he disembarked.

His return to active duty had to be agreed with the Medical Officer before he could rejoin his unit. When he did he was greeted with surprise by his CO. "I didn't expect you back so soon," he said. "But I'm pleased to see you. With your experience in action we could use a good man like you up at Tank HQ."

The following week he was promoted to Captain and moved to headquarters behind the lines.

He wrote to Rose every week, telling her how much he missed her and couldn't bear the wait until they could be together again. He wrote with humour and passion about places he visited on his days off, people he worked with, meals he'd eaten in restaurants and assured her that he was so far behind enemy lines that the rumble of gunfire sounded like rolls of distant thunder. He sent her drawings of old buildings, cosy cottages and grand chateaus, postcards he picked up and pressed flowers he thought she might like. He didn't tell her about the Gothas flying overhead strafing the supply carrying convoys along the roads, the number of tanks and men lost or the awful toll of death and destruction.

She wrote back asking him to keep safe and think of her often. She told him about the buds and new leaves on the trees, snowdrops and daffodils coming into bloom, early morning sunrises and Cissie and Glyn's wedding plans. She said she loved him very much and was counting the days until he came home. She sent books she thought he might like, cigarettes and chocolate.

She rushed to collect the post each morning and Hope didn't miss the envelopes in Peter's handwriting.

"I see Peter writes often," she said. "And you seem very alive, these days. Is it what I think it is?"

Rose blushed. "Would you mind?" she asked.

"Mind? No, of course not. You make him happy and that's all I want for him. I couldn't wish for a better daughter-in-law."

Rose gasped. "Daughter-in-law? He hasn't proposed yet."

"No, but he will," Hope said. "Peter will do things properly. He always has. It's his way."

Reassured, Rose smiled. "And will Uncle Silas approve?"

Hope laughed. "Uncle Silas will be happy because I'm happy," she said, "and he'll approve because it will make Peter happy too. No. It's your ma and pa you need to worry about. I'm not sure how Violet will take it."

Rose's happy mood evaporated like water on a hot stove. Aunt Hope was right. Ma still saw Peter as the street-boy he'd been. A ragged guttersnipe who'd bettered himself thanks to Hope and Silas's generosity. She'd want better for Rose. She didn't see Peter's quiet strength, courage, patience, independence of spirit and determination to earn his own living.

Pa would approve if it was what she wanted, he'd always been more approachable than Ma, but she'd be harder to convince. Peter would need all his intelligence and unique resourcefulness to charm her, Rose thought.

When Cissie left the hospital at Easter to prepare for her wedding, Rose decided it was time to plan for her own future, which she hoped would include marriage to Peter.

"I'm going home for a few days," she said to Hope over breakfast. "The hospital's not the same with Cissie gone."

Hope smiled. "Yes, and I daresay you want to discuss your own plans with your mother." She poured Rose another cup of tea. "Best to speak to her face to face," she said.

Rose sighed. At eighteen she'd need her mother's permission to marry, unlike Peter, who was twenty-one and could do what he liked.

Hope replaced the teapot on its mat. "My sister's headstrong, stubborn, opinionated and has a competitive streak where me and my family are concerned," she said, "but she loves you very much and your happiness means the world to her."

"I know," Rose said. "She'll need time to get used to the idea. I want to prepare her before Peter comes home."

"Well, you can tell her that both Silas and I approve, although I'm not sure how far that will go in your favour."

Rose left the following morning and arrived in Great Yarmouth as the April sun warmed the streets and flowers along the Promenade were coming into bloom. Walking through the familiar streets lifted her heart. She didn't care what her mother thought, she loved Peter and he said he loved her. That's all that mattered.

Violet greeted her warmly. "I was so pleased to get your letter," she said. "You've come at the right time of year. The town's looking lovely and the weather's brightening. How long are you staying?"

"Just a few days."

Violet looked her up and down. "Any special reason for this visit?"

Rose shrugged. "No. Well, yes, perhaps, I mean with Cissie going home I thought it was time I paid a visit."

"Ahh," Violet said. "That all? Good." She kissed her. "Well, your room's ready. I have a million things to do but no doubt you can find something to amuse yourself until dinner."

"Yes. Thank you," Rose said.

Once she'd left her things in her room Rose went out to walk along the Promenade. She stopped by the railings to look out over the sea and remembered standing there with Gabriel, telling him she wanted to be a nurse. How long ago was that? So much had happened since then it felt like a lifetime ago. Then she thought of William. He was never far from her thoughts but here, at home, standing looking out to sea, brought a flood of memories. Usually thoughts of him brought on a deluge of icy shivers but today a warm glow filled her body. Perhaps it was the April sunshine, she thought, was that enough to make her feel so good? Or was it knowing Peter loved her and her future lay with him?

She watched the ebb and flow of the tide, the boats going to and fro, people walking on the sands. Life looked so normal yet she knew different. Every day men were risking their lives. She'd seen the evidence of it in the hospital, men whose lives would never be the same, men like Glyn who'd marry Cissie and live a life neither of them had ever expected.

Rose walked slowly back to the hotel just as the telegraph boy arrived on his bicycle.

Her heart sank. Thoughts of the terrible news it might contain raced through her mind and sent a frenzy of fear pounding through her body. Surely losing William was enough? Not Gabriel as well. Her mother wouldn't be able to bear it. A stone of dread and foreboding formed in her stomach. "I'll take it," she said.

"It's addressed to the missus," the boy said.

"I'll take it to her," Rose said, thinking at least she'd be there to ease the pain. The boy shrugged and handed her the brown envelope. She took it in, calling her mother as she did so.

Violet saw the dreaded envelope in Rose's hand. "No," she said, deep fear raising her voice to a shriek. She shook her head. "No. Not Gabriel." Terror filled her eyes. Her trembling hands covered her mouth. "You open it. I can't—"

Rose's hands shook so violently she fumbled with the envelope as she tore it open and withdrew the telegram. "It's not Gabriel," she said. "It's William."

Chapter Thirty Six

William sat on the edge of the hospital bed replaying the events of the last few months in his head.

He'd woken up with no memory of where he was or how he got there or even how long he'd been there. At first confusion fogged his brain. People spoke to him but he didn't understand what they were saying. He couldn't move. His arms, legs and chest were heavily bandaged.

"Where am I?" he asked. Everyone stared blankly at him until, one day, another man came and stood by the bed staring at him. Tall, dark and swarthy, William guessed him to be in his thirties. Dressed in Arab garb he appeared intimidating, despite his wide smile.

"Where am I?" William asked again.

"Ah, English," the man said. "You speak English."

"I am English," William said. It was the one thing he was sure about.

"I am Ahmed. I speak English," the man said.

Ahmed, the English speaker, told him that some fishermen had found him washed up on the beach. They'd brought him to the hospital.

"You're very lucky, English," Ahmed said. "You could have died." He told William his shoulder was dislocated, his collar bone and ribs broken, his legs badly gashed and he'd been suffering from pneumonia. "You very battered," he said. "We mend you. Like new soon."

Over the weeks the bandages were removed and William's arm put in a sling. Ahmed came every day to talk to him. "I speak good English, yes?" he said. "Beautiful English lady she teach me." Pride shone in his deep brown eyes. William had the impression that

Ahmed had taught the beautiful English lady a thing or two in return.

As his body recovered, fragments of memory returned. He remembered being on the ship but not why or where. Ahmed brought him a bag with his possessions, rescued with him. He went through them, his wallet, some photographs, some paperwork, not much else, all damaged by water. All that had survived the sea was his silver cigarette case and a few English coins.

Time went on, each day the same and William still felt lost. His leg healed but he found he'd lost the use of his right arm. "It will come back in time," Ahmed told him. "Very badly injured."

There was nothing he could do but sit, watch and wait as the weeks rolled by.

Early spring sunshine shone through the widows, sultry heat gathered in the wards, the smell of sweat, blood and bodies filled the air.

Then he had a visit from a man who introduced himself as Oliver Saintly, an envoy from the British Embassy.

In his early forties, tall, blonde with an upright military bearing, he sniffed as he approached William's bed. "Ahmed asked me to come," he said. "Wouldn't take no for an answer, but I'm not sure what I can do for you."

William had perked up. "I'm a British citizen," he said. "You can arrange for me to go home."

"Sorry, chum. No can do," Oliver Saintly said. "Seas around here are full of enemy ships, mines and U-boats. Arranging passage is like asking for sunshine in the deepest cave. You can ask but you're not likely to get it."

He pulled up a chair and sat down. "You're here for the duration, old boy. Best I can do is let your family know you're safe." He took out a notebook and pencil. "Address?"

William thought but the address escaped him. "It's in Norfolk," he said.

"Ah. Norfolk. Know it well," Saintly said. "Lovely part of the country. My wife's family live there." He licked the end of the pencil. "Address?"

William shrugged.

"Never mind. We're assuming you were shipwrecked. What ship were you on? Any paperwork?"

William reached for his bag of possessions, lifted it down and spread them out on the bed. "It's not exactly—"

He didn't get any further. Oliver Saintly picked up William's cigarette case. His brow furrowed into a frown. He turned it over to read the inscription. "Where did you get this?" he asked.

"A gift," William said. Seeing it, broken fragments of memory surfaced. "In the sea, a boy, drowning. I saved him, I think," he said.

"And who is this AJD?"

William thought hard. It took a while for it to come to him. "Davenport," he said. "Boy's grandfather or something. Sorry I can't remember any more."

Oliver Saintly's face lit up, his lips spread into a broad smile. "Anthony John Davenport. He's my father-in-law. The boy you saved was my son. I owe you his life." He looked again at the cigarette case. "We were on holiday in Norfolk. I remember it well. Madness taking the boat out when the weather was so uncertain. I tore them off a strip I can tell you. They could have both drowned if it hadn't been for you and your family." He handed the cigarette case back to William. "I bought this for you. You must be William Stone. Your family have a hotel in Great Yarmouth. We're so grateful to you." He put his notebook and pencil away and stood up. "I'll let them know you're safe and don't worry, I'll have you on the next boat home. Least I can do," he said.

Later that day William was moved to a private room on the top floor with a view over the bay. There were washing facilities and two orderlies came to wash and shave him and help him dress. A basket of fruit arrived with clothes, toiletries, sweetmeats and an English newspaper. It was a week old but to William it was something from home and reading it the jigsaw pieces of his memory came together to build fragmented pictures of his life.

Oliver Saintly came the next day and talked to him about his family and what he knew of them. "You were in the Royal Navy," he said. "Your ship sunk off the coast. You must have tried to swim ashore. Damned brave thing to do."

"I remember the ship," William said. "What happened to the rest of the crew?"

"Some were picked up by other ships," Oliver Saintly said.

"Many lost?" William asked.

Saintly nodded. "Too many," he said.

That was a few days ago. This morning Ahmed had come to help him dress and get ready for the journey. He put the remains of his possession in his pockets. He still felt weak, his right arm was in a sling and his wrist bandaged.

"You look very handsome, English," Ahmed assured him. "Very tickerty boo." He laughed. William visualised the 'beautiful English lady' teaching these odd phrases he came out with.

Oliver Saintly himself came to collect him. He carried a small bag. "I've brought you a few things for the journey," he said. "Clean shirts, toiletries, something to eat." He opened the bag and William saw a couple of packets of almond biscuits he'd told Ahmed he liked and a bottle of rum. "And some English money in case you need it." He handed William a bundle of notes.

The English money, Oliver Saintly's kindness and the thought of going home overwhelmed him. "I don't know how to thank you," he said, tears misting his eyes.

"No need," Saintly said. "My debt to you is far greater than I can ever repay."

The memory of the small boy floundering in the sea surfaced in William's mind. "Thanks anyway," he said, feeling humbled.

"You'll be going on a merchant ship. I know the skipper," Saintly said. "He'll take care of you. When you get to Liverpool there's a First Class rail ticket waiting for you. There are two changes but it's all listed on the ticket. It's booked in your name. Pick it up at the Booking Office."

Oliver Saintly shook Ahmed's hand. "Thank you for bringing Mr Stone to our attention," he said.

Ahmed beamed with pleasure.

William went to shake Ahmed's hand but the older man hugged him instead. "Goodbye, English," he said. "Have a safe journey."

"I'll never forget you," William said. "And your kindness to me."

"When this war is over you must come back to Tangiers, beautiful international city," Ahmed said. "Bring your lovely English wife."

"I'm not married."

Ahmed's eyes sparkled. "Then we shall have even more fun," he said.

Saying goodbye brought sadness and a maelstrom of emotions crashing over William, but he was anxious to get home. Oliver Saintly saw him off and wished him well. "If there's anything else, let me know," he said.

On the boat home William had a lot of time to think. As his memory returned he thought of Ma, Pa, Rose, he thought a lot about Rose, but most of all he thought about his future. He couldn't see himself settling down, getting married, raising a family on land as a farmer or a fisherman. He'd seen some of the world, now he wanted to see the rest. He'd enjoyed the camaraderie of shipmates, using his skills and learning new things. He couldn't go back to the way things were before he joined the Navy. His last experience hadn't put him off sailing, on the contrary, he was more determined than ever to make a career of it.

He tried to lift his arm, but failed. It hung uselessly by his side. "It will get better," Ahmed had said. "But it will take time."

William sighed. What use would he be as a sailor with only one arm?

Chapter Thirty Seven

As soon as Rose heard that William was safe and coming home she applied for extended compassionate leave so she could stay home and nurse him if he needed it. Violet too had put the Military Medical Officer, Major Maitland, on stand-by should William require medical assistance.

"You don't know what he's been through," the Major said. "He'll need to take it easy for a while."

Florence and Joshua were allowed to stay home from school on the day he was due to arrive. Rose went with an Officer on convalescence to the station to collect him. As soon as she saw him walk out of the station, carrying his bag, all the old certainties returned. It was William. He was real. He was home. Suddenly everything was right with the world, her world. Her beloved brother was home. He was safe. It had been so long. He looked pale and far too thin, deep lines criss-crossed his face, his blonde hair had grown down to curl on his collar, stubble darkened his chin. She couldn't remember seeing him looking so unkempt, but she put that down to four days on a boat and several long hours on trains.

"I've missed you," she said, hugging him.

"I've missed you too," he replied. He held her at arm's length, with his one good arm. "You've blossomed," he said. "Is there a reason for that?"

Rose blushed. "Must be seeing you again," she said. Her other news could wait. She wasn't sure how he'd feel about her and Peter. That was another hurdle she'd have to overcome.

The Officer driver picked up William's bag and opened the car door for them. Sitting beside William

Rose watched him as they drove past familiar landmarks. He sat silent, staring out. A shaft of sunlight broke through the clouds sending its rays to light his face. A rush of love filled Rose's heart. This was her brother, who'd been lost and was now returned to her.

Violet had closed the bar to residents so the family could have some time together and drink to his safe return. A 'Welcome Home' banner stretched across the hotel entrance. No one in Great Yarmouth could be unaware of Violet's delight at having her eldest son home. "We'll have a party and invite all his friends in a few days' time," she said. "But first let's see how he is."

Rose knew she wanted to keep him for themselves, for a while at least. "My only regret is that Gabriel isn't here," Violet said.

William smiled when he saw the banner stretched across the hotel entrance. Suddenly everything felt familiar. It was a good feeling. He was home. He hadn't realised how much it meant to him or how much he missed it.

"Hello, Ma," he said when he walked in.

Violet gave him a hug and a kiss. "Good to have you home, son," she said, her eyes shining with tears. She stood back to look at him. "Was it terribly bad, the hospital and everything?" Deep concern filled her eyes as she ushered him into the bar.

William took a deep breath as images flashed through his mind. "Let's just say I'm glad to be home." He sank gratefully into one of the cosy armchairs.

Joshua and Florence greeted him enthusiastically. Florence kissed him. "You need a shave," she said, rubbing his chin with her soft, gentle hand.

"I know," William said. "But I only have one good arm. Will you do it for me?"

She giggled. "Don't be silly," she said. Then she kissed him again. "I'm pleased you're home," she whispered in his ear, and his heart swelled with love. How could he have forgotten this sweet little girl who was so like Rose and Ma?

Joshua wanted to know about the ship he came home on. "Was it very mucky?" he asked.

"It was fine. I was jolly glad to be on it," William said.

They wanted to know about his time in the hospital and the journey home but Violet said, "Plenty of time to hear about that. Let him settle in first. " She opened a bottle of wine. William said he'd rather have rum, so she poured him a generous measure.

"Gabriel sends his love," Violet said. "He tried to get leave, but it's difficult, there's some sort of big push on, he said. He'll be home as soon as he can."

"How is he?"

"Delighted to hear that you're safe."

"Good." William looked around the bar taking in the decorations, the pictures, the big comfortable furnishings. There was a sort of permanence about it, which he found comforting.

After about an hour of drinks and talking, the family telling him all the local news, Violet said, "You look exhausted. Rose has got your room ready. You can have a lie-down before dinner."

"I'd like to wash up and have that shave Florence has so rightly pointed out that I need," he said.

"I'll help with that," Rose said. "I'm actually quite adept with a razor."

Upstairs he sunk onto the bed.

"How are you really?" Rose asked. "I sense there's something…"

He shrugged. "I'm all right in so far as I'll mend, but an experience like that – it changes you. Things that seemed to be important before appear trivial and stupid. I feel as though it's all been a terrible waste of time. I've been thrown back to the beginning and I have to do it all over again. It's all a mess, Rose. A terrible mess."

"It hasn't been a waste of time if you've made a difference," Rose said. "And you have. You've stood up for what you believe in. That's something to be applauded."

He sighed. "Yes. I suppose you're right. Well, can't change it now. So, what about this shave?" She went and got a bowl of hot water, shaving soap and brush, a razor and a towel from the supplies provided for the patients. She made him sit on a chair and wrapped the towel around his neck. She lathered the soap and brushed it onto his bristles.

"Are you sure you know how to do this?" he said as she held the razor to his throat.

She laughed. "Sit still and let me do the talking." She started to shave him. "Do you remember Cissie?" she asked.

"Cissie? A nurse. Worked with you at the hospital?"

"Yes, that's right. Well, she's getting married."

"Good for her. Anyone I know?"

"You remember your friend Glyn? Welsh chap you brought him with you on your first leave."

"Glyn?" He thought for a while then the memory returned and he realised it was another part of his life he'd forgotten. "I remember him but I don't know what happened to him."

"He was picked up by another ship. Brought home injured. Well Cissie's going to marry him."

"Injured? How badly?"

"Badly enough for a Medical Discharge. Cissie's going to look after him."

William sighed. Rose wiped the razor on the towel. "I'd like to see him again," William said. "He was a good friend."

Rose put her finger under his chin and lifted it to shave his neck. "That's not all," she said.

"Something else?"

"Keep still." She drew the razor over his neck towards his chin. "I'm going to marry Peter."

He pushed Rose's hand away with his good arm, sat upright and wiped the suds from his face with the towel. He stared at her as though he'd never seen her before. "You and Peter? Since when?"

"Since forever," she said, "but we only realised it when he came home on leave. Oh do be pleased for me William. I'm depending on you to back me up when I tell Ma."

"Ma doesn't know?"

"No. I came home to prepare the ground before Peter gets here. He hasn't actually proposed yet, but he will and I don't want her to fly off the handle the way she does without thinking it through. Then we heard you were coming home and I didn't get the chance to mention it."

William laughed. "Rose, my darling sister. You are unbelievable." He was stunned. His first day home and the world had gone mad. Rose and Peter. He wasn't sure how he felt about that. He'd always liked and admired Peter, but even so. "You'd better tell me all about it," he said. "And I thought coming home would be too dull after fighting the war."

She told him about falling in love with Peter. "I love him and he says he loves me. What else is there?"

"Are you sure, really sure? You're not mistaking familiarity with love. I mean, you've known him since—"

"Forever and if you don't want to appear at dinner half shaved you'll sit back in this chair and let me finish." He sat back in the chair. She lathered his face again and carried on shaving him. "He makes me happy, William. Please say you're all right with it."

"It'll take some thinking about."

Rose stepped closer with the razor poised, her eyebrows raised and a gleam in her eye.

William wasn't deterred. "Are you really sure? It's a big step, marriage. It's the rest of your life, Rose."

He saw the tension ebb out of her shoulders. "Which I want to spend with Peter. It's not a passing fancy. I want to have his children."

William swallowed. What was it with women, he thought. Always wanting to settle down and have children when there's a whole world of adventure out there to explore. This was way out of the scope of his experience. She was serious and Rose, when serious was a force to be reckoned with.

"You've inherited Ma's stubborn streak and you're just as headstrong, and determined as she is. I'm not sure she appreciates that, but I do. If it's what you want, Rose, I won't say owt against it."

Rose smiled and carried on shaving him.

"I suppose you get used to doing this, in the hospital," he said.

"I've got used to doing a lot of things for men in hospital," she said.

"I'm not sure what I think about that either," he said. "Didn't really think about it until I was there myself seeing what nurses had to do."

"No. You prefer to think of us as young innocents unaware of the ways of the world, but I've grown up a lot in the last two years."

"We both have." He laughed. "God. We were innocents weren't we, Rose, two years ago?"

She laughed. "As new-born babes." She finished shaving him and wiped the last of the lather off his cheek. "There," she said. "You'll do."

"You too," he replied without thinking and realised he really was home.

Chapter Thirty Eight

Violet had invited Major Maitland to dinner as she wanted him to assess William's health. "He can recommend a Medical Discharge," she told Rose.

Over dinner, served in the family suite, William told them about his journey home on the merchant ship but nothing else. Rose and Violet talked about people they knew in town and plans for the coming week.

The children were full of chatter and questions for William, and Rose and Violet were just happy to have him home.

"Joe Jennings is home," Rose said. "He's back working in the boatyard. I'm sure he'd love to see you. You were friends."

"Joe?" William smiled. He remembered him, as he remembered a lot of things from when he was growing up. It was just the more recent things that eluded him. "I'd like to see him too," he said. "I'll take a walk round there tomorrow. I expect old Lenny's still there as well."

"He is," Rose said. "Hasn't changed. Still the same old Lenny."

"What about the rest of the family?" William asked. "Uncle Silas, Uncle John, Peter? Have you heard from any of them?"

Rose shot him a glare across the table. He gazed back, innocence in his eyes.

"I spoke to Hope on the telephone," Violet said. "She said they're all well. She was delighted to hear that you were coming home."

"What's Peter doing now? Still in the Gunners?" Rose didn't miss the mischievous smirk on William's face. His eyes, still filled with innocence, met hers with an untroubled gaze.

"I believe he's in tanks now," Rose said.

"Of course, you will have seen him earlier this year. He was home, injured wasn't he? Was it serious? No. Couldn't have been or he'd still be home. He went back didn't he?" Violet managed to say all that while dishing up the potatoes.

A blush crept up Rose's face, like a glass filling with red wine. "I've been writing to him," she said. "We got to know one another quite well while I was in London."

Violet's eyebrows rose.

"I always liked Peter," William said. "Knew he'd go far. Good head on his shoulders. Lucky the girl who gets him." He scooped some cabbage onto his plate. Rose kicked him under the table.

"Ouch," he said.

"What's that?" Violet said.

"Nothing. I just dropped something." William dived down to rub his leg. "Dangerous this dinner table."

When dessert was served the Major asked William about his stay in hospital.

"Bearable," William said, then changed the subject.

"Come to my office in the morning," the Major said. "Best to have a full medical examination." He nodded to William's arm. "I'd like to know more about that."

After dinner Rose cleared the plates. William helped.

"Thanks for that," she said when they were alone.

"What, telling Ma what a great catch Peter was? I thought I was helping."

She saw the same innocent look in his eyes she remembered from childhood. It was how he looked when he'd done something he knew he shouldn't and got away with it. "I was going to tell her in my own time."

"Still, couldn't hurt could it?" He kissed her cheek and walked away. She sighed. He was the same, adorable William and she couldn't be cross with him for long.

The next morning William went to the Major's office. William gave him the medical notes he'd brought with him from the hospital. "They were in Arabic," he said. "I had a chap translate them."

The Major read them briefly then examined William. "Hmm," he said, when he saw his legs. "Scars seem to be healing well." Then he examined his chest and back which too were heavily scarred. "Blisters?" he asked.

"Yes, jellyfish, salt burn or something."

He removed the sling from William's arm and lifted it shoulder high. "Any pain?" he asked.

"No."

"Clench your fist."

William tried. His fingers moved but only slightly.

"Hmm. Well, there's movement, so the ligaments are still attached. It will get better, but it will take time. You'll have to keep moving it. Any other weaknesses? Legs?"

William lifted one foot. "Not too bad, but I was glad of the seat on the train. Don't think I could have stood for long."

"I can give you some exercises to do," the Major said. He made a note on a piece of paper on his desk. "It says in your notes about memory loss. How bad is that?"

William sighed. It was his memory, or lack of it that worried him most. "Comes and goes," he said. "I can remember some things well, coming home helped that. I vividly remember growing up here, birthday parties, days out on the beach, the family, people, anything in the distant past, but it's the recent memories I find difficult. Can't remember much about the ship, or my time in the Service."

"Hmm. Well, that's not unusual," the Major said. "Your mind's blocking out anything that might trigger the memory of a bad experience. It's your body's way of protecting itself. You're lucky. Some people only remember the bad experience. It plays over and over again in their minds. They can't get rid of it."

"Will it come back?"

The Major shrugged. "It might, it might not. Sometimes it's best to forget things that don't agree with us. Makes for a happier life." He walked round his desk and picked up a pile of papers and a pen. "I'll recommend you for Medical Discharge," he said. "It'll be up to the Admiralty but, with your injury, I can't see any problem."

"I don't want a Medical Discharge," William said. "I want to go back to the Navy."

"But your mother said—"

"My mother wants to keep me at home. I can't see myself working here as a waiter with one arm, can you?"

The Major laughed. "No. But I can't see you as a sailor with one arm either."

William grinned. "Nelson only had one arm. At the end."

The Major chuckled, then he sighed. "I'll sign you off for a month and we'll see what happens." He shook his head. "Your mother won't be pleased."

William was determined to get fit enough to convince the Major to recommend his return to duty. Every day he rose early to run along the Promenade or to the boatyard to see Joe and Lenny. He walked around the town, but it held no charms for him. He exercised every day, trying to coax his arm's muscles back into use. Some movement in his arm returned, but not enough for him to be signed off as fit.

Over time he grew a little stronger. Physically he was getting better but his mind remained in turmoil. Whenever he stopped to gaze out to sea, watching the clouds scudding across the sky, and the waves washing the shore, he thought of the men on ships, men he'd served with, men he wanted to serve with again. The sea was where he belonged.

Chapter Thirty Nine

A few days after William's return Rose was on her way back from her morning walk into town to return some of the bunting Ma had borrowed from the shopkeepers. The pink glow of daybreak spread across the horizon. She never tired of watching the sun rise. She thought of Peter and wondered if he was watching it too. She imagined him waking before dawn, getting ready for the day ahead. She wondered if he slept, or if the bombing kept him awake. It didn't stop just because the daylight was gone. She thought of the day ahead of him and shuddered. She prayed again to keep him safe.

When she reached the hotel she met the postwoman. "Lovely morning," the postwoman said. "You can't beat watching the sun rise over the sea. This is my favourite round."

Rose smiled and agreed with her. "It looks as though we're in for a grand day," she said.

"Aye. Maybe some April showers later." The woman sniffed the air as though smelling for rain. She handed Rose the letters. "Have a nice day." She smiled, mounted her bicycle and rode away.

Rose grinned. It was a good start to a good day. She looked forward to spending time with William, even if he wasn't in the best of spirits because of his injury. At least he looked better than when he arrived. Ma had seen to that. She'd made sure his favourite meals were served and that he got enough rest. She was happier too, the light had come back into her eyes and her step had lightened since William arrived home. Rose knew she missed Gabriel and worried about him but having William home seemed to make that worry less. Her belief that the war would end soon was all that kept Ma going.

Glancing through the post, mostly letters to the patients and staff, her heart leapt when she saw a letter from Peter, redirected by Hope. His letters were like him, full of heart, determination and passion. He wrote with wry humour about the places he visited and people he met, bringing them alive for her. Reading them she felt she was there with him.

She felt a stab of guilt thinking about him. With the fuss about William coming home she hadn't told Ma about her feelings for Peter and that she wanted to spend the rest of her life with him. It would be a shock. Ma hadn't seen him for years and still thought of him as that skinny boy who came for the holidays with Hope and Silas. She wouldn't know about the man he had become.

She'd have to broach the subject gently, but determinedly. It was William's homecoming that had driven it from her mind, but now that he'd been home for a few days and Ma was in a good mood, perhaps the time was right. She'd do it today. Then she'd write to Pa and tell him, so he could support her as she knew he would. Butterflies fluttered inside her. Whenever she tried to talk to Ma they fell out. Ma never saw her point of view. She knew her mother loved her and only wanted the best for her but that best probably wouldn't include a boy who'd lived on the streets, no matter how well he'd done for himself since.

She sighed and looked at the rest of the post. A letter from Cissie made her smile and she looked forward to hearing all her news.

Inside she handed the other post to Violet, who was setting out breakfast with Joshua and Florence.

Violet flicked through them and put them on the side ready to take up to the office to be distributed. She noticed Rose held two back.

"Anything interesting?" she asked, pouring Rose a cup of tea.

"One's from Peter," Rose said. "Aunt Hope sent it on. The other's from Cissie, a friend I worked with."

"If Hope sent the letter on she must think it's important," Violet said, glancing up from the tea she was pouring.

"It's important to me," Rose said. "I told you I saw him in London and we've become close." Heat rose through her body.

"Really? How close?"

Rose saw the clouds gathering in her eyes but didn't foresee the storm to come. "I love him," she said. "He loves me. We want to get married."

If Violet had been struck by lightning she couldn't have looked more shocked. "Peter? He's a boy. And you're far too young, both of you."

Anger burned inside Rose. Why did her mother have to treat her like a silly five-year-old who didn't know her own mind? "Oh I see. He's old enough to fight and die for his country, but not old enough to decide he wants to marry me?"

Violet hesitated. "I didn't mean that. I just…" She sighed. "Oh Rose, these war time romances. They don't last. It's just the thrill of a man in uniform, fighting for our country. When he comes home you'll see things differently. Things will change after the war. You'll see. There'll be so many new opportunities open to you. You don't want to get tied down so young…"

Rose's irritation turned to fury. She stood up, the chair she was sitting on scraped the ground and crashed to the floor. "I love him. I want to marry him. Nothing you do or say will change my mind. I'm sorry if you don't approve…" Rage and sadness rose up inside her. She bit her lip to stop the tears that threatened to overwhelm her at her mother's unreasonable attitude. Joshua and Florence sat silent staring at her. "I'm sorry if I disappoint you," she said. She picked up her post and stormed out.

Outside she stood by the railings overlooking the sea, trying to gather her thoughts. She'd been so nervous it had come out all wrong. She'd hoped Ma would be pleased for her. She should have known better than to blurt it out. She was in the middle of blaming herself when William came back from his morning run.

"What's up, old girl?" William asked. "You look terrible."

"I've just told Ma about me and Peter. It didn't go well."

William chuckled. "Well, what did you expect? Ma probably had a suitor picked out for you years ago. Someone insufferably rich, boring and old enough to be your grandfather. Don't mind her. She just needs time to get used to the idea that we have lives of our own and want to make our own decisions."

"I don't want her to hate him because he wants to marry me," she said.

William put his good arm around her. "This is the Peter, who can charm the birds out of the trees. The bright intelligent boy who everyone regards as some kind of family saviour. Why would she hate him for loving you?"

"She thinks he'll take me away from her and I'll live in penury for the rest of my life."

William laughed. "Well, one day someone will and I can't see Peter living in penury. Not with Uncle Silas behind him."

Rose giggled. "That's true," she said. She took a breath. "It's not that she hates him, she doesn't. It's that she thinks I'm having some sort of romantic fantasy because he's away fighting the war, but it isn't. I love him for himself, for all that he is and I've never wanted anything more in my life than to be with him."

"Then you shall, Rose. Ma will never deny your happiness for long. She can't."

"You always make me feel better," Rose said. "I'm so glad you came home." She kissed his cheek. "Do you really think she'll come round?"

"Of course she will. If not you can always elope. Couples do that you know, in Gretna Green."

She took his arm and together they went into the hotel. Rose went up to her room to read her letters. She read Peter's first. It comforted her. Reading his letter brought him closer and love for him filled every part of her body. I'll marry you whether Ma likes it or not, she thought. She was about to read Cissie's letter when she heard a knock on her door.

"Can I come in?" Violet said.

Rose sighed. She'd been rude to her mother and she'd have to apologise. She braced herself for the tongue lashing that was bound to come. "Come in," she called.

Violet opened the door and came in.

"I'm sorry," Rose said. "I didn't mean to be rude but I love Peter and he loves me and we want to be together."

Violet sat beside her. "I know you think you love him now. He's easy to love, a valiant soldier fighting for his country, and handsome enough to turn a young girl's head, but marriage is quite a different proposition."

Hearing Violet's words Rose thought of Ferdie Giggs. She could have been describing him, and Rose had thought herself in love with him on the strength of one kiss in a dark alley when they'd both been drinking. But Peter was different. She loved him with a passion that had grown deep inside her over years. How could she convince Ma of that?

"No, Ma. It's not just because he's a soldier fighting for his country. I see enough of them in the wards to know my feelings for Peter are different. I've loved him since he came into our lives, a dark-eyed boy, filled with solid silent pride and bursting with bravado. It's him I love, not who he is or what he's doing. It's him, the kindest, dearest, sweetest man alive."

Violet took her hand. "You're very young. You have a life ahead of you, things will change after the war, you'll see. Things can be different. I don't want you to rush into anything you may regret."

"Like you did with our father?"

Violet bristled and Rose wondered if she'd gone too far. A chill iced Violet's voice as she said, "I made mistakes, I'll admit it, but I can't regret having you and William. I just don't want you to make the same mistake I did."

"I won't, Ma. I love Peter, I trust him and I won't marry anyone else."

Violet huffed. "Well, let's wait and see shall we. Like I said, once this war is over you'll see things differently."

Chapter Forty

Cissie's letter, as well as news of her new job at the hospital, contained an invitation to her wedding in Wales. William was also invited. '*I want you to be my bridesmaid,*' she wrote. '*You are my best friend, please say you will.*'

How could I refuse? Rose thought.

Cissie wrote to Rose telling her how the women of the village had put their clothing coupons together for material for the dresses. She was sending Rose some dusky rose taffeta, so Rose could make it up into a dress suitable for a bridesmaid. When the parcel arrived Violet helped and Rose was delighted with the result.

'*Come for the weekend,*' Cissie wrote. '*We can put you both up.*'

Rose grabbed at the chance to spend a few days away from home with William. Perhaps it would give Ma time to think about me getting married, she thought.

The Friday before the wedding William and Rose travelled to Wales together. Cissie met them at the station. "I'm delighted to see you," she said. "Accommodation is all sorted. Rose is with me and William, you'll be staying with Glyn."

"How is he?" William asked. "It's been a while since…"

"He'll be thrilled you've come," Cissie said. "He doesn't remember much about…well you know." She smiled and her eyes crinkled with optimism.

That evening Rose, Cissie, her mother, aunt and a several women from the village sat in Cissie's mother's best parlour eating and drinking the couple's health.

William and Glyn went to the pub with some of his friends.

When William first saw Glyn the years rolled away. He recalled their first tour of duty together, the shore leaves in London and other cities and the close friendship. He was glad to see him looking so well.

"You're a dark horse," he said. "Stealing my girl from under my nose."

"And I can never thank you enough for introducing us, boyo," Glyn said, in his lilting Welsh accent. "Can't help it if you was too slow off the mark."

"Good luck to you," William said. "How are you, really though?"

"Good. Better now I've a life with Cissie to look forward to. Come and have a drink." He ushered him into the pub. William noticed the hesitation in his speech and movement.

The barman brought them two beers, without being asked. "On the house," he said.

"Thanks," William said, surprised at his generosity.

"It's nowt compared to what you lads are doing for us," he said. "It's appreciated."

A warm glow washed over William. "It's a great place you've got here," he said. "I bet it's good to be home."

Glyn smiled. "Best place in the world." He raised his glass.

"To coming home," William said and they both drank deeply, each thinking of their own home and how lucky they were to be there.

"I don't know much about what happened," William said. "I only heard recently about the rest of the crew. I wondered if you'd survived."

"I survived pretty well," Glyn said. "Of course it's different. I can't do the things I did before, but I've found other things I can do which give me as much pleasure. I can't regret what happened, I've no time for regrets, they serve no purpose. I have a good life now, a life I want to live to the full with the girl of my dreams." He raised his glass. "I'm a lucky man."

"You are," William said, raising his glass too.

"How are you, yourself?" Glyn asked. William still wore a sling on his wrist, not being able to fully control his arm. "I heard you was missing and found again. Cissie told me. Must've been bad though?"

"I'm alive," William said. "And this," he tried to lift his arm. It moved slightly. "Is only temporary. I'll be back aboard before you know it." The look in Glyn's eyes told him he didn't believe a word but he didn't pursue it.

"What about your future plans?" William said. "How will you manage?"

Glyn took a swallow of beer while he thought. "We'll do pretty well," he said eventually. "Cissie's carrying on working and I've my pension and two mornings a week at the local school teaching music. I couldn't be happier." He smiled and William saw the sparkle in his eye that told him Glyn was where he should be; happy and looking forward to his future.

"Sounds, wonderful," William said. "I'm pleased for you." And he meant it. Glyn was a remarkable guy who deserved the best. His love of music was well known and William thought he'd be good at teaching it. "They're lucky to have you," he said.

The evening passed in a flood of drinks, laughter, gossip, introductions and general catching up. Glyn's brother, who was best man, his father, one of Cissie's brothers, Cissie's father, home on leave for his daughter's wedding and some friends who, like Glyn's father and brother were miners and in a reserved occupation, joined them.

By the end of the evening the party became rowdy and loud, inhibitions lost in the ocean of drink passing over the bar that night. Songs were sung, stories told and anecdotes of lost youth and old men's reminiscences related. It brought to William's mind fond recollections of good times in the ward room with shipmates and all he was missing being ashore. He also noticed Glyn's hands shook, he fumbled with his glass a couple of times, almost dropping it, and fell off his chair once. Nothing was said and William put it down to the drink, but he wasn't too sure it was.

Meanwhile the girls were having fun catching up with the gossip. Rose had forgotten what fun being with Cissie could be and her family were fun too. Cissie's mother and two aunts, cheeks glowing from over-indulgence, led the shrieks, giggles, hoots and snorts of laughter and loud chatter that filled the room. All Rose's worries about Peter and her mother drifted away. Several of Cissie's younger friends talked about their hopes of getting married in the not too distant future. Rose wished it was her getting married in the morning.

The next morning they dressed in a flurry of excitement, last minute panics and worries about everything going all right. Cissie looked beautiful in a cream lace dress once worn by her grandmother, remodelled to update it and altered to fit. Rose helped Cissie put her hair up, weaving sprigs of lilac into her blonde curls.

"Do I look all right?" Cissie asked, breathless as they waited to leave. Rose had never seen her so nervous.

"You look amazing. Glyn's a lucky man," Rose said.

"Thanks," Cissie said. "You'll be next."

Rose sighed. If only she could be sure of that.

Rose only relaxed when they walked into the chapel decorated with flowers that the WI had spent the previous day arranging. Cissie carried a bouquet of pink and white sweet peas and peonies. Rose, in dusky pink taffeta, carried a posy of rose buds.

The organ music rose to the rafters as Cissie walked down the aisle on her father's arm to meet her future husband. Tears stung Rose's eyes as they exchanged vows. The love between them shone on their faces. She heard it in the sincerity of their voices and the conviction in the words they spoke. If one good thing's come out of this war, Rose thought, it's Cissie and Glyn finding each other.

Rose noticed William was very quiet on the train on the way home. He hadn't said much since seeing Glyn and Cissie off on their honeymoon. She wondered if everything was all right. "Good to see them so happy together, wasn't it?" she said. "At one time I thought you and Cissie might…"

"What? Me and Cissie? No. That was never on the cards. I like her, don't get me wrong, like her a lot, but not like that, not to…I'm glad she and Glyn got together."

He sat quiet for a while. "He's not right, you know. Not himself. Not the man I knew. He's changed."

"I expect he has. We've all changed. You'll have changed too."

"No. I don't mean merely changed, I mean…he's not well. Didn't you notice?"

"Yes I did. He suffered a terrible head injury. It's bound to affect him. Cissie will look after him."

"He makes her feel needed you mean? Is that why she married him? Out of pity? I'd hate anyone to marry me out of pity."

Rose gasped. "You sanctimonious prig," she said. "You're wrong. She didn't marry him out of pity. She loves him despite his injury, not because of it."

"You're sure of that are you?"

Rose's mind spiralled back to the first time William brought Glyn home. "I think she fell in love with him the first time she met him," she said, her voice filled with wistful remembrance. "When he stood up in that cafe and sung that song in Welsh. She only wrote to you so she could find out what he was doing. I don't think it was you she was after, it was him."

William looked stunned. He shook his head. "You mean I was being used?"

Rose nodded.

His face broke into a smile. "I'll never understand women," he said. "Devious creatures."

A little while later William said, "I don't think I could live like that, though. He's half the man he used to be. That must be hard."

Rose thought of all the men lying in hospital wards who'd go home half the men they used to be.

"Sometimes there's no alternative," she said softly. "The ones I've seen are glad to be alive."

William hung his head. "It's this arm. It's not getting any better and I don't want to be an invalid for the rest of my life."

"You're not an invalid. You've got one gammy arm. You're still able to work and do something useful."

"But I can't go back to sea, unless…"

"Unless what?"

"Major Maitland said he knows a surgeon who may be able to fix my arm. Apparently it's the shoulder. It'd mean an operation and there's always a risk…"

"How much of a risk?"

"He says it may not work, it may result in permanent damage. There are no guarantees, but I want to try, Rose. I want to be made whole again."

"Oh William. You know we love you just as you are, one arm or two. It doesn't matter to us."

"It matters to me."

Rose nodded. She remembered how, even as a child, William had to be the best. Always had to win at games, always had to prove himself. "Whatever you decide I'll support you," she said. "You know that."

He smiled and patted her arm. "Thanks." He sighed. "What about you, Rose? Do you have to go back to London? How long can you stay in Norfolk?"

Rose brightened at the prospect of going back to work. "I have to go back tomorrow," she said. "They're expecting me at the hospital on Tuesday."

"Glad to be going back?"

Rose smiled. "Very glad," she said.

Chapter Forty One

The next morning Rose returned to London. A week later William was admitted to hospital for the operation on his shoulder to restore the use of his arm.

June brought summer sunshine, warm breezes and long sultry nights. Shadows lengthened, grass grew vivid and green, trees spread their leaves and flowers blossomed. Birds chirped on sunny mornings in English gardens. Old men played cricket on village greens and ladies enjoyed light-hearted, perfumed evenings on paved terraces.

In Belgium, guns continuously blasted their deadly barrages across barren, cratered ground churned up by heavy artillery, shells and mortar bombs. Fighting continued and men died. Peter was sent back to the Front.

He wanted to marry Rose. It wasn't a light-hearted or rushed decision. He'd always known there was something special between them, a connection he kept at the back of his mind through the years growing up. He recalled the pleasure he felt in her company, how at ease he felt with her, how she lifted his spirits and made him feel that life was worth living.

He knew that if he ever got married it would be to someone like Rose, but the possibility had spun away from him, as distant as the stars shining in the night sky. He'd seen himself as not worthy of her. Now something had happened. She'd kissed him and said she loved him.

That kiss had awakened in him a deep burning passion to hold her, love her and keep her forever by his side. She filled his dreams and thoughts of her made his waking moments bearable in the hell that daily surrounded him. He wanted to make Rose his wife, but he wasn't going to rush her into it. He had too much respect for her. She had to want it as much as he did. Anything less would be unworthy of them both.

He planned what he would do with all the care and patience he brought to all his undertakings. He applied for leave. Once that had been granted he wrote to her stepfather, Gabriel, telling him of his intentions and asking for his blessing. He chose a ring, a single, perfect diamond that sparkled like her eyes. By the time he crossed the Channel on his way home he knew exactly what he was going to do and how he was going to do it.

When he arrived in Dover he stopped over for one night in a small inn so he could wash the mud from his boots and have his uniform cleaned and pressed. He wanted to arrive in London looking his best. He rehearsed what he would say. He didn't want to push her into anything she wasn't ready for. He steeled himself. Facing German guns appeared nothing compared to what lay ahead of him today. Either way it would change his life forever.

By the time the train arrived In London he was ready. He took a deep breath and went to meet Rose, the love of his life. Memories of her when they were growing up filled his mind. There'd never been anyone but Rose, he thought.

He waited across the road from the hospital until her shift ended and she came out.

She walked with her head down, distracted. She didn't see him at first. He stood smoking a cigarette, watching her with mounting pleasure, revelling in the easy sway of her walk, the way her head tilted, the serious look on her face. She looked up to cross the road and saw him.

He took a last long draw, threw the cigarette down, ground it out and strode across the road.

"Peter!" Her face lit with joy. She threw her arms around his neck and pulled him close. He wrapped his arms around her, swinging her off the ground.

"I'm so happy to see you," she whispered in his ear. "Why didn't you tell me you were coming?"

He set her down. Looking into her face a sudden rush of tenderness and desire rose up inside him. He touched her cheek. "Wanted to surprise you," he murmured.

"Well, you certainly did that."

"Shall we walk?" he said.

They walked along beside the river until they came to a place they could sit. The evening sun dappled on the water, its glow warmed the air. A light breeze stirred the trees. Boats passed silently by. Rose kissed him again. "You look serious," she said. "Is there a problem?" Worry creased her brow and Peter felt a stab of guilt.

"No," he said. "It's just…your letters. They kept me going, gave me a reason to hope, something to live for. When I read them it felt as though I'd found diamonds in a handful of mud. Hearing from you brought home nearer and made everything worthwhile. But I need to know."

"Know what?"

"Did you mean what you said, or were you merely writing to a lonely soldier risking his life to fight a war nobody wanted? Did you feel sorry for me? Was that why you wrote?"

Rose looked aghast. Her jaw dropped. Shock and confusion paled her face. "No," she said. "Is that what you thought? That I said I loved you because you were going away? Some dippy, stupid thing to say in case you didn't come back?" Her eyes sparked like a summer bonfire as her bewilderment turned to anger, then panic. "I'd never say that, never, if I didn't mean it. And as for feeling sorry for you…" Her fury gathered momentum. "I've never felt sorry for you in my entire life. You've always been far too self-sufficient for that, you, you—" Tears quivered on the edge of her lashes before falling to run down her cheeks.

He pulled her into his arms and kissed her with all the pent-up passion he'd been holding back, gripping her tightly, breathing in the sweet, warm smell of her, his lips on hers, never wanting to let her go. "I just had to be sure," he said when he finally released her.

He slipped to the ground on one knee. "Rose Addison Stone," he said. "You are the most beautiful, intelligent, wonderful girl in the world. I've loved you for as long as I can remember. I want to spend the rest of my life, however long it may be, making you happy. Will you do me the honour of marrying me and make me the most fortunate and blessed man alive?"

Rose giggled with relief, her good nature restored. "Of course I will," she said. "I can't wait."

He took a small box out of his pocket and opened it to reveal the diamond ring. "I can change it if you don't like it," he said.

Rose gasped. Her eyes widened. "Not like it? I love it."

He took the ring out of the box and slipped it on her wedding finger. "I hope you'll wear it as a sign of our love," he said. "So you don't forget me."

Her eyes moistened. "I'll never forget you," she said and kissed him again just to prove it.

Lost in his embrace all thoughts of obstacles flew from her head until she remembered. "Oh Lord," she said. "What about Ma? She won't be pleased."

Peter laughed, nothing would spoil this moment; it was his to keep forever. "If I can face the hailstorm of German bullets and bombs I can face your mother," he said.

"When?" she said suddenly gripped by fear.

He grinned. "Tomorrow."

"I'll come with you."

"No. I need to go alone. It's the proper thing to do, to show due respect and allow her the freedom to speak her mind rather than be confronted by the two of us."

Rose pulled a face. "She'll insist we wait until the war's over," she said. "I don't want to wait."

"Neither do I," Peter said. "Trust me."

So she did.

Peter caught the first train to Great Yarmouth the next morning, arriving at the hotel before lunch. The first person he saw was William, home to convalesce after his operation.

"I can guess what you're here for," William said, a beaming smile on his face. He slapped Peter on the back. "Good luck to you."

"Thanks," Peter said. "So you approve?"

William nodded slowly. "I do," he said. "Rose needs looking after and there's no one I'd trust more than you to do that. She's always had a thing for you,

you know, right from the beginning. Never could understand it."

Peter chuckled. "Must have been my dirty face, ragged clothes and stubborn refusal to fit in."

"Yes, that must've been it." William laughed. "Seriously though, I hope you'll both be very happy. If she's not you'll have me to deal with."

"Understood," Peter said

They heard Violet's approaching footsteps. "I'll leave you to it," William said. "Good luck."

When Violet heard she had a visitor waiting to see her she hadn't known what to expect. Her heart raced when she saw Peter. She hadn't seen him for several years, not since they were children and always thought of him as a skinny boy a bit too big for his boots, who came for holidays with Hope and Silas.

All her preconceptions shattered when she saw him. Standing before her was a tall, dark haired man in Tank Corps uniform. Handsome and self-assured, he had a scar on his cheek, Captain's pips on his broad shoulders and two wound stripes on his sleeve. A battle-hardened warrior whose build suggested he could take care of himself. A force to be reckoned with. My God, she thought. No wonder Rose was so taken with him.

"Aunt Violet," he said, approaching her. He kissed her cheek. Amusement danced in his dark, coal-chip eyes. "I'm happy to see you."

Violet's breath caught in her throat. She struggled to gather her thoughts.

"We have to talk," he said. He had an air of authority about him and she saw Silas's influence in his manner. She had no doubt about why he'd come and she wasn't sure how she was going to deal with it.

"Come this way," she said and led him into the bar which had yet to open. "Can I get you a drink?"

"No, thanks, but don't let me stop you."

"Thank you." Violet helped herself to a gin. It was too early but she thought she might need it. "How are you? How is it, over there?" she asked to give herself time to think.

Peter smiled. "It's hell," he said, "but we're not allowed to talk about it. It's the inevitability of death that's the worst. Not something you'd understand unless you've been there and seen it, lived with men who witness the carnage all around them and don't expect to see tomorrow."

"Is it inevitable? For you I mean?" His words put a different complexion on things. She'd never thought of how the men must feel facing death, only the effect on the women left behind.

He shrugged. "It's what we face every day. You get used to it."

"Why do they do it?" Violet said, almost to herself.

"They do it because they have families at home, mothers, wives, sisters, daughters they want to protect from what would happen if we don't win this war."

"I suppose we're protected from the reality here, living our comfortable lives. The inconvenience and shortages are the worst we have to put up with. Even Gabriel never says…" The thought of Gabriel brought tears to her eyes.

"I expect you know why I've come," Peter said. "I want your permission to marry Rose. I love her, as I know you do. I want to protect her, as you do. I want to make her my wife before I go back, so that if anything happens to me she'll be looked after. With my pension she'd have enough to allow her to live however she chooses."

Violet was humbled. She'd got Peter all wrong, she'd mistaken his motives, never thought beyond her own need to keep Rose close. She hadn't bargained for the man he'd become.

"I want your permission to marry your daughter, Violet. Will you do that for me, for Rose?"

"As you did that favour for me so many years ago," Violet said, thinking again how different her life would be if it hadn't been for him. She might never have married Gabriel…

Peter laughed. "No. I've been amply rewarded for that. I want your permission because it will make Rose happy. It's something you can do for her."

Violet thought back to the conversation she'd had with Gabriel last time he was home on leave, shortly after Rose had returned to London. She'd told him what Rose had said about wanting to marry and that she'd told her to wait until the war was over. Gabriel had stroked his chin. "You can't rationalise other people's choices, Violet," he'd said. "Peter's a good lad. Everything he has he's earned by his own efforts. You can't say that about everyone and if Rose loves him…"

Then Violet had recalled how Gabriel's parents felt about their marriage before they met her. Now they were happy with the union because their son was happy. Why couldn't she be just as happy for Rose? "I only want the best for her, a good marriage, stability and yes, money. What's wrong with that?" she'd said to Gabriel.

"The world's changed, my darling," he'd told her, taking her in his arms. "I've seen it. Your history counts for nothing. It's what you do, how you treat your fellow man that counts. I've seen it in the trenches. It's not money that makes men, it's fortitude, courage and a willingness to put others first. Peter has all those attributes and he's Rose's choice. You can't change that."

Peter held her gaze, waiting for her response. In his eyes she saw honesty, respect and passion. She sighed. "You have my permission," she said. "Rose would never forgive me if I refused. I do believe and hope that you'll both be very happy." As she said it she realised it was true. Peter, solid, dependable, courageous, would be good for Rose and she could see now why she'd fallen in love with him. Then she consoled herself with the thought that Rose would be marrying an Officer after all.

Chapter Forty Two

Rose walked the ward in a daze that morning. She couldn't concentrate, her mind filled with thoughts of Peter speaking to her mother.

"Well, you might as well go home," Sister said when she heard of Rose's engagement and wedding plans. "You're about as much use here as a chocolate teapot." She hugged Rose. "I'll miss you," she said.

"I'll be back," Rose said. "He's a soldier serving overseas and I want to keep working as long as they let me." She felt a glow of pride as she said it.

"Good luck to you," she said. "We're losing too many trained nurses when they get married. This war's changed everything. Now anything's possible. I'll put in a good word for you." She sanctioned a week's leave for a home visit. "I wish you both well."

Rose couldn't contain her excitement when she told Hope.

"I'm utterly delighted," Hope said when Rose told her, "but not surprised." She hugged her soon-to-be-daughter-in-law. "I know you'll make Peter happy. He needs someone like you and I'm glad you found each other. I'm only sorry Silas can't be here. He loves you both and would want to wish you well."

Olivia hugged Rose excitedly when she saw the ring Peter had given her. "Golly gosh," she said, eyes shining with delight. "Now you'll be my sister."

Sean too hugged her when he heard the news, but his affection was expressed more modestly.

"Thank you all so much," Rose said when Hope welcomed her into the family. "I couldn't ask for better in-laws."

"So when will you be able to marry?" Hope asked. "It's difficult, with all the men being away."

"I'm going home today to arrange everything," Rose said. "I was hoping you'd all come with me. We want to get married straight away. No one knows how long this war will last and we want to be together now, for as long as we can."

"Of course," Hope said. "How lovely, a June wedding. Silas and I were married in June. I hope you'll both be as happy as we are."

"I only hope Ma feels the same," Rose said.

By the time Peter telephoned Rose, Hope, and the children were already packed to go with her to Norfolk. They travelled by train, arriving that evening.

"I'm sorry Silas isn't here," Hope said when she saw Violet. "But I know he'd wish them well."

"Gabriel's not here either," Violet said. "It's such a shame. It doesn't seem right, Rose getting married without Gabriel here to give her away. I wanted them to wait, but…"

Hope laughed. "Like you'd wait for anything when you were that age." She sighed. "It's the same for a lot of families," she reminded Violet. "But life must go on, or else what is it all for?"

With Violet's approval Peter applied for a Special Licence and then went to see the vicar at the local church. "I've only got a few days' leave," he told him.

The vicar nodded. "I'll be happy to marry you," he said. "And jolly proud to do it." Peter didn't miss the wistful look in his eyes when he said, "I'll put in a prayer for your safe return."

Peter asked William to be his best man.

"It'll be an honour," William said. "Have you got the ring?"

Peter gasped. "Oh Lord," he said.

Violet came to the rescue. "Here, take this," she said, removing the ring she wore on her right hand. "It's Ma's wedding ring. Uncle John gave it to me after she died. It's fitting that Rose should have it."

"Of course it is," Hope said. "It's what Ma would have wanted, for her first granddaughter."

"If you're sure?" Peter said.

"I'm sure," Violet said and looked happier than she had for a long time.

That evening Peter and William went out for a drink with some of the convalescing officers while Hope, Violet, Rose and the girls decided on dresses and hats.

Violet and Hope, as mothers of the bride and groom, vied for the position of wearer of the most elaborate hat. Violet won hands down.

The morning of the wedding Rose dressed in the dusky pink taffeta she'd worn to Cissie's wedding. Sprigs of orange blossom were pinned into the curls of her deep chestnut hair. She carried a bouquet of myrtle and pink carnations.

Violet and Hope wore varying shades of blue. Florence, acting as bridesmaid, dressed in a frilly pink frock, her eyes sparkling with excitement. Joshua, dressed in his Sunday best and acting as an usher, kept fidgeting and running his finger around the collar of his shirt.

Olivia, who at eleven years of age was beginning to take an interest in fashion, wore a slim-line summer frock in pale lilac which swished around her calves.

Major Maitland, in his best dress uniform, stood ready to stand in for Gabriel to give Rose away.

"I don't know what people will think, rushing into marriage like this," Violet said.

Rose knew exactly what her mother was hinting at. "I don't care what people think," she said. "Peter and I love each other. That's all that matters."

After much fussing about, nervous tension and near hysteria on Violet's part, the bridal party were ready to depart. Rose gasped as the bedroom door opened and Gabriel walked in.

Violet shrieked and ran into his arms. "You made it? How did you get here in time? Oh. Isn't it marvellous." Her beaming smile said more than words.

Gabriel laughed and kissed her, then kissed Rose. "I wouldn't have missed it for the world," he said.

Rose's heart almost burst with happiness. She hugged him. "I'm so pleased you made it," she said. "It wouldn't be the same without you."

"How did you do it?" Violet said. "How did you know?"

"Peter wrote to me. I came as soon as I heard. Thought he might have trouble convincing you, Violet, and that he might need my support. Still, it seems he has won you over without it."

Violet smiled. "He has a way with him," she said, and blushed. "How could I refuse when I saw how happy he made Rose?"

"Plus the Captain's pips on his shoulder," Rose said. "They helped didn't they, Ma?"

Violet's blush deepened. "Well, you can't blame me for wanting the best for my daughter can you?"

"At least you're happy for me aren't you, Pa?"

Gabriel nodded. "I am, Rose. Peter's a good man. I know he'll take care of you. I wish you both well."

They had five minutes before the bridal party were due to leave, and Rose didn't mind being fashionably late, so Gabriel opened a bottle of champagne he'd managed to bring with him so they could all drink to a long and happy life before the service.

At the church, walking down the aisle on Gabriel's arm, Rose saw the two men she loved most in the world waiting for her; Peter, the man she'd grown to love, half-a-head taller than William, her twin brother, her other half. Her mind filled with the tangled ties that bound them, stretching back to childhood. She tried to imagine a life without Peter in it but couldn't. It was as though it was meant to be.

As they exchanged vows Rose's heart filled with love for this enigmatic man standing next to her. Now, in a simple, solemn ceremony, witnessed by friends and family, their lives would be joined forever.

Afterwards, at the hotel, Violet had laid on a feast fit for Royalty. They drank champagne, and shared a wedding cake made by Martha. They danced to music supplied by a trio of convalescing officers.

"Are you happy?" Peter asked as he held Rose in his arms.

"It's the happiest day of my life," she said.

Later they drove off in the hotel car which Violet loaned them so they could honeymoon up the coast. At least they'd have some privacy for their one night together before Peter went back to the Western Front and Rose returned to work at the hospital.

Chapter Forty Three

Over the next months, summer turned to autumn. Rose noticed the thinning of the leaves on the trees and the golden glow of afternoon sun as it sunk over the skyline. Mist rose over the river and clouds filled the sky. Working at the hospital, seeing men who'd come in with terrible wounds recovering in both body and spirit, gave her some satisfaction but she missed Peter more than ever. Every day she thought of him, still at the Front, and prayed to God to keep him safe.

During the first months of autumn she began to feel queasy in the mornings. She lost her appetite and felt tired in the middle of the afternoon. The ward Sister was first to notice how often she was sick in the morning and insisted she see a doctor who confirmed it. She was expecting their first child. She could hardly believe it.

Her hands trembled as she wrote to Peter telling him he would be a father next spring.

When Peter read her letter in a short respite waiting for the next onslaught across the battlefield, he had to read it twice before the news sunk in. His jaw dropped. He couldn't believe it either. Him a father! It was the best thing that could ever happen and his love for Rose deepened. He wrote back that he couldn't wait to come home and see her.

Rose travelled home to tell her mother in person. Violet's eyes widened.

"You're making me a grandmother?" She wasn't sure how she felt about that but a new baby in the family was something celebrate. "It's wonderful. Congratulations." She hugged Rose with genuine affection. Thank God I don't have to have it, she thought.

Hope guessed from seeing Rose's early morning dashes to the bathroom and the way she pushed her breakfast plate away without eating anything, that she might be in the family way. Still, she was equally thrilled when Violet telephoned with the news. "Who'd have thought we'd be sharing our first grandchild,' she said when she heard.

"Well, if I have to share with anyone I'd as soon it was you," Violet said laughing.

When the Armistice came in November it was greeted with shock and disbelief by some, sheer relief and jubilations by others. All over the country people poured out onto the streets, joining together to celebrate. Factories spilled out, crowds crammed the streets, the sounds of works hooters, sirens, and rockets filled the air. Bands played, church bells rang, people danced in the roads, shouting and laughing.

Jubilant masses came out to rejoice. The men would be coming home. The war to end all wars was over. The Great War was at an end. A great surge of euphoric patriotism filled the air.

After the initial shock, disbelief and euphoria, Violet, Major Maitland, the children and as many of the convalescing officers who could make it, went out to the Promenade. The whole town had turned out to watch the parade led by the cadet band. The procession snaked through the town followed by shop and factory workers, fishermen, bank clerks, and every able bodied man and woman all dancing a conga in the street.

William, Joe Jennings, Lenny and the other men from the boatyard celebrated with a bonfire on the beach and enough beer to float a battleship.

In London, Rose was working in the pharmacy. Being five months pregnant she couldn't work on the wards. Her status had been reduced to that of a volunteer, but she did visit the wards taking books and newspapers, so she still felt she was making a contribution.

When she heard the news she was overcome with elation. It meant Peter would be coming home. Her whole body glowed with unrestrained joy when she went with the other staff, and as many of the patients who could manage it, to push their way through the celebrating crowds standing on Westminster Bridge and watch the fireworks over the Thames.

Hope went with Olivia and Sean to visit Alice and her children at the Hope and Anchor. "This means John will be coming home," Alice said, the relief after three years of sustained work and worry clear on her face.

In Devon Alfie and Jenny opened the pub. Farmers, land girls, shopkeepers, dairymen and everyone in the village turned out for the celebrations.

"Does this mean you can give up your job for the Ministry and become a full-time landlord?" Jenny asked.

Alfie kissed her. "I can," he said, "and I can't wait."

A pandemonium of rejoicing filled the streets in every part of the country. Bonfires were lit, street parties organised, laughter and joy erupted everywhere, mixed with a sense of disbelief and unreality. It was a day anyone who experienced it would never forget.

The men at the Front, war weary and exhausted, couldn't believe it was over when the news filtered through.

By Christmas the number of casualties coming into the hospital were decreasing. Men were gradually returning from overseas, although it would take months for the demobilisation and repatriation of the thousands of troops. Rose found she tired more easily these days so she decided it was time to go home.

Saying a fond farewell to Hope and the children was a wrench, but they promised to visit soon.

"Don't worry, we'll all be there when the baby comes," Hope said. "We wouldn't miss the birth of my first grandchild for the world."

Arriving back in Great Yarmouth Rose felt happier about coming home than she had for a long time. She felt settled about her future. With the hotel emptying of patients, the departure of Military personnel and William home it was just like old times.

Christmas Eve she stood outside the hotel looking over the bay. The moon was full and the sky drenched with stars. William joined her.

"I don't need to ask what you're thinking about," he said. "Any idea when Peter's coming home?"

"He'll be here as soon as he can," she said. "But I was just thinking how different things will be this coming year. No more war."

He put his arm around her. "Different lives for both of us from now on," he said.

"You'll be going back to sea?"

"As soon as my shoulder's better, but not before my nephew is born."

Rose laughed. "You're sure it's a nephew, not a niece?"

"I'm sure."

She shivered in the cold night air. He removed his jacket and put it round her. "Big day tomorrow," he said. "Come on, let's go in and see if there's any of Martha's cake left."

Rose grinned. Things aren't so very different after all, she thought, following him into the hotel.

They celebrated their nineteenth birthday quietly, with Violet, Joshua and Florence. They went to church for the Christmas Day service. On the way back they ran into Lenny and Joe from the boatyard, each carrying gifts. Violet invited them in for drinks.

"We knew it was your birthday," Lenny said, "and seeing as how Amos was lost at sea…" He unwrapped the parcel he had carried in to reveal a dummy, just like Amos.

William gasped. "It's amazing. Thank you, Lenny. I'll try to take better care of this one." He took the dummy and it said, "Look, Rose, it's me again."

Everyone laughed. Even Violet had to admit that it was just right.

Joe sheepishly unwrapped his parcel which turned out to be a superbly carved crib for Rose's baby. "Lenny helped," he said.

Rose caught her breath. "It's beautiful. I love it." She kissed his cheek. "Thank you, Joe, I'll treasure it."

"Least I could do," said a bashful Joe.

After lunch they walked on the beach and gave thanks for not having to worry about the war.

"It's time to rebuild," Violet said. "I have plans for the future."

Rose smiled. Ma's plans always involved a great deal of expense. She felt sorry for Gabriel who'd be presented with them as soon as he returned home.

Peter wrote and told Rose he was going to resign his commission. Working in the Tank Corps and his love of buildings had given him an interest in design and he planned to go into business with his friend Buffy who was an architect. '*People will need houses and the country will need re-building,*' he said.

Gradually, over time the men came home. John managed to be demobbed first. He applied for early release due to being needed at home to run his business. A thankful Alice greeted him. Amy, Alexander, John Junior and Emily all hugged and kissed him. Hope, Olivia and Sean joined them for Christmas Day.

"How was it?" Hope asked when they were alone in the kitchen.

"It was hell," John said. "But I'm glad I went. I learned a lot about myself while I was there. You never know how you'll cope, but I found that I can do whatever I'm called upon to do and stand with the other men. I can live with myself knowing I've done my best. It's something I would have wondered about if I hadn't gone. Now I know I need never doubt myself again. Still, I'm glad to be home. I'll appreciate what I've got even more and I'll be a better man for it."

He'd bought them all presents from his time in France and it was the happiest Christmas the Hope and Anchor had seen for a long time.

Gabriel arrived home in January to a jubilant reception. At the hotel Violet quickly immersed him in her plans for refurbishment, rebuilding and re-fitting to make it the best hotel on the coast. Rose, William, Joshua and Florence all pitched in with ideas to attract the summer visitors who would come flocking back to the resort, looking forward to the future.

Silas arrived home, weary from his time overseas. Hope found him quieter and more prone to contemplation than before. She saw specks of silver in his raven-dark hair. Some of his spark had gone.

"Do you know what impressed me most over there?" he said. "The sheer guts and bloody-minded resilience of the ordinary Tommy. Men who've spent their lives working in factories, shops, offices, on market stalls and farms, who were bombed night and day and yet, when they were called upon, were willing to do what they had to do. I don't know if it's self-respect, pride, discipline or not wanting to let the other chaps down, but whatever it is it makes me damned proud to be British."

"It's what we all feel," Hope said and knew it was true.

His outlook had changed too. "I'm going to close the club for refurbishment," he said, "and make some changes. When we re-open it'll be a place where ordinary men and women can come to enjoy themselves. The old order is changing. It's the hard-working men and women in the street we need to cater for. A place of entertainment for everyone, that's my aim."

Hope kissed him and when she lay in his arms that night thought again how lucky she was to have married him.

After a turbulent Channel crossing on a blustery March day, Peter arrived in Dover too late for the last London train. He'd never been more pleased to be back in England. Rose was waiting for him, but there were still too many miles between them.

He stopped overnight at a small inn, thankful for the chance to sleep, wash, change into fresh clothes. He telephoned Hope and Rose to say he'd go straight to Norfolk in the morning. He couldn't wait to see Rose again. Thoughts of her and the child she would have filled every waking moment.

He caught the first train out from Dover to London, changing at Kings Cross for Great Yarmouth. Dawn broke clear and sharp. He watched the sun rise over the hills, the fields turning green and trees coming into leaf as the early morning light spread over the countryside. He hadn't realised how much he missed the peaceful tranquillity of green fields and clear blue skies. He thought of the child they were bringing into the world. The wonder of it never ceased to amaze him. With everything fresh and new it felt right. Love for Rose and the child she carried radiated through every part of him.

Rose, excited at the thought of Peter coming home, had felt a bit out of sorts that morning, so took a walk along the Promenade for some fresh air. When she felt the first spasm of pain, she ignored it and walked on to Nesta's boarding house. Nesta took one look at her contorted face when the next pain came and called Violet.

"She's young and healthy," the doctor said, when he was called. "Shouldn't take too long."

Peter arrived at the hotel in time to pace the floor with Gabriel while they waited for his child to be born.

As soon as Hope heard Rose was in labour she got Silas to drive them all to Norfolk.

Rose and Peter's son was born that evening, on the day before Good Friday.

When Rose held her baby in her arms everything felt right with the world. The tiny scrap brought her more joy than she'd felt in her whole life. Nothing could ever be as perfect again. All thoughts of doing anything other than loving and protecting him for the rest of her life left her mind. He had Peter's eyes and the shadow of his dark as night hair, she noticed and loved him all the more for it. This child they'd made together would do wonderful things, she decided.

Peter kissed her. "I'm so happy and so proud of you," he said. "Both of you." He touched the sleeping baby's cheek, the deepest love and admiration shone in his eyes.

Hope and Violet celebrated the birth of their first grandchild together each vying to be the proudest grandmother. Silas and Gabriel handed out cigars and brandy to 'wet the baby's head'.

"I've never seen anyone so proud and pleased with himself as our Peter," Silas said to Hope. "You have to give him credit. He's done us proud."

"As I always knew he would," Hope said, recalling the criticism and comments made when she took him in.

Even William cooed over the baby. "Wow, I'm an uncle," he said. "I'll teach him to sail and all he needs to know about the sea. He's amazing. What are you going to call him?"

Rose looked at Peter. "You tell them," she said.

Peter puffed up with pride. "We thought we'd call him David William Silas," he said. David was Peter's father's name.

Hope gasped and kissed Peter, Silas shook his hand and William slapped him on the back. "Good choice," he said, an ear to ear grin on his face.

Gabriel opened the champagne, they all drank to "David William Silas Quirk."

"What an adventure we've all been through these last years," Hope said.

Peter took his son in his arms. Holding him his heart flooded with love for this tiny scrap. This was what all the fighting had been about; their children and their future. He was moved in a way nothing had ever moved him before. "Thank God it's all over," he said. "At least he won't be called upon to go through what we've been through."

"Thank God," they all said.

"Here's to the war to end all wars," Silas said.

Rose looked at her son in the arms of the man she loved and a great wave of tenderness, pride and hope washed over her. She raised her glass. "To new beginning," she said, "and lasting peace."

They all raised their glasses and drank to "New beginnings and lasting peace."

About the Author

Kay Seeley lives in London. She has two daughters, both married and three grandchildren, all adorable. She has been a writer for several years, writing novels, short stories and poetry.

A Girl Called Rose, is her sixth novel and the third in the Hope series. Kay Seeley's three previous novels, *The Water Gypsy, The Watercress Girls* and *The Guardian Angel* were all shortlisted for The Wishing Shelf Book Award. *The Guardian Angel* was a #1 best seller. Kay has had over fifty short stories published in women's magazines including *The People's Friend Magazine, Woman's Weekly, Take-A-Break Fiction Feast* and *The Weekly News*. Her stories are available in her three short story collections: *The Cappuccino Collection, The Summer Stories* and *The Christmas Stories.*

She is a member of The Alliance of Independent Authors and The Society of Women Writers and Journalists.

Acknowledgements

Once again I thank my family for their unstinting support. I also need to thank my beta readers and Helen Baggott for editing, all of whom have helped make this a better book.

My thanks also go to writing friends for their invaluable support and encouragement. Researching and writing about The Great War reminded me of my grandfather who served in two World Wars. They should never be forgotten.

Once again thanks to Jane Dixon-Smith for the amazing cover.

But most thanks of all go to my wonderful readers who make it all worthwhile.

If you've enjoyed this book, or any of Kay's books, she'd love it if you could leave a review. Reviews enable other readers to find books they too will enjoy.

Please feel free to contact Kay through her website www.kayseeleyauthor.com She'd love to hear from you.

If you enjoyed this book you may also enjoy Kay's other books:

A Girl Called Hope

In Victorian London's East End, life for Hope Daniels in the public house run by her parents is not as it seems. Pa drinks and gambles, brother John longs for a place of his own, sister Violet dreams of a life on stage and little Alfie is being bullied at school.

Silas Quirk, the charismatic owner of a local gentlemen's club and disreputable gambling den her father frequents, has his own plans for Hope.

When disaster strikes the family lose everything and the future they planned is snatched away from them. Secrets are revealed that make Hope question all she's ever believed in.

Can Hope keep them together when fate is pulling them apart?

What will she sacrifice to save her family?

A captivating story of tragedy and triumph you won't want to put down.

This is the first book in the Hope Series

A Girl Called Violet

Violet Daniels isn't perfect. She's made mistakes in her life, but the deep love she has for her five-year-old twins is beyond dispute.

When their feckless and often violent father turns up out of the blue, demanding to see them, she's terrified he might snatch them from her.

She flees with them to a place of safety where she meets the handsome and charming Gabriel Stone. He shows her a better way of life, but is he everything he appears to be?

Violet decides to stop running and finds the courage to return to London to confront the children's father. There she finds a far greater evil than she ever thought possible.

How far will Violet go to protect her children?

Set against the background of two very different worlds in Edwardian London's East End this is the second book in the Hope Series.

The Water Gypsy

Struggling to survive on Britain's waterways Tilly
Thompson, a girl from the canal, is caught stealing a
pie from the terrace of The Imperial Hotel, Athelstone.
Only the intervention of Captain Charles Thackery
saves her from prison. Tilly soon finds out the reason
for the rescue.

With the Captain Tilly sees life away from the
poverty and hardship of the waterways, but

the Captain's favour stirs up jealously and hatred
among the hotel staff, especially Freddie, the stable
boy, who harbours desires of his own.

Freddie's pursuit leads Tilly into far greater danger
than she could ever have imagined. Can she escape the
prejudice, persecution and hypocrisy of Victorian
Society, leave her past behind and find true happiness?

**This is a story of love and loss, lust and passion,
injustice and ultimate redemption.**

The Watercress Girls

Annie knows the secrets men whisper in her ears to impress her. When she disappears who will care? Who will look for her?

Two girls sell cress on the streets of Victorian London. When they grow up they each take a different path. Annie's reckless ambition takes her to Paris to dance at the Folies Bergère. When she comes home she takes up a far more dangerous occupation.

When she disappears, leaving her illegitimate son behind, her friend Hettie Bundy sets out to find her. Hettie's search leads her from the East End, where opium dens and street gangs rule, to uncover the corruption and depravity in Victorian society.

Secrets are revealed that put both girls' lives in danger.

Can Hettie find Annie in time?

What does the future hold for the watercress girls?

A Victorian Mystery

The Guardian Angel

When Nell Draper leaves the workhouse to care for Robert, the five-year-old son and heir of Lord Eversham, a wealthy landowner, she has no idea of the heartache that lies ahead of her.

She soon discovers that Robert can't speak or communicate with her, his family or the staff that work for his father. Robert's mother died in childbirth. Lord Eversham, a powerful man, remarries but the new Lady Eversham is not happy about Robert's existence. When she gives birth to a son Robert's fate is sealed. Can Nell save him from a desolate future, secure his inheritance and ensure he takes his rightful place in society?

Betrayal, kidnap, murder, loyalty and love all play their part in this wonderful novel that shows how the Victorians lived – rich and poor. Inspired by her autistic and non-verbal grandson, Kay Seeley writes with passion and inspiration in her third novel set in the Victorian era.

A love story

A #1 Bestseller

Kay's Victorian Novels are also available for Kindle in:

The Victorian Novels

BOX SET

Romance, mystery and suspense come together in these heart-pulling tales of love, loyalty and sacrifice. Beautiful evocative writing and compelling characters bring Victorian London to pulsating life. These three historical novels and their feisty heroines will grab you by the heart-strings and won't let go until the last page.

Contains:

The Water Gypsy

The Watercress Girls

The Guardian Angel

You may also enjoy Kay's short story collections:

The Cappuccino Collection

20 stories to warm the heart.

All the stories in *The Cappuccino Collection*, except one, have been previously published in magazines, anthologies or on the internet. They are romantic, humorous and thought provoking stories that reflect real life, love in all its guises and the ties that bind. Enjoy them in small bites.

The Summer Stories

12 romantic stories to make you smile

From first to last a joy to read. Romance blossoms like summer flowers in these delightfully different stories filled with humour, love, life and surprises. Perfect for holiday reading or sitting in the sun in the garden with a glass of wine.

The Christmas Stories

6 magical Christmas Stories

When it's snowing outside and frost sparkles on the window pane, there's nothing better than roasting chestnuts by the fire with a glass of mulled wine and a book of six magical stories to bring a smile to your face and joy to your heart. Here are the stories. You'll have to provide the chestnuts, fire and wine yourself.

Printed in Great Britain
by Amazon